THE DIVIDE

a novel

Kaitlyn Kroner

THE DIVIDE

CREATESPACE EDITION

Cover Design: Indie Solutions
Edited by: Indie Solutions
Formatted by: Ready, Set, Edit

Dedication

For those who believed in me and pushed me toward my dreams.

CHAPTER ONE

"Why won't you work?" I muttered under my breath. My fingers delicately turned the dial on the lock—hitting the numbers slowly and carefully—then skated up to the latch and yanked. The latch caught on the lock. Again. The damn thing just wouldn't open. As I groaned and leaned my head up against the cool surface of the locker, I imagined myself banging my head a couple of times but decided against it. School had let out twenty minutes ago, and I had been working on the stupid thing ever since. It wasn't *my* fault I was given a defective locker. For the third year in a row. Why did *I* have to get the same one every year? As I took a deep breath, trying to calm down the frustration that was brewing inside of me, I lifted my head and glared at the locker. One more time. I turned the dial and lifted the cold metal handle; it still wouldn't budge. I peeked around to find the hallway completely empty before looking back at the locker, fisting my hand, and punching it. Spikes of pain shot up through my arm, but it never opened.

"You might have won the battle, but I *will* win the war," I said to the nonresponsive metal piece of crap. Picking my heavy backpack up from the floor, I slid my arms through the straps and heaved it onto my back. The backpack weighed a ton; it felt more like bricks were inside of it than books. I took one last glance at my locker, glaring at it with invisible lasers shooting from my eyes, before turning away and making my way down the hall.

The sun shone brightly as I stepped out through the doors. The warm rays hit my face for only a few seconds before the cold wind whipped it away. Pulling my jacket in closer, I shoved my hands deep into the jacket pockets and ducked my head. I tried to cover my ears as best as I could with my jacket, not wanting a repeat of this morning when I'd forgotten my hat and come to school with frozen ears.

The trek home sucked. The bitter wind pushed against my back, catching on any exposed skin and covering my body in goose bumps. Tears kept forming in my eyes as the wind whipped across my face. My nose tingled, and I had to keep sniffing so snot wouldn't drip down. If it were summertime, I would have taken my time getting home. I was never in a rush to get there, but I hated walking in the winter. These were the days I wished vehicles were still used. There were a few vehicles left after The Great War, but they were only used during special circumstances. The only way to visit a different region was to walk or take the community train. And trains weren't cheap, so most people stayed in their own regions.

After The Great War that had wiped out hundreds of thousands of lives a hundred and fifty years earlier, the country had been split up into six different regions and was under the control of a new nation: Lorburn. A Leader had been formed to take control of Lorburn, along with a council, who'd considered themselves to be Ambassadors. They had been leading us ever since. The council would vote on laws, but it was the Leader who made the ultimate decision. And each Leader passed down the control to their child, making sure only one family could ever rule. In my opinion, this was ridiculous. But no one ever asked for my opinion.

Each councilman had a region to control and answered to the Leader. The Leader mainly kept to Gildonia, where he lived and ruled with his unhappy family. How did I know they were unhappy? Because I was his unhappy daughter.

I hated Gildonia. I wasn't sure how they did it in the other regions, but Gildonia separated the people. They put the wealthy on one side and the poor on another. They *literally* built a wall to keep both citizens separated. It wasn't right. I remembered reading a passage in my history class about how they used to separate people by color. Thankfully, we didn't stoop to that level, but learning about segregation in history really made me livid that we were doing it all over again. This time against all who were underprivileged. My father was to blame. The wall had never been there until he started to rule. He despised the poor and I could never understand why. They were just human beings, like the rest of us. After the war, instead of going forward, we went backward. Way backward.

Gildonia was the largest and richest of the regions, with oil and farmland being its main produce. Inonia was the second largest; coal was an enormous product and helped the region bloom. Centonia and Minonia were both about the same size and located right next to water, which brought in our seafood delicacies. Baronia was known as the prison region. Instead of having a place to keep prisoners in every region, Baronia was made into one large prison. The poorest of the regions was Destonia. I didn't understand how the people of Destonia survived. The land was barren, and they didn't have enough money to take a train to get supplies. I wanted to bring up a solution to my father, but I knew better. My father never took me with him when he went to other regions, so I've never been outside of Gildonia, but I would have loved to be near the water. It was something we didn't have. Of course, I didn't know how to swim, but if I could sink my toes into sandy water, I could die happy. When I was younger, I'd read as much as I could on oceans, lakes, and even ponds and had this sense of adventure take over, but there was no way I'd ever be able to leave Gildonia.

I should have been happy with what I had and where I lived, but I wasn't. Knowing there were people out there who had nothing made it hard for me to enjoy anything of value. I wanted to help the poor. It seemed I was the only one who wanted to help them. At school, I tried to get a group set up and start a food drive; of course the administration sent a note home to my parents, and I never tried again. I had to endure listening to classmates make fun of those less fortunate, about the clothes they could afford, the limited jobs that were available to them, and the lack of education they received. Kids who came from nothing weren't allowed to attend my school. They had to go to a secondary one, where the supplies were limited. How could anyone learn if they didn't have enough supplies?

Suddenly, the sound of yelling broke through my thoughts. As I crossed the street, I looked up at the construction site ahead. A miter saw screamed into the air, mingling in with the yelling. Metal rigs were set up against the theater and men were walking around on top of the roof, while others were working on the ground. One night, a few weeks earlier, somebody or somebodies had set fire to it. My dad assumed someone from outside of the wall had sneaked in and done it. He claimed people on the other side were jealous of everything we had, so he put out a notice. Everyone who lived over there would lose half their paycheck until the theater was fixed. It sickened me. It wasn't right. Especially since I knew who had set the fire, and they came from very wealthy families. I wanted to tell my father, but two things stopped me. One, I would be known as the rat, and school would be horrible. And two, my father wouldn't have cared anyway. One word would keep popping up in my head when I bit my tongue from telling the truth—coward.

Shaking my head, I looked at the theater. Half of the theater was blackened from soot while the other half was missing. I grimaced and looked away as a gust of cold wind whipped through me, causing me to stumble. The wind was strong, and I had to pull my hands out of my pockets to grab on to the straps of my backpack. Every time the wind whisked by, it felt like a hand covered in ice was slapping me across the face. Chills danced up and down my spine, causing one long shudder to erupt from my body. It didn't help that I was in stockings and a skirt. *Stupid uniforms.* Another gust whipped through, pushing my heavy backpack to the right and as I tried to balance myself, my foot slipped off the curb and I tumbled sideways. I slammed into something hard, bounced off, and fell forward hard onto my hands and knees. Tears formed at the back of my eyes as my palms and knees started to sting. Gulping in a few deep breaths, I willed the tears back—*stupid wind*—and leaned back onto my feet, gently removing my hands from the ground; pebbles and debris were embedded into my skin. A piece of glass stuck out of my right palm and I slowly removed it, wincing as blood trickled down my hand. I wiped my hands together to get the pebbles and debris off. Then I looked up. The something hard I had slammed into was staring down at me.

"I'm sorry," I said breathlessly, looking into deep green eyes. I wanted to get up off my knees—I could feel a large rock pinching into one of my knees—but I was afraid to move. The man standing in front of me was enormous. He had to be doubled—maybe tripled—my height, and definitely had to be doubled my weight, in muscle. At only five foot three and a hundred pounds, there wasn't much to me. But the man in front of me had a lot to him; his legs were long and looked like they went on forever, he had a light tan and a long-sleeved shirt on, but it was tight enough on him that you could make out a six-pack, and it wasn't until my eyes reached his face that my jaw dropped. Literally dropped. He was gorgeous. And when I say gorgeous, I mean *gorgeous* gorgeous. He had a strong square jaw, a small scar above his full lips, and dark brown hair covering his head. As I looked back into those green eyes again, I sighed. *I'm an idiot. Who sighs like that?*

"You should watch where you're going," he said. His eyebrows pinched together as he glared down at me.

"The wind caught my backpack wrong and I stumbled," I said. "I didn't mean to bump into you." God, he was gorgeous. I could have started naming the babies we would one day have.

"You're going to blame this on the wind? You people are always blaming everything on someone or something else." He rolled his eyes. He still looked gorgeous when rolling his eyes. I could look into those gorgeous, rolling green eyes all day. It wasn't every day I stumbled across such a fine specimen.

"Well, the wind is pretty strong today, and my foot caught the curb." I pointed over to the curb lamely.

He shook his head. "Right. Maybe next time you should watch where you're going," he repeated sharply. He crossed his arms. I could see a muscle tick in his jaw as he clenched down on his teeth.

I frowned while I fumbled with the straps to my backpack. I looked down at the ground, hoping it would give me answers to why he seemed so angry, it didn't have any, before clearing my throat and looking back up at him. "I've already apologized."

His lip curled. He gave me one long look before walking away. I sat there, on my knees, in disbelief that someone would appear so angry over this. It wasn't a big deal. "There's nothing to get mad about!" I yelled after him. He just shook his head and continued to walk away. I could feel a flush creep across my cheeks, tingling dancing along my neck. Why did I feel embarrassed? I didn't do anything. I scratched my head before remembering how dirty my hands were and let out a sigh.

Laughter drifted over as I stayed kneeling on the ground. I peeked around and spotted a couple of guys laughing, nodding their heads toward me. The beautiful stranger I ran into walked past them without a word. The others continued to laugh. My chest tightened, and I forced myself to look away.

I sat there on my knees, dumbfounded. How could someone that gorgeous be so mean and get upset over something so small? I shook my head. There were more important things to get upset about. Maybe he'd had a bad day. *Maybe he's just a dick.* But I did have those days, where I only had to drop my pen and I'd end up with a meltdown. Everyone had those days. But that didn't mean he had to be a dick about it. *There go the names for our non-future children.* Slowly standing up, I brushed off my knees the best I could while murmuring the different ways he could shove his head up his ass. I frowned as I stared at my ripped stockings and the blood dribbling down my leg. I took a deep breath and looked back toward the ground then moved forward.

I took a quick peek behind me and glared; I could feel the temperature rising in me, even with the cold wind that kept spitting in my face. The laughing morons were still watching me, but now the stranger I bumped into was smirking. I could feel the flush burn further into my face. I curled my hands around my middle and shuffled my feet forward. His gorgeous-meter had started at ten but was now at two. Okay, maybe more like eight. Maybe he was decent, and maybe it was just buried under his asshole attitude. *And maybe fairies are real if I'm going by that logic.*

By the time I looked back up, I was quite surprised that I was standing in front of my house. My house was a good fifteen minutes from the theater; I must have power walked when I was thinking of all the different ways I'd have liked to *jab* the handsome jackass with a hot *poker*. I stared up at the large house. The house stood two stories high with an unfinished basement. On the outside, two large windows decorated each side of the front door. Two large white pillars stood alongside the windows, with five stairs leading to the front door. I detested this place. In the windows, I could see people running about getting everything set up for tonight. Dread bloomed in my stomach and I took a deep breath. *I can do this. I will walk through that door and get myself ready for tonight. I will not embarrass my father. Otherwise, there will be repercussions, and I don't want that.* I nodded to myself and willed myself up the stairs.

Opening the door, I could feel the warmth of the house caress my body, my limbs instantly relaxing. I closed my eyes and took a deep, satisfying breath. My body was frozen and my ears started to burn, but I didn't care. The smell of warm vanilla wafted through the house; smelling delicious. And cozy.

"Mia, shut the damn door," my father snapped.

The coziness evaporated as I opened my eyes to find my father glowering at me. Chills ran up my spine. There went the warmth. I quietly shut the door, wishing I didn't have to see him until later tonight.

"What the hell did you do to your stockings?" My father flicked a look of disgust at my torn stockings then back to my face. I could *so* feel the love in that.

Looking down at my torn stockings—I'd completely forgotten I'd fallen—I should have remembered and sneaked in through the back door, but had it really been my fault that the wind was brutal and decided to take it out on me, and then I'd met the most gorgeous man I'd ever seen, only to find out that his personality was about as pleasant as stabbing myself in the face? "I, uh, fell," I finished lamely.

"How many times have I told you to take care of your things? There is a rip going all the way down your leg. You look like you belong with *them*." His face contorted into a sneer at that last word.

I looked around and could see the judgment that decorated the party planners' faces like they had much to prove. I rolled my eyes at them and mentally flipped them off, but was careful to stop before making my way back to my father's heated face. Blood drained from my face. "I didn't mean to. I stumbled over the curb and couldn't catch myself in time." Sweat sailed down my back as I clutched my chest, feeling my heart race against my breasts.

My father narrowed his eyes at me, and I could see his hand closing and opening. Swallowing down the panic that started to crawl its way up my throat, I took a small step backward. *Please, not now.* "I won't let it happen again. I promise," I finished quickly.

"Your promise means shit," he said. "Go get yourself ready. I don't need anyone coming in and seeing how much of a disgrace you are."

Tears pricked at the backs of my eyes, but I wouldn't cry. I never cried, and I was getting off easy. Taking a deep breath and slowly letting it out I started to walk toward the stairs. "Yes, Father." My voice shook as I slowly walked by him, trying to go as quietly as I could.

My father's hand grabbed my arm and gripped it tightly as I passed. "Make sure this never happens again." My head bounced up and down as I nodded, and I kept my gaze on the wall. His nails bit into my arm as he squeezed for a full silent minute; I bit my lip from crying out. When he finally let go, I all but ran up the stairs and into my bedroom; shutting my door as softly as I could before I finally let out the breath I'd been holding.

I dropped my backpack on the floor and leaned up against the door. My room was my safe haven. The walls were a light yellow, the bedding the same yellow with butterflies drawn on. The dresser was a deep mahogany, the same as my desk and beauty station. It was simple and that was what I loved about it, and the fact that my father never stepped foot in it. I didn't know why he never came in, but I wasn't complaining.

I frowned at the pile of dresses laying on my bed; I didn't want to attend the stupid party tonight. My father insisted on throwing a party for some type of law that he was putting into place. The only people who actually knew what it consisted of were the councilmen. They were probably waiting for it to be put into place before letting anyone know what it actually contained, that way no one would have the chance to openly complain. Once a law was put into place, it was illegal to openly complain or protest about it. It was annoying to be around a bunch of rich socialites trying to win my parents' attention.

I walked to my bed and sat down, picking at my stocking; blood had crusted on my knee. My door squeaked open, and I could hear footsteps enter. The door closed, but I kept my eyes on my stocking. I already knew who it was. It was the only person who ever came into my room: Agathy.

"We need to get you ready," Agathy said, her voice floating closer to me.

"Can't I pretend to be sick? I really don't want to go." I looked up and gave her puppy eyes, and pouted my lips. Agathy just rolled her eyes.

"No, you have to go. Up, up, up." Agathy went to the bathroom that was adjoined to my room, and I could hear the water turn on in the shower. "Mia!"

"I'm coming, I'm coming." I sighed and moved slowly toward the bathroom. I loved Agathy. She was our chief maid—more like a mother to me—she had practically raised me. She was the only one who gave me birthday and Christmas presents; of course I would have just been fine with spending time with her. She took care of me after my father had a round with me, she held on to me when I needed a shoulder to cry on, and she was there for me whenever I needed her. If it meant living on the other side of the wall, I would have done it if it meant I could live with her.

Steam was already filling up the bathroom by the time I walked in. The mirror was fogging up, but I could still see my reflection: my strawberry-blonde hair was high up in a ponytail, my soft, clear water-blue eyes staring back at me, and my thin pink lips frowning.

"Such a beautiful girl," Agathy said, coming up behind me. She was the same height as me, but a little on the plumper side. Gray streaks swam throughout her hair, and her eyes were dark blue, like the color of a storm brewing.

I shrugged my shoulders. "If you say so." I didn't believe it. My sister had been the beautiful one. When she was still alive. She'd had perfect, curly blonde hair and deep brown eyes, she'd looked just like our mother, except for the eyes—my mother had midnight-blue eyes. There had been this delicate and precious look about my sister. She'd always been able to talk her way out of trouble and get people to do her work. But she had always been kind. Never hurtful.

"Come on, come on. We need to get you ready." Agathy squeezed my shoulders and led me over to the shower. She left me alone, closing the door behind her as I undressed and stepped in.

The hot water felt amazing on my body after being out in the cold. My toes burned, but I didn't care. It was the good type of burn. I lathered my hair up with coconut shampoo and rinsed, repeating with the conditioner. I covered my body in bubbles with strawberry shower gel, wincing when my knee started to sting from the cut. After I rinsed off, I just stood in the downpour, shutting my eyes: green eyes materialized in front of me. I wanted to see a smile. *Or a grimace, for when you kick him where it hurts. Since, I don't know, he was kind of a dick to you.* I nodded my head. He needed a good kicking.

"Mia!" Agathy banged on the door, and my eyes flashed open. "Are you finished yet?"

"Yeah," I yelled out. Why couldn't I stay in the shower longer? Like an all-night type of deal? Watch my fingers prune along with my body type of shower. I shut my eyes, imagined myself kicking the dude where it hurts, and turned off the shower. Pulling open the glass shower door, I grabbed a towel and wrapped it snugly around my body. Making my way over to the door, I grabbed the handle and held in a breath: this was it. No backing out of it. *Like I had any choice to begin with.* I wanted to shut myself in the bathroom, but I didn't. Letting out the breath I was holding, I opened the door to see Agathy arranging the different dresses on the bed, with matching shoes. I bit my lip. Tonight was going to be a long night.

CHAPTER TWO

"Mia, stand up straight," my mother slurred in my ear. I could smell the alcohol roll off her tongue; I grimaced from the burning smell. I rolled my eyes but straightened my shoulders back.

After I was finished getting ready, I had walked downstairs and my brows disappeared into my hairline. The house had been transformed, and it looked ridiculous. The place was decorated in gold and silver: gold balloons bobbed up and down from the ceiling while silver streamers surged out of every available nook. Confetti was thrown all over the floor and tables. It honestly looked like an angel had walked into the house, glanced around, and decided to throw up on everything. Guests didn't seem to mind the obnoxious display. They mingled and crowded the once very empty house. So many people littered the rooms. If I were claustrophobic, I would probably have passed out. But at least I got to stand next to the door all night greeting people. The downfall: standing next to my already drunk mother and listening to my father drone on about how grateful he was that Mr. and Mrs. So-and-so shown up. Did I have better things to do? Probably, like read a book or file my nails. But did I have a choice? Nope. I was itching to move around and eat. The only good thing about these pointless parties was the food; I usually stuffed my face and packed a plate full to sneak up to my bedroom.

"Can I go now?" I asked my mother. I smiled sweetly at her, hoping her uncaring, drunk personality would decide I could leave. She narrowed her eyes at me in response. *So that's a no.*

"Aedan! How are you?" my father asked. I tried hard not to glare at my mother before turning my attention to the man standing in front of my father. The man was a little on the short side with light peppered hair and dark blue eyes. Wrinkles appeared at the sides of his eyes and mouth. Standing next to him was a tall, slim woman, who I assumed was his wife. White streaks flashed throughout her long brown hair as if lightning streaked through sand. As she looked at me, her soft brown eyes warmed the way a mother's eyes should when looking at their child. Except I wasn't her daughter, and the only temperature in my mother's eyes was ice cold.

"This must be your beautiful daughter, Mia," she said, her voice flowing like honey. She stepped in front of me and clutched my hand, covering it with both of her soft ones. "I've heard wonderful things about you."

I tried not to roll my eyes. I knew for a fact that no one talked nicely about me, except for Agathy, but no one ever talked to Agathy like she was an actual person. It would have been more realistic if she'd said, *I've heard you're such a disappointment,* or *I can't believe they spawned you* than *I've heard wonderful things about you.* I stretched a fake smile across my face. "Hello."

"Mia," my father said, "this is Aedan and Aileen Wibert. Aedan, as you know, is the Ambassador of Inonia."

The fake smile stretched even further on my face. "It is nice to meet you both," I said, finishing with a curtsy. I kept my head bowed and counted the long ten seconds before I could get out of the godforsaken position. I didn't work out. I hated working out. And when one curtsied, one was doing a type of squat. I didn't do squats. Beads of sweat started forming on my temple and my legs started to buckle. After ten excruciating seconds, I stood straight back up. *Don't forget to push out and flaunt your boobs so your back is straight.*

"Right, right," Aedan said, without breaking eye contact with my father. "Andrew, we have to talk. Things are getting dangerous with the rebels. They are out of control. People are start—"

"Aedan," my father chided, as though he were talking to a child. "We'll talk later. For now, let's just enjoy ourselves." He patted Aedan on the back. "Now, where is your son?"

Aedan glowered. He wasn't happy with my father's dismissal. "He's back home. He's buried in coursework. You know how it is."

"That's too bad," my mother chimed in, her words slurring at the end. "I would have loved it if Mia and Jake had gotten together."

Still holding my hands, Aileen slightly squeezed my fingers at my mother's comment. Clearing her throat, Aileen smiled at my father. "Would you mind if I took Mia with me? I don't have the first clue of where to go in this massive place."

"Of course," my father said. My mother mumbled something but it was so incoherent I figured it was because of the alcohol. My father shot her a look and she pressed her lips together. Looking back over to Aileen, my father faked a smile. "Mia, show Aileen around."

"Yes, Father," I said. "Would you like to see the Great Room?

Aileen smiled. "I'd love that." She let go of my hands, and before I had a chance to move, she looped her arm with mine. I smiled dutifully at my father and dropped the smile the moment we were out of sight.

Aileen walked slowly as she murmured her approval of all of the decorations. *One. Two. Three. Stop. One. Two. Three. Stop. One. Two. Three. Stop.* Aileen kept stopping us after three steps. At this rate, we would get to the Great Room by midnight. Of course, Aileen never noticed my irritation. That or she didn't care. When the Great Room came into view, I almost jumped up and down but I didn't get the chance, as Aileen kept walking past it. I looked back toward the Great Room as we walked farther from it.

"Umm...we passed the Great Room," I said.

Aileen smiled down at me. *Thank you, height, for making me so short.* "I figured when you slowed your steps as we walked past."

I tilted my head to the side. "I thought you wanted to see the Great Room?"

Aileen waved me off with her free hand. "I've been here plenty of times before. I know how to get around."

That was news to me. I'd never seen her before, and I had lived here for almost eighteen years. "Okay. So where are we going?" There were only two more rooms down this hall: the kitchen and the library.

"I was thinking the library would do just fine." We moved our way around guests and into the library. Only a few people were mingling in the room. Aileen kept moving toward the back of the library, dragging me along with her. Unease tickled at the pit of my stomach.

Aileen let go of my arm the moment we were out of earshot. She walked toward the last bookcase, gliding her fingers across the books. "It has been so long since the last time I was in here."

I stood there awkwardly. Scratching the back of my neck, I wondered if I could sneak out before she noticed.

"But I remember it just like it was yesterday," she whispered. I started to tiptoe backward until the next words stopped my progress. "Your mother and I were in here looking for a book on magic. Of course, we don't believe in magic. We just wanted to see if others believed in it. Anyway, we were all the way back here, searching through books endlessly. Your mother had to eat and pee a lot." Aileen smiled over at me. "She was pregnant with you. And your sister kept running up and down the aisle, giggling."

My heart throbbed at the mention of my sister. "You knew my sister?" I tried to keep my voice neutral, but it ended up coming out wobbly.

Aileen nodded her head. "I did. She was a wonderful child. She was always happy. Of course, this was years ago, way before the incident."

I flinched at the word incident. Slight tremors started to swim up my body. "I don't remember you." It was true.

Aileen kept her attention on the books. "That's because the last time I saw you, you were only four."

"Oh." I walked over to the only empty wall in the room and leaned up against it. "Why'd you stop coming over?"

"Your mother and I had a falling out." Aileen shrugged her shoulders. "But that was years ago." She pulled out a book and started flipping through pages. "So, Mia, how's school going?" Closing the book, she put it back and pulled out another one.

I shrugged my shoulders. "School is school."

"Do you like school?" Aileen flipped through the book slowly, making sure she went through each individual page before she closed it, returned it, and took down another one.

I nodded my head. "It's okay, I guess."

"Why would you guess? I bet you're a bright student." Aileen closed that book and started another. I furrowed my brows as I watched her. *What the hell is she doing?* I watched as Aileen did her routine on the next book, and then the next one. "Well?"

I shook my head out of the daze of watching her. "Huh?" I asked. I could hear other voices, but they were all the way down at the other side of the room. The library was enormous. It was a two-story library accessible from three entrances and was approximately twenty-nine feet by twenty-seven feet. One way to enter was the way we came in, from the Grand Hallway. Another entry point was on the second floor, which enters into the upstairs landing. The third entryway was through a hidden bookcase in the middle of the library. At least that's what I'd read about. Of course I'd never actually been able to find that last entry point. The central part of the room had a seven-foot fireplace with a mirror sitting above it; reflecting the staircase. The entire room was surrounded by bookcases on both floors.

Aileen chuckled. She closed the book and repeated her system with the next one. "Why wouldn't you like school?"

"It's not that I don't like it. I love to learn. I just don't really have many friends, and a lot of the kids don't like me." I rubbed my hands over my arms. "Lunch can be lonely."

"That's great that you love to learn. And don't worry about having friends. Once you run Lorburn, you will have many friends."

I gritted my teeth. *Because having friends only because you run something is so cool.* "I don't really see people sucking up to me as friends. If I did, then I would have friends now."

Aileen cursed as she put the book away and grabbed another. "You'll find having followers will come in handy one day."

I bit my lip to stop myself from commenting on that. I watched, as though I were mesmerized, as she went through three more books. Getting more frustrated, I finally asked, "What are you doing?"

"I'm looking for something I hid a very long time ago." She fumbled through two more when she let out a disgruntled sigh. "It's not here. How is it not here?" She walked back and forth, scratching her head.

"What was it?" I asked.

Aileen stopped suddenly and looked at me. She looked like she had aged ten years just by flipping through books. She shook her head. "It's nothing. Don't worry about it." Walking over to the two armchairs that faced the back bookcase, Aileen sat down. She patted the seat next to her and I reluctantly took it.

"Have you been mated?" she asked.

Worry seeped in and out on her pale face, and I tried very hard to not think much into it. “No, not yet.” Or at least I didn’t think so.

“I’m surprised,” she said. “You turn eighteen in just a few months, don’t you?”

“February fourteenth.”

“Three months away, and you don’t have anyone to mate with?” She tried to act surprised, but I didn’t believe it.

“My father hasn’t told me if I’ve been mated yet or not.” I wasn’t looking forward to that talk. I didn’t think it was right that my parents had free rein over whom I was to marry. My father had passed a bill the day I turned thirteen: parents of any child born into the council determined whom the child married. The child had no say in it at all. It was a way for my father to make sure I didn’t marry someone he didn't approve of. I was seventeen and in three months, I would be eighteen and would have to present the person I was mated with to the people of Lorburn. Of course, we'd wait to get married until I was twenty, and in the meantime I would learn everything there was to learn about Lorburn and its regions—it wasn’t like I didn’t already know most of it. I would never have a day to myself again. So I was looking for these next three months to go as slowly as possible.

“That’s a pity,” she said, except she didn’t sound like she thought it was a pity at all.

"What were you looking for?" I blurted out. Aileen kept glancing from bookcase to bookcase, tapping her finger against her lips.

Instead of answering my question, she leaned into me and lowered her voice, "You need to be very careful."

I frowned. "What do you mean?"

"There is a movement happening. Terrible people are trying to take over. They will come after you. I promise you that. And there will be nothing you can do to stop them. Trust no one. Rely on no one. Be vigilant. And whatever you do, listen to your gut. If it is telling you to run, you run."

Goosebumps trailed up my spine. The uneasiness was back swimming in the pit of my stomach. "What movement?" I tried to keep the skepticism out of my voice.

A small, sad smile formed on her lips. "I can't tell you. I wish I could. I wish I could have helped both you and your sister long ago."

My body stiffened. "How could you have helped? You don't even know what happened."

She continued on like I hadn't said anything. "Thankfully your sister is at peace and is happy. But you—" she reached up and cupped my face "—things are about to happen, and you're going to experience more pain than you ever have felt before."

I cleared my throat. Anger bubbled up in my chest, and I wanted to shove her hand off of me. "You're crazy." I moved my head away from her soft hand and stood up from the chair. Rushing out of the library, I could hear my name being called, but I didn't stop until I had made it through the kitchen and out onto the back patio. I hurried down the stairs and made my way to the back alley, slamming the metal gate closed and sliding down it. Blood pounded in my ears while black dots danced in my vision.

I buried my head into my hands and tried to breathe in and out, but my breath kept catching. I willed the tears away. I was not going to cry over something that had happened in the past, no matter how much it pained me. I knew better than to cry. If I showed weakness in front of my father, he would make it that much more painful.

I lifted my head and brought my knees to my chest, wrapping my arms around my knees and setting my chin on them. A cold breeze blew by, causing me to shiver; goose bumps covered my arms. *I should have brought out a coat.* My dress didn’t cover much of my upper body. I was wearing a long, silky denim-blue dress. It clung to my hips and breasts and dropped down to my feet. It was a halter dress, exposing my entire back and stopping at the top of my butt. The front covered from my neck down, so my breasts never showed. I loved it. I was wearing four-inch silver heels to help make up for my height. My hair was up, and a thousand curls cascaded down my back like a waterfall.

A pair of old boots appeared suddenly in my vision. I looked up, my eyes connecting with a pair of green ones. As gracefully as I could, I stood up, holding on to the metal gate for support as I teetered. Green eyes raked over my body, and my body shivered from the intensity of the stare.

As his eyes reached mine, I could see the heat coming from them.

I cleared my throat. "Like what you see?" I tried to still my shaking hands. I didn't want to show how nervous I was. Or cold.

An eyebrow rose. "What happened to the school uniform?"

I motioned toward the dark sky. "It's nighttime. I don't usually wear my school clothes at night."

His eyes raked over my body again. "So you wear that instead?"

"Uh…I…uh, no," I muttered. Another gust of cold wind brushed by and my body shivered in response.

"Why are you dressed like that? You do realize it's freezing out, right?" he asked. "It's supposed to snow tonight."

I rolled my eyes. *Of course I know it's freezing out,* I thought. I could feel it. "My family is throwing a party."

His eyes narrowed at me. I might have been wearing shoes that helped my height tremendously, but he was still much, much taller than me. "That dress looks like it could pay my rent for the next year."

Guilt rolled about in my stomach. "I doubt it."

He rolled his eyes. "Right." He raked his eyes over my body again, and this time, when he looked at me, disgust filled his eyes. Anger bubbled up in my chest.

"What?" I asked defensively.

"You look kind of sleazy."

My jaw dropped. "No I don't." I looked down and smoothed out my dress. "This dress is elegant and makes me feel beautiful."

"Keep believing that," he said, "and you will never know what beauty really is." He gave me one last glance before continuing down the alley.

"You're an ass!" I yelled after him. I pulled up my dress and ran after him, my feet screaming in protest. My heels kept slipping on the loose rock, and I had to lean my elbows out to balance myself. As I caught up next to him, I grabbed his arm. "You can't just make comments like that to people you don't know. It's mean." Like he didn't already know that.

He shrugged off my hand as he kept walking. "I'm pretty sure I can damn well say anything want."

I grabbed a hold of his arm again. "No, you can't. Well, I mean, you can, but it gives you a bad image. Do you really want to have a bad image?"

"I honestly don't care," he said. He shrugged his arm away from me at the same time my shoe caught on a rock. My body dropped to the ground like a sack of flour, while my sad, pathetic arms flailed out as I tried to catch my balance. My knees and hands skidded on the rocks and dirt. *Twice in one day, how awesome.* The cuts on my hands from earlier broke open, and I could feel the one on my knee breaking open too. I gritted my teeth and looked back up. He didn't even stop to see if I was okay. He just kept walking.

"Jackass," I yelled after him. He lifted his hand and flipped me off. *The nerve of this guy.*

Standing back up, I tried to dust the dirt off the front of my dress as best as I could before I carefully made my way back over to my house, making sure I didn't slip on anything else. As I opened up the gate, I took my time walking up the patio stairs and peeked through the small window of the back door. After determining it was all clear, I quietly let myself back into the house and slipped through the back staircase and up into my room. Locking the door behind me, I let out a breath I hadn't realized I had been holding in. I turned on my bedroom light and walked over to my full-length mirror. A frown formed on my lips as I assessed the damage. My dress was ruined. There was a small hole in one of the knees and scratches in the other. It would be impossible to fix because of the silky material.

I grabbed my pajamas and headed into the bathroom and changed quickly. I stuffed my dress all the way at the back of my closet, hoping no one would ever find it. Shutting off my bedroom light, I curled into my bed and I could hear the music and voices of the party downstairs float into my room; I hoped my parents weren't looking for me. As I lay my head down on my soft pillow, my mind rushed to the man with the green eyes. He was such a jerk. Or more like an ass. I knew individuals like him despised us but come on. I hadn't done anything. And it wasn't fair that

I actually felt something stirring in my stomach when his eyes raked over me. And then he opened his mouth. His stupid, stupid mouth. His yummy-looking mouth. I groaned. Couldn't my hatred of him douse my lust? Was it lust, though? Could seventeen-year-olds lust? I glared into the darkness of my room. After school tomorrow, I would see him, and when I saw him, I would lay it all out straight, that he couldn't be rude to me. Or anyone. I smiled. Yes, I would tell him how it was, and he would listen. How could he not listen? *I'm delusional,* I thought.

I closed my eyes, my chest feeling a little lighter. Tomorrow was going to be a good day. Maybe I could get us some hot chocolate while I talked to him, show him I was generous. Maybe some cookies too. My smile grew more as I pictured how tomorrow would go.

CHAPTER THREE

"Stupid locker," I muttered under my breath as I tried to pry it open. I should just give up and beg to get a new one, but I wouldn't lose to a nonresponsive object. Looking around quickly, I made sure no one in the crowded hallway was looking in my direction before I turned back and glared at the pain-in-the-ass obstacle, fisted my hand, and slammed it into the metal contraption. I ignored the sharp pain in my hand as the door popped open. *Finally!* Smiling, I looked around; only a few people had turned in my direction at the noise, but they went back to whatever they were doing. I shoved my backpack onto the top shelf and reached forward on the very bottom shelf, sliding my hand until it hit a small wooden box. I slid the rough box out and opened it. Inside, in a tight ball, was a roll of money.

When I was thirteen, my father had started giving me money at the beginning of each week. Unless I was being scolded or punished, my father never talked to me, so it had been strange when he'd summoned me to his study on my thirteenth birthday. He'd sat me down and told me that he would be giving me money each week, and that I could do whatever I wanted with it. My eyes had grown to saucers as he continued talking about this new deal between us. He'd never just sat me down to talk normally, let alone be nice to me. He'd told me I'd get the money only if I followed two rules: I was to never tell anyone about this arrangement and I was to keep out of the way and stay out of trouble. I didn't remember what else he'd droned on about because I'd been too shocked he was actually giving me something, like a human being. So I'd hid my money in a shoebox under my bed. I'd ended up breaking rule number one. My mother had somehow found out about our little arrangement and she'd torn my room apart looking for the money. My father had chastised me, but he'd continued giving me the money, so I'd decided to keep it on me until I came up with the bright idea of keeping it hidden in the school. I'd asked Agathy if she could find something I could store it in, and the next day she'd given me a small wooden box with a key. It had worked perfectly, and I had been able to hide it without anyone ever noticing.

I never used a dime of the money though. I was saving it for the day I would run; that was my goal. Since the day he gave me the money, I had been planning my escape; I was going to flee on my eighteenth birthday. I didn't tell anyone, not even Agathy. If my father ever found out she had helped me with any of it, he would do something detrimental, and I would never forgive myself. So I kept it secret. When I was fifteen, I'd found a small abandoned lodge deep in the woods. It was a good three-hour hike to get there. Rust and mildew freshened the air of the lodge, but it was an excellent place to start hiding items I would need when I escaped. So for the past year and a half, I had been loading up that place a little at a time. I didn't see my future here in Gildonia. I saw my future out there in no-man's-land, making my own way by teaching little kids. I would be abandoning my family, but we weren't much of a family to begin with. My mother was a drunk and my father was abusive. There was no way I'd not take a chance.

Trying to block the sight of prying eyes, I hovered close to my locker as I unrolled the money from the rubber band and slipped out a few bills. I grabbed enough to pay for two hot chocolates and two cookies before rolling the rest of it back up, placing it back in the box, and slipping it all the way into the back. I stuck two books in front of the box to help keep it hidden. As I stuffed the bills deep inside my pocket and slammed the locker door, I turned without looking up and hit a solid chest. I looked up into blue eyes, and my heart skipped a beat. I rubbed my hands down the front of my pants to help smooth them and wipe away the sweat that was building on my palms.

Tyler smiled and crooked a brow. "Hey, Mia." I tried to smile, but it came out lopsided. I'd known Tyler since I was a little kid. We'd grown up together, but we were never friends. I had always had a crush on him and wrote about him in my diary. And yes, I always put his last name with my first name to make sure it sounded good. And it always did. But Tyler never gave me the time of day. He was too busy with his friends or flirting with the pretty girls. The only time he talked to me was to tell me to make sure I didn't hover over my tests so he could cheat off of them or to ask me to write him a paper. And of course I helped him. He was beautiful. You couldn't be beautiful *and* smart. At least *he* couldn't. I couldn't fault him for that. He was just slightly taller than me, and he had luscious platinum-blond hair and perfect ocean-blue eyes. The kind of eyes you wanted to get lost in. He was on the skinnier side, but it worked perfectly for his frame.

"Hey," I said. I could feel the burn slowly creep up my neck, and my ears started buzzing. He was so good-looking that I lost my train of thought and all senses. I could feel my fingers slide against my jaw as I tucked a loose piece of hair behind my ear.

"What are you up to?" Tyler deposited his hands in both of his front pockets and leaned up against the lockers.

"Um, nothing," I said. I had this natural way of coming off awkwardly. I didn't talk to boys often, so I blamed it on that.

"Doesn't look like nothing." His blue eyes danced with mischief.

Nervousness staggered up my spine. Had he been watching me the whole time? "I, uh, was thinking about getting some hot chocolate." I nibbled on my lip while I waited for his response. I didn't know what I was more worried about—him asking what I was keeping in my locker or him already knowing, which would mean I'd need to find a different spot. But was Tyler the type to steal? *I wouldn't put it past him.*

"By yourself?" A smile formed on Tyler's mouth. It was the kind of smile that could get him out of any kind of trouble. It was a beautiful smile.

I nodded. "Yup." Clearly he knew I had no friends. I looked around, watching students as they started to clear out of the building either going home or hanging out with friends. I glanced back at Tyler, who raised his eyebrow. "So, what are you up to?" I asked as nonchalantly as I could. So, of course, it came out the opposite way.

"I'm going with you to get some hot chocolate."

"You are?" I could feel the excitement course through my body. Tyler had never asked to hang out before. He didn't exactly ask now, but I wasn't going to let him inviting himself bother me.

"Of course," he said, "and the others are going to be there." He grabbed my hand, and we started walking toward the exit of the school. I tried to smile at the fact that he was holding my hand, but the thought of seeing his friends put a frown on my face.

I hated his friends. And I knew hate was such a strong word that shouldn't be used, but I did hate them. They were terrible people. They couldn't have a good day unless at least ten people were miserable. And they would make them miserable. But did they ever get in any trouble? Nope. It was because all of them were the epitome of beauty. And when you were the epitome of beauty, you got what you wanted when you wanted it while everyone else looked the other way. Tyler might have had his faults, but he was nowhere near as bad as Mandy and Sarah. Just thinking of their names sent chills down my spine. George at least tried to be a decent guy. He was Tyler's best friend. He was just a little bit shorter than Tyler, but he didn't let his height get in the way. He still excelled at everything. He had dark chocolate-brown skin and light hazel eyes. Girls would throw themselves at his feet, but he never seemed interested in any of them. He spent most of his time hanging out with Tyler or beating everyone in sports. Sarah was taller than me but shorter than the boys, with long, curly red hair and mossy green eyes. She was so skinny everyone assumed she never ate. She probably didn't. She and I had been best friends when we were little until Mandy came along. Mandy had transferred from Inonia, and she and Sarah had become instant best friends, throwing me out like a piece of trash. Mandy was stunning. She was tall with long, curly blonde hair, dark brown eyes, and boobs that every girl wished they had. She was as skinny as Sarah, but she ate all of the time. I always imagined she threw up after every meal, but she was lucky enough to just have the perfect body and be able to eat whatever she wanted without gaining a pound. I, on the other hand, could eat a piece of pizza and gain like twenty. Probably not that much, but that was how it seemed to me. One last thing about Mandy: she was in love with Tyler. Everyone knew it. If you were within ten feet of Tyler, Mandy would give you a look that said to move or have your eyes gouged out. I liked my eyes, so when Tyler came asking for a paper, I made sure there was enough space between us. If Mandy had seen us holding hands, she would have broken my spine.

"Mia?" Tyler said, breaking through my thoughts.

"Hmm?"

"I didn't see you at the party last night," he said. I slipped my hand from his, mourning on the inside, and zipped up my jacket as we walked outside into the cold. Wind blasted in our faces, making me blink back invading tears. Snow clouds started to take over the sky; it would definitely snow tonight.

"You were there?" I didn't remember seeing him as I greeted everyone.

"My family arrived late," he said. "I asked where you were."

"Oh." I think I might have swooned. He had asked for me. *Eek!*

"Your father said you were sick."

My father had actually covered for me? Who was this guy? "Yeah, I had a terrible headache."

"That's what your father said. He said your *maid* had informed him you had taken ill and had to go lie down." He said maid like the word itself disgusted him.

A frown formed on my lips. "Yup." I thanked God for Agathy. I didn't know what I would do without her.

"I was hoping that we could have hung out last night. I wanted to get to know you and your family better."

"Really?" I asked. This was the first time he had ever brought up wanting to get to know me. All the time we'd known each other he never once wanted to hang out. So what had changed?

"Yeah," he said. "I think we should hang out more. It would look good for both of our families."

I nodded my head. Something didn't sound right when he said it like that. "Okay."

We were so close to the shop I could smell the chocolate from here. My mouth almost had drool coming out, but with Tyler right next to me, I tried to keep cool and not drool. I didn't get chocolate very often.

As we walked through the doors, heat rushed at us. My face burned from the change in temperature.

We made our way to the counter, and Tyler ordered his stuff, paid, and then moved over to the table where his friends were sitting. I ordered a small hot chocolate, reminding myself to get another one before I left, and a small chocolate chip cookie. I paid and reluctantly went over to sit with the dreaded group. The three of them looked up at me in disbelief as Tyler patted the seat next to him. Mandy sneered at me as I took the seat.

"What's she doing here?" Mandy asked. *Ah, this is going to be fun.*

My spine felt like liquid as I tried sitting up. I could face her. She was just a pretty face and horror on the inside. "I was invited."

Mandy smiled down at me. "Right, well, maybe you should find another table to sit at."

"I invited her," Tyler announced. Mandy shot him a look between hurt and disbelief. I sipped my hot chocolate to keep my mouth busy. "I was thinking we should invite her with us tomorrow night."

"What?" Mandy shrieked. I winced at the high pitch of her voice. If it were to get any higher, she could shatter windows.

Tyler ignored Mandy and caught my attention. "We're escaping this place and going on an adventure to the other side." A playful smile lit his face.

"Why?" I asked. Why would any of them want to go over there?

"They have bars there that serve eighteen and over," George's low voice spoke next to me.

"Um, I'm not eighteen." I straightened in my chair. And neither were they.

"Don't worry about it," Tyler said. "Mandy and Sarah can help you look older. Plus, they don't check IDs."

I sat in uncomfortable silence while they waited for my answer. Mandy and Sarah didn't look happy with the announcement; Mandy's eyes kept shooting daggers at me like it was my fault Tyler invited me. "I don't know." I looked down at my cup of hot chocolate.

"Oh, come on," Tyler said. "Haven't you ever wanted to see what it was like out there?"

"How about we don't bring her," Mandy snapped at Tyler.

"I want her to come," Tyler said. It came out more like a whine than anything.

"Don't pressure her," George said. I looked up in time to see George and Tyler exchange a look I couldn't decipher. It was like there was this secret and I was at the center of it.

"I'm not," Tyler said finally, glaring at George. "So, what do you say, Mia?"

Setting my cup down on the table, I scratched my head and bit my lip. "I'm not sure." How would I be able to get out of the house? "Breaking rules isn't really my thing."

Tyler smirked. "We will sneak out and sneak back in. No one will ever know. I promise."

I bit down on my lip even harder. I watched as my finger made its journey up and down my cup. This was what I wanted, to hang out with Tyler. But why did my gut beg me to say no? I always listened to my gut. Then again, this was Tyler; the guy I'd been hoping would see me as more than a person he could cheat off. If I wanted any chance, I had to do this. "Okay." The moment the words were out, I had an intense feeling that I was going to regret the choice.

Tyler's smile grew so wide that it reminded me of the Cheshire Cat's. "You have no idea how happy you just made me."

Butterflies danced in my stomach while Mandy scowled at me. "What time are we leaving?"

"Midnight," Tyler said. "We'll meet you at the back of your house, so make sure you are there at exactly midnight." Tyler drained the rest of his hot chocolate. "Well, we have things to do—" he gave a meaningful look at George "—so we should get going. I'm glad we got to hang out." He picked up my hand and laid a soft kiss on it. My heart pounded roughly against my chest as he rose from his seat. "See you tomorrow night, Mia." He winked, Mandy snarled, and then they were gone.

My hot chocolate was now warm. My stomach churned at the thought of sneaking out. Should I really sneak out with people who didn't like me? Looking down at my hot chocolate, I contemplated: I did want to be with Tyler, and he did seem to really want me there. I bit the side of my thumb, trying to keep the apprehension out. I could do this. I could sneak out for one night. Tyler did say no one would ever notice. There was no way we would get in trouble.

I ate my cookie as I thought of what I should wear. We were going to a bar, and I needed to not look seventeen. But did I own anything that would make me look older? I wasn't quite sure.

I wiped my hands together to get rid of the crumbs and stood up. Throwing out my half-full cup, I bought another small hot chocolate and chocolate chip cookie and walked out into the cold, brisk air. I was happy I had something warm to hold on to in this cold weather. Snow started to tumble down, leaving small flakes on my hair and jacket.

As I approached the theater, I could hear the drilling and sawing of the machines. Men were working and yelling at each other to hurry up before the snow really started to fall. I peeked over the fence, trying to locate my mystery guy, but I couldn't see him. So, I moved up onto my tiptoes to try to get a better view.

"Looking for something?" His voice boomed from behind me, making me jump and almost dropping the hot chocolate.

I turned around and tried to slow the racing of my heart. "Hey…I uh…I got you something." I pushed the cup toward him.

His eyes narrowed at my outstretched hand. "I didn't ask for anything."

"I know," I rushed on. "But I got you something since it's cold out, and it will warm you up." I smiled at the last part. *Show him you're friendly. That you do nice things.*

He just stared at me. "What is it?"

"It's hot chocolate," I said. "I was hoping that we could talk, too."

He just continued to stare at me, not taking the cup. "Why?"

"Well, I just wanted to get some things straight, and I—"

He cocked his head then shook it. He flicked his gaze toward the sky, like he was trying to communicate with someone up there, and flicked it back toward me. "I don't have time to listen to you babble."

I narrowed my eyes at him. "I'm not going to babble."

He raised an eyebrow. "You have a look on your face that plainly show that you're about to babble. And, if you haven't noticed, I have work to do."

My arm started to slightly shake. "I'm not going to babble." I nodded toward the cup. "I got you something warm to drink."

He rubbed his eyes. "I don't want anything."

"But I already bought it," I said.

"Then you drink it," he said. "If you're done babbling, I have work to do."

"Wait," I said. It was pointless to keep trying to carry a conversation with him, but I needed to. I couldn't exactly pinpoint why I needed to; I just had this feeling. Maybe I was just so lonely from having no friends. Maybe it was the fact that he had a type of freedom I'd never had. But either way, I wanted to keep talking to him. I had to prove to myself that no matter who the person was, deep down they were good. "I already drank mine. This one is yours."

His face tightened as his lips pursed. "Like I said, I don't want anything."

"But it's cold out. This can keep you warm." I leaned in. I ignored the shaky arm. I licked my bottom lip, waiting for him to take the cup.

He opened his mouth then shut it. He did this several times before walking away. I gaped at his retreating back. *Oh no.* Racing after him, carefully keeping the liquid in the cup, I grabbed his arm. "Why are you being rude?"

He groaned and rubbed his face. "You can't take a hint?"

"A hint about what?" I smiled at him when he looked at me. He just shook his head.

"I don't want to talk to you," he said, "and I don't want anything from you."

I could feel a sinking sensation in my stomach. "Why? I don't understand."

"I'm not interested."

"Interested?" I quirked my head at him. My eyebrows pinched together.

He looked around before turning his full attention on me. "You're not my type."

Type? "What does that have to do with anything?"

"You are offering me something to drink after stalking my job." He motioned with his hands around the area. "And I'm telling you, I'm not interested."

I laughed. "That's not what I was doing. I bought you a drink as a peace offering."

He smiled condescendingly. "Sure you did."

"No, really," I said as I watched him press his lips together and nod his head. My posture stiffened. I squinted at him. He didn't believe me. "You don't believe me."

"Nope."

"Why not?"

"I honestly don't have time for this." He rubbed the back of his neck. "Maybe you should go stalk someone else."

"I'm not stalking you," I said through gritted teeth.

He shook his head and walked away. I watched him walk through the opening of the wall to the theater. I wasn't stalking him. How he came up with that ridiculous idea, I didn't know. I looked at my outstretched arm holding the now cold hot chocolate. That had been a waste of money. I shuffled over to the dumpster lined up against the wall and tossed the cup in, then made my way past the opening of the wall and peeked inside. He was looking at me, giving me a pointed stare. I rolled my eyes and shook my head before walking the rest of the way home with a clenched stomach.

"Mia?" Agathy asked.

I curled into the fetal position and burrowed into the middle of the bed, covering my head with my comforter. I was not a morning person. I would have loved to just sleep until noon, but even that might have been too early. "Hmm?"

"Time to wake up." I could hear her moving around in my closet.

"But I don't have school today." My fingers clenched tightly onto the fabric, knowing Agathy would try and wrestle it away from me.

"I know you don't," she said, "but your father has a very important meeting this morning and wants you out of the house."

"He's having it here?"

"Yes, and he specifically said you were to be gone when the council arrives."

I rolled my eyes under my closed lids. "Can't I just stay in bed all day? I wouldn't leave it at all. No one will know I'm here." A day of sleeping, I liked the sound of that.

"Mia," she warned.

I groaned. I let go of the comforter and pulled myself out from under it. Agathy stood at the end of the bed, holding out clothes. "Where am I to go?"

"Your father has given you money to treat yourself for the whole day," she said. "Why not meet up with someone and do something fun?"

"Because I don't have friends and fun is foreign to me," I said dryly. I slowly made my way out of bed, hating how the sun had to rise every morning.

"That's not true." She handed me my clothes as I zombie-walked by her. "What about the young man who asked where you were the other night?"

"Tyler?" I pushed my way through the bathroom, setting my clothes down on the counter and turning on the water in the shower.

"Yes."

"I don't know." I couldn't exactly tell her that he usually only talked to me when he wanted to cheat and that *now* he wanted me to sneak out with him. And plus, I honestly didn't know how to get in touch with him in the first place. I could ask my father, but I doubted he would give me the information. "It's fine. I'll just go to the library and then maybe the café afterward."

"Check out more books?" I could hear the smile in Agathy's voice. She knew how much I loved reading. Especially all the books from the old days: the pre-war books. Those were the best.

"Maybe."

"Well, hurry up and get ready," she said. "Your father wants you out of the house in an hour."

"Yes, ma'am!" I saluted her and smiled. She waved me off and closed the bathroom door as she left. I quickly undressed and hopped into the steaming hot water.

The shower helped wake me up, but only a little bit. I got out, dressed quickly into the jeans and pink sweater that Agathy had put out, dried my wet hair and put it up in a ponytail, and applied a little bit of makeup—a little bit of light pink eye shadow for my eyelids and a little mascara. I never was the type to wear too much makeup. I didn't find the caked-on look appealing. I didn't think guys did either, but that didn't stop them from "hanging" out with the girls who looked that way. Leaving the bathroom, I grabbed the socks that sat folded on my bed and slipped them on followed by my cute knee-high boots. As I grabbed my jacket, I left my bedroom and the smell of bacon assaulted me in the hallway; my stomach growled angrily.

The kitchen staff were in the middle of cooking when I made my way down. My nose led me to the large platter of bacon sitting on the counter. Bending down, I inhaled the smell of the deliciousness mouthwatering piece of art. Food was my art; I didn't care much for paintings. I picked up a piece of the crispy masterpiece and jammed it into my mouth. "Mia! The food is not for you!" Charlie, the head cook, swatted my hand away from the food and led me out of the kitchen.

"I can't eat?" My stomach growled in protest.

"No," he said as he walked back into the kitchen.

Looked like my first stop was going to be the café. As I staggered to the front door, I kept peeking behind my shoulder; a look of longing appeared on my face from not being able to have any of the delicious food. Voices rose from my father's study, stopping me in my tracks. After looking toward both ends of the Grand Hallway, and getting the all clear, I sneaked up to the door of the study, placing my hands on the wall and positioning my ear against the door.

"You can't ignore this, Andrew." I recognized the voice, but I couldn't pinpoint where I'd heard it before.

"I'm not ignoring this, Aedan. It's just not that important," my father said. I could hear footsteps move back and forth and could imagine my father pacing around the office.

"It is important," Aedan said. "The rebels are growing and growing fast. The people are angry with you. Everyone is angry with you. Half of them want you to fight, and the other want you dead. And you're doing nothing about this uprising."

"We will be able to stop the rebels," my father said, dismissal lacing his words.

"We've lost contact with our spies. We don't know where Kieran is or what he plans on doing next. We can't get people to join the army. You won't even make people join. You're just sitting in this big house, doing nothing. Kieran could slaughter us all." Confusion clouded my mind. Who was Kieran? What uprising? Wasn't everyone getting along? My father had held a press conference weeks ago telling everyone there was nothing to worry about. He'd said more, but I hadn't been paying attention. I had been paying more attention to why bees were yellow and not pink. But in my defense, it was a pretty big debate going on in my head about the colors of bees. Now I wished I had been more attentive at those conferences.

"I'm not afraid of Kieran."

"You should be," Aedan said. "We all should be. They are coming for you and your family. What do you think they'll do to your wife? Your daughter? You saw those pictures of the women who got in their way. You might as well take your wife and daughter out back and shoot them before Kieran makes his way here, or they will have wished they'd died before he got his hands on them. And what about the people of Lorburn? How do you think they feel? Mostly everyone hates you. Don't you think they would be attracted to the promises Kieran is throwing out there? Some already have. The people are divided."

"Aedan, I promise nothing will happen. We've been friends for how long? Twenty, thirty years? When have I ever let something terrible happen to our people?"

"They won't only be attacking you and your family, Andrew."

"And that is why you are so worried. You would be the next target if something happened to my family. But you have to trust that I have everything under control."

Aedan muttered something, but I couldn't catch it. I tried to lean in closer, as I couldn't hear anything else. They were either taking a breather or whispering.

As I moved away from the office door and toward the front door, I couldn't help think of the worry in Aedan's voice. I bit my thumb nervously and leaned my back up against the wall, waiting for Agathy to show up, and stared down at my shoes. Why would there be an uprising? Didn't they know how dangerous it would be to go against the Lorburn's army? Who were these rebels? *There is a movement happening.* Aileen's voice popped into the back of my head. *They will come after you. Listen to your gut. If it is telling you to run, you run.* Was this what she meant? Was this the movement she was talking about? The rebels?

"Mia?" Agathy's voice broke through my thoughts. I blinked a couple of times and shook my head. Agathy stood in front of me with a look of concern. "Are you okay?" I nodded my head, but the look didn't drop from her face. She handed me my light-green bag. "Here you go. The money is in your wallet. You have enough to get food for the day and do whatever you would like."

My jaw dropped. Thoughts of rebels and running vanished from my head. My father had never given me that much money before. If he'd wanted me out of the house before, he would make me rely on the money he gave me every week. "Really?"

Agathy nodded. "Really. Now go out and have some fun."

I slid my black wool jacket on and draped the bag onto my shoulder and over my head, that way it was lying across my chest. "I'll see you later," I said. Agathy was looking down the hallway. It was the first time I'd ever seen her look distracted. Something was bothering her. I wondered if she had been like that earlier.

"Yes, yes." She patted me on the head and moved me out the front door.

I walked down the steps and moved toward the café. I pushed my hands deep inside my jacket pocket to keep them out of the cold. Snow covered the streets and lawns from the downfall the night before; snow was still sprinkling onto the ground. It was beautiful. It always brought me peace. *You might as well take your wife and daughter out back and shoot them. They will wish they'd died.* I shivered at the words. It wasn't a very peaceful thought. Would these rebels really hurt innocent women? Why wasn't my father taking Aedan's words seriously? Did he truly not believe the rebels and this Kieran guy were that dangerous? With the way Aedan was talking about them, I would want to hide in my secret lodge.

"Hey!" a familiar, deep voice yelled out.

I looked up and squinted through the brightness of the snow. I could see my new mystery jerk walking toward me. He didn't look happy. *Look who's stalking me now.* He slipped his hands in his back pockets as he stood blocking my way. I took him in; he was wearing navy-blue jeans, the same boots, and a black hoodie under a black leather jacket.

"What are you doing?" he asked.

I looked up at him and narrowed my eyes at him. "Walking."

"Why?"

"Umm, because I have legs that work? And why do you care?"

He rolled his eyes at me. "You shouldn't be here."

"Well, I live here." I started to get annoyed. "And you can't tell me where I should or shouldn't be." As I moved around him, he stepped in my way again, blocking my path.

"You don't have any friends, do you?"

I glared up at him. "I do too have friends. And why do you care? Wasn't it just yesterday when you brushed me off?" I raised my eyebrows and placed my hands on my hips. "Don't you have someone else to annoy?"

"One, I don't think you have any friends; I've never seen you with any. Two, you seem like the loner type, but not the *I want to be by myself* loner type, more like the *no one wants to be friends with me* loner type," he said. "Plus, you shouldn't be walking around alone."

I wondered if his middle name started with *A* and ended with *hole*. "Just because you've seen me alone three times doesn't mean you know if I have friends or not. And I walk around alone all of the time." I moved to the right to get around him, and he blocked me again. Crossing my arms, I glared up at him. This was getting ridiculous.

"I've watched you for longer than three days. I noticed you on my first day of the rebuild of the theater." My heart decided to accelerate along with his words. "It always struck me as odd that with all the money you had, you had zero friends." My heart decelerated back to normal as the blood started to boil in my veins.

"Wow. Who peed in your cereal?" I started to walk past him. "And it brings me back to my question, now who's stalking who?"

He grinned. I would have been impressed that his lips could form that shape, but I was too annoyed by his irritating, sadistic, happy attitude. "My bets are still on you stalking me," he said, strutting next to me down the street. Who was this guy?

I looked over at him and narrowed my eyes. "Are you a twin? Do you have a twin who is all brooding and you're the jerk?" I said. I forced my legs to pick up the pace, but he just continued along with me. "Why are you walking with me? You just called me a loser, by the way."

He threw his hands up in front of him. "Hey, I didn't say loser. That came out of your mouth. I was just telling it like it is. And maybe because I'm walking to the same place you are."

I rolled my eyes. "You don't even know where I'm going. Shouldn't you be working?"

"We just got canceled for the day, something about the weather," he said. He motioned around to all the snow.

I peeked over at him. Maybe this was his happy stage. I think I might have preferred his grumpy stage.

My stomach growled loud enough for the other regions to know I was hungry. I grabbed my stomach with my hands. *We are almost to food—just hold on.*

"Hungry?" he asked.

Damn. I had hoped he hadn't heard that. "Yes, I'm actually on my way to get something to eat."

"What, no food at your big house?"

"Shouldn't you be leaving?" I didn't want to be around him anymore.

"I should."

I slipped my hand out in front of us, animated two fingers as legs, and made the walking motion. He pushed my arm down and away from him.

"Are you trying to kick me out?"

I shrugged my shoulders. "All I'm saying is that you brushed me off yesterday. You took an innocent hot chocolate event and made me into some creepy, lovesick child who would stalk her prey."

He laughed. "Did I hurt your feelings?"

"Look," I said. "We could argue all day whether you did or didn't. I have a feeling no matter what I say you won't believe me. So move along. Go home. Leave me alone." I hurried my steps, leaving him behind.

I opened the doors to the café and inhaled all of the wonderful smells that were drifting through the place. The café was enormous. On one side were all of the food vendors and on the other side was the seating area. I got in line for pizza and felt a little drool trying to make its way out as two delicious slices of extra cheese landed on my plate. Picking up the tray, along with an orange soda, I checked out and picked a table next to the window so I could watch the snow drift down. I slipped my bag and jacket off and set them on the chair next to me. I closed my eyes and moaned as I took a large bite of the pizza; letting the mozzarella sizzle in my mouth.

A chair scraped across the floor, and my eyes popped open. *Oh, come on!* He picked up a burger and took a bite. He chewed while staring at me. I kept my eyes on him, not wanting to break this staring contest we seemed to be having. I took another bite of pizza as he took a sip of his soda.

"Are you going to moan like that again?" He pointed to the pizza that I was currently holding. "Or do you moan for more than just pizza?"

I rolled my eyes. I was not going to let him get to me. He took another bite of his burger as I took another one of my pizza. It was like some weird, food-eating stare down. It was a pity that he was such an ass, because he was striking. Dropping my pizza on my plate, I licked my fingers. "So, why are you here?"

He stared at my fingers and then at my face. He shrugged his shoulders. "Because I'm hungry."

"I mean why are you sitting with me?"

He smiled and I couldn't remember how to breathe. It was a beautiful smile. The kind of smile I doubted he showed very often. His smile reminded me of a rainbow, very seldom seen, but when it appeared, it stopped you in your tracks. "There's nowhere else to sit."

His smile disappeared as he took another bite of his burger. I cleared my throat and looked around, there was barely anyone here. Most likely because of the weather, not a lot of people liked the cold. I raised my eyebrows. "I'm pretty sure if you looked around, you might find an open spot. Like anywhere."

"Nah, I'm good here." He finished the rest of the burger, the whole time keeping his eyes on me. I rolled mine and returned to my pizza.

I would just ignore him. He could sit there all he liked, but I wouldn't have to think he was here. I could do this.

"So why are you out on a day like this?" His voice sent fingers of warmth up my spine. I loathed that my spine decided to work against me.

"Because I decided I didn't want to stay in bed all day and do nothing. I wanted to spend my Saturday wandering around with an annoying voice in my ear," I said dryly.

He smiled again. "You know, if it weren't for the fact you live on this side of the wall, I might like you." I cocked a brow at him, and he shook his head. "And don't let that get to your head. When I said like, I meant more like of an acquaintance like. You are definitely not my type."

"I believe we covered this yesterday." I tried to keep the sting of his words from hitting my esteem and kept my eye on my pizza. "Anyway, you're not my type either."

He laughed. It was full and masculine and gorgeous. So, of course, I hated it. "Whatever you say."

I looked down at my second piece of pizza. My appetite disappeared. "Well, I think I'm done here." Picking up my tray, I dumped its contents into the trash and grabbed my jacket and bag; putting it on before I walked out in the freezing cold. If I ever saw him again, it would be way too soon.

As I opened the door, the cold wind hit me in the face and I winced and felt tears pounce in the corner of my eyes. Tears were always pouncing in my eyes from the cold.

Burrowing further into my jacket, I headed in the opposite direction of my house—moving slowly as the wind shoved up against me. I slipped a few times on pieces of ice but was able to catch myself each time—except for the last one. When I moved one foot forward, it slipped out from under me, my body landing hard on the ground. Not only was my butt sore, but my pants were now soaked by the snow. I would be walking around with wet pants, and I wasn't allowed to go home.

"You're kind of a klutz," he said, coming up from behind me.

You have got to be kidding me. "You're kind of a stalker."

He stood in front of me. "Nope. The gate's this way." He held his hand out to me. I stared, wondering what trick he was going to do. He tilted his head at me. "Do you need any help?"

Probably. But would I accept his? With my luck, I would try to get up on my own and end up slipping the whole time, never finding traction. I would make myself look like an even bigger fool than I already had. As I slipped my petite hand into his large calloused one, he hefted me up without any trouble. Quickly, I took my hand back.

I looked at the ground as I started to move. "Thank you," I mumbled.

He came up beside me. "What? I didn't quite catch that."

I groaned. "Thank you." I made sure I said it loud enough, so I wouldn't have to repeat myself again.

"You're welcome." He shoved his hands into his front pockets. "So, where are you headed?"

"The library." I really wanted to drop my pants. The water from the snow was so cold on my butt I would have given anything to dry off.

"Why?" he sounded genuinely confused.

"I like to read."

"Why?" I glowered at him, and he smirked. "You're such a grouchy person."

"I am not. You make me grouchy." I focused back on my feet: one foot in front of the other.

"So, what's your name?"

"Why would I tell you my name?" I asked suspiciously.

"I could just call you Grouchy." He smirked again. "That could be your nickname. You're Grouchy and I'm Gregory."

Gregory was a nice name. Too bad it didn't fit with his personality. "You can call me whatever you like." I smiled bitterly up at him. I pushed past him and up the steps to the library. My hand was on the door when he yelled out behind me.

"Try not to stalk me tomorrow."

I turned toward him, flipped him off, and made my way inside the library.

CHAPTER FIVE

I woke with a start drenched in sweat—clothes clung to my slimy body. I couldn't remember much of the dream, mostly that I had been running from something. Trying to clear the sensation of the dream, I shook my head and noticed my alarm clock had been blaring; so that had woke me up. My fingers skated over the buttons until the I hit the right one, and the alarm went silent. It was still dark out. Looking at the time, the red numbers blared eleven thirty. I groaned. I wanted nothing more than to stay in my warm bed. Why had I agreed to sneak out to the poor sector?

As I turned on the lamp next to my bed, I stared down at the three library books I had checked out earlier. When I arrived at the library, I had spent the rest of the afternoon reading, and finally, around five, I had checked out three books and made my way back home. Agathy never told me how long I was supposed to stay out, but I'd figured I could just sneak in through the back way and up to my room without anyone noticing. Though, when I'd arrived home, my father and the council were gone, out to dinner. Agathy made me a sandwich for dinner and then left to go home while I ate in my room and continued reading before taking a nap. And now I was staring down at my books, wondering if it was even worth sneaking out. *Probably not.*

I sighed and slipped out of bed. Throwing on jeans, a white tank top, and a black sweater, I put my black boots back on and wrapped a scarf around my neck. Making my way into my bathroom, I brushed my teeth, applied makeup to my face, and fixed my hair. By the time I was finished, my clock showed I only had three minutes to get to the back alley. Slipping my bag around my shoulder and my jacket on, I turned off the lamp and the room plunged into darkness. It took a few seconds for my eyes to focus in the dark, before I was able to tiptoe over to the door and open it as quietly as I could, sliding out, and shutting it just as quietly. Treading softly down the stairs and out the back door, I kept it unlocked so I could sneak back in. Snow was no longer falling, but there was still enough covering the ground.

As I opened the gate and walked out, I pulled my hood up to cover my ears from the biting wind. I planted my hands in my pockets and looked around. No one was here. Were they even coming? I let out a breath, watching the white cloud form in front of me. My nose started to run from the cold, so I kept sniffing so it wouldn't leak. It was so cold out that I had to bounce up and down to keep myself warm.

It felt like I'd been standing there for hours, but it had really only been ten minutes when I figured they weren't coming. They were probably playing a trick on me, and I had been stupid enough to fall for it. Just as I turned to open the gate, I heard voices floating down from the end of the alley; squinting over, I could see four bodies walking this way. Mandy and Sarah's laughing floated closer to where I stood frozen outside of my house. As they got closer, I could see Mandy draped around Tyler and Sarah leaning close to George.

"Mia!" Tyler yelled as they came within ten feet of me. Wincing, I peeked up at my house, but no lights came on, thank God.

"Hey," I said, trying to pull of being nonchalant. It didn't work with Mandy giving me a nasty smile as indication.

Tyler pulled himself free of Mandy and put an arm around me, walking us down the alley. "I'm glad you decided to come with us."

"I wasn't sure you guys were coming," I said. It felt awkward walking with his arm around my shoulders. I'd always thought I would love it, but I didn't. *Maybe it's because of the nerves?*

"Mandy and Sarah took forever getting ready," he said, "but we're here now. Are you ready to explore the outside?" He said the "outside" like it was some mystical place.

"Tyler, I want a drink!" Mandy whined behind us.

Tyler laughed. "Don't worry. I'll get you one as soon as we get there."

"Where are we going?" I asked. I didn't want to be too loud, even though they were being loud enough to wake up the dead.

"To this little bar that I've heard all about."

"From who?" I was almost a hundred percent positive these four would never make friends with anyone from the other side.

"Don't you worry about that," he finished with a wink.

As we moved farther and farther away from my house, dread began to bloom in my stomach. My gut kept telling me to go back home and get back into bed, but I didn't want to look like a little kid to them. Especially not to Tyler. We walked for about fifteen minutes—the four of them talking so loudly that I was sure we would get caught before we even made it out—before we made it to the brick wall. Tyler stopped in front of it, and I looked up. The brick wall was twenty feet high to prevent anyone from climbing it.

Tyler pulled his arm from my shoulders and dragged his hands across the wall, following it all the way to the right. Mandy and Sarah followed him while George and I just stood there. I looked over at George, and he mirrored the same expression that was on my face: doubt. There was no way we could get over the wall.

"George, Mia, come on," Tyler yelled from somewhere to our right.

George looked at me and shrugged his shoulders, and then he started to walk over to where the others were. I took a deep breath and walked after him. *I should go back. They won't miss me if I go back. But if I go back, Tyler will think I'm a chicken.*

"What do you think?" Tyler beamed as George and I made it over.

Looking down toward where Tyler was pointing was a rather large hole, big enough for each of us to crawl through to the other side. I glanced back up at Tyler; he had such a satisfactory smile on his face. "I, uh, I don't think we should be doing this." I did *not* want to crawl through a hole in a wall.

Tyler's smile never dimmed. "Mia, don't worry. We'll be fine."

I watched as Tyler, Mandy, Sarah, and George climbed through the hole. I took a deep breath and let it out. If I went through that hole, I was officially breaking rules. "Okay," I said, ignoring the warning signs that were bouncing around my head. Bending down, I got on my hands and knees and crawled through. After I came out on the other side, Tyler hid the hole with a trashcan. I got up from my knees and wiped the dirt off my pants.

"Okay, listen up," Tyler said. "We're only a few minutes away from the bar. Act like you belong here and we'll be fine."

Everyone nodded their heads, including reluctant me, and we were off. Rounding the corner of the alley, we made it onto the streets and I stopped moving. My mouth gaped open as I stared around at my surroundings. I never knew how bad this side looked. Debris littered the ground from the collapsed buildings, wood planks covered the broken windows to keep either the cold or people out—most likely the latter—some people stood around a large trashcan, where a fire was burning, while others were huddled up against the building to stay out of the wind, tattered blankets covering their bodies. The smell hit me the most. It smelled like garbage, sewer, and death mixed together. How could people live like this? How could my father let people live like this?

"Mia!" Tyler yelled. I turned toward the sound of his voice. The four of them were nearly at the end of the block. Quickly, I took one more glance around before I ran to catch up with them, ignoring the glares from Mandy and Sarah.

"You okay?" Tyler asked. I nodded my head and followed them as they started walking.

I wasn't okay. I was disgusted. I was disgusted with my father. I was disgusted with how the poor had been left to fend for themselves, and this was how they found warmth.

"There it is! There it is!" Mandy squealed. Looking up from the broken road, a dilapidated building stood in front of us. This was it? This was what all the fuss was about? It was not impressive. Why they wanted to go there was beyond me.

"Mandy, Sarah, make Mia look older," Tyler said. "And hotter."

I winced at that last part while George gave me a sympathetic smile and Mandy rolled her eyes. Sarah pulled out a ridiculously low-cut shirt and threw it at me, at the same time Mandy took out her makeup.

"What am I supposed to do with this?" I asked, holding up the shirt.

"Put it on," Sarah said.

I looked around. There was nowhere to change. I turned my back to the group and took off my jacket, which I regretted immediately as the cold wind whipped through my sweater. Unbuttoning my sweater, I sadly took it off but made sure to keep my tank top on; there would be no way in hell I was taking it off. I slipped the low-cut shirt over my head and pulled it down; the tank top just showed at my breasts, keeping them hidden. Slipping my jacket back on, I held on to my sweater, not sure where I was going to put it, and turned around. Sarah snatched the sweater out of my hands and deposited it in the bag she was holding while Mandy pulled my face toward her so she could apply the makeup. *I'm going to look like a whore.* After she prodded my face for what seemed like hours, she pushed my face away and put the makeup back in the bag. Looking in the only glass window I could find, I took in my appearance: I looked older, but definitely not in a good way.

"Let's go," Tyler said, walking away and toward the bar. Everyone followed. *This is it.* I bit the inside of my cheek as I followed after them, trying to keep up.

Stopping in front of the rundown bar, the walls made of brick with some of the littering the ground, Tyler turned around and smiled. "This is it. Let's have some fun, shall we?"

Mandy and Sarah beamed, and George grunted. I felt sick to my stomach. The smell was once again the first thing that hit me as we walked in; alcohol and smoke filtered through the air. Wood tables were scattered throughout the room with mismatched chairs. The place was packed and we had to push our way over to the only empty table in the place. There were way too many people in here. Music blared through the room, and conversations were being yelled. Tyler, Mandy, Sarah, and George looked like they were about to have the time of their lives. Scooting closer to me, Tyler draped his arm around the back of my chair.

"What can I get ya?" an old scraggly voice asked. I looked up to see an old man with shaky hands holding on to a small notepad.

"Five whiskeys," Tyler said. The old man lifted an eyebrow but just wrote down the order and walked away.

My eyes followed the old man to the back of the bar. He started taking out glasses and pouring the drinks. As I started to look away, my gaze locked on to a pair of angry green eyes. Gregory. He returned my stare, but he was not happy to see me. Raking my eyes over him, I took in his black jeans, black boots, and black t-shirt. Someone liked black a little too much. He needed some color splashed in there. When my eyes made their way back up to his, a tall brunette girl caught my attention. She was leaning in on his side, his arm wrapped around her waist. How had I not seen her before? I looked back up at his face and narrowed my eyes at his raised brow.

"Hey," Tyler whispered in my ear. I jumped and broke the staring contest Gregory and I seemed to have been having. "I'm glad you came along."

"Yeah," I said. "How long are we staying?" I tried to keep my attention on Tyler and not look over at Gregory with his slut. *That's very rude to say.* But if it's true, it's true.

Tyler smirked. "Relax. It's going to be a fun night. I promise." His voice sent chills scattering up my spine, and not the good kind. "You have really pretty eyes. I've never noticed them before." I could feel the heat coming from Mandy's glaring hitting my body.

"Thanks," I whispered. Tyler was so close to me that I could see tiny spots of gray in his blue eyes. I tried to swallow, but my mouth was too dry.

Tyler leaned all the way in until his lips touched mine—I was so stunned I didn't move. His lips were soft and kept moving, trying to encourage mine to move with them. As I pushed his shoulders back, I moved my head back until the kiss ended. Swiftly, I turned my attention to the bar and let out a sigh of relief when I didn't see Gregory. Of course, I didn't end the kiss because of Gregory. He just happened to be here. I ended it because we were in a bar, and I didn't want my first real kiss to be in a bar. Though, it was kind of too late. I turned my attention back over to Tyler. "I'm sorry."

"For what?" He smiled. "I'm not."

I tried to smile back but was saved when the old man came shuffling back. He set the drinks down on the table, five cups filled with brown liquid. "Twenty."

"Twenty what?" Tyler grabbed one and started drinking.

"Twenty dollars," the old man said, placing his hand out and waiting for the money to be put in his hand. Tyler reached into his pocket and gave the man a fifty.

"Keep the change," Tyler said, smirking.

"Where's the bathroom?" I asked before the guy could move on to another table.

He nodded his head in the direction toward the bar. "Back there."

"Thank you," I said. As he walked away, I stood up and walked in the direction of where the old man had nodded. I tried to pass people without touching them, not wanting to accidently bump into the wrong person. I could see two doors to the right of the bar, and as I got closer, a rough, calloused hand grabbed on to my upper arm and dragged me further into the back. Turing toward the hand, I ran right into a solid, muscled chest. I slowly moved my head up, my eyes roaming up from his chest to his strong neck, and then finally resting on those deep green eyes.

"Why are you here?" Gregory asked.

Instantly, I narrowed my eyes at him. "I'm having a drink."

"I can see that. But why are you *here*?" His hand tightened on my arm. I winced, but he never let go.

"Because they serve drinks here."

Gregory moved us even farther back, where no one was around. I wondered if I screamed if anyone would come and help me. "Okay, *princess*, why did you leave your sector?"

At least he didn't call me Grouchy. I didn't know which name I hated more. "Because they don't serve 'special' drinks to people my age there." I smiled at the look he gave me when I used my fingers to quote the word special.

Gregory shook his head. "Do you know how unsafe it is for you to be here?"

I tried to pull my arm from his hand but couldn't. "How is it unsafe? You guys come to our sector all of the time, and it's safe there. Remember the stalking you did earlier today?"

"That's different," he said. "People here would do anything to make a buck, including holding five idiots hostage. And I wasn't stalking you."

Ignoring his comment, I tried pulling my arm out of his grasp. "Can I have my arm back?" I snapped.

"Only if you leave now." He tightened his grip.

"I can't leave," I said through gritted teeth. "I'm here with people."

"Do you mean sucking face with people?"

"Jealous?" I asked innocently. Tapping my foot and raising a brow, I waited for his answer.

"Of course not," he said, "but I thought you would be more of a prude. What really surprises me is that you do actually have friends." He leaned in close until his lips whispered up against my ear. My body tingled when his lips moved from talking. "Or are they actually people who could possibly be using you? But would you even notice it? I would put my money on no. Because, like I said earlier, you're a loner who no one wants to be friends with." It felt as though a rock dropped to the bottom of my stomach, but it was probably just my racing heart.

Tears formed in my eyes. I leaned back as I tried blinking them away. Gregory's face showed no signs of emotion, until he saw the tears lining my eyes; what looked like guilt flickered across his face. "Please let go of my arm." Turning my head away from him, I hurriedly blinked back the rest of the tears. Gregory's hand slowly released my arm, and as soon as his fingertips stopped touching my skin, I hurried back to the others.

Tyler was going on and on about some guy in our class, but I hadn't heard a word since I sat back down. I kept my head down and my focus on my hands. I didn't want to think that Tyler was just using me for something, whatever that could be. But why would Tyler just invite me somewhere out of the blue? I looked at the full glass in front of me.

"Hey, pretty lady," a rough, scraggly voice said in my ear. Looking to my left, I nearly jumped out of my seat. A man, maybe in his thirties, crouched down next to me. He had three rather large scars all parallel with each other down the right side of his face. A menacing smile spread across his face as he looked me up and down. "You new here?"

"What business is it of yours?" Tyler asked. He leaned over me and came face-to-face with the guy. Probably not the smartest thing to do.

"What business? What business?" He laughed and looked over his shoulder to four other guys. *Great, he has friends.* "Well, you see here, this is our table." He gestured to us. "And will you look at that? People are sitting here."

"We were here first," Mandy said. She flipped her hair behind her. "Go find somewhere else to sit." Her gaze flicked up and down, and a look of disgust captured her features.

The guy stood up and crossed his arms, putting his full attention on Mandy. "No, what's going to happen is you all will vacate the seats and leave. Or at least the little boys will. I bet we could have tons of fun with you girlies." My body shuddered. I did not want to have any type of fun with these men.

"No," Tyler said.

The guy leaned over me toward Tyler. I tried to shrink back as best I could. “Do you not understand the words that are coming out of my mouth?”

“I’m very well aw—”

“Then you will get your asses out of our seats now,” he boomed. He slipped a knife out of his pocket and started picking at his nails with it.

My body stilled. The man was playing with the knife too close to my face. One little slip and I could get hit. “We’ll leave,” I said. I wanted to scoot farther away from but I stayed perfectly still.

The guy turned his face toward mine and smiled sadistically. “I’m glad to see you have a thinker on your hands.” He put his free hand on my face, causing me to flinch, and ran his thumb over my cheek. “Pretty little thing, maybe you could stay and keep me and my buddies some company.”

I wanted to hurl his hand away, but I didn't. “No, thank you.”

“That’s a bummer,” he said, licking his lips.

Bile rose in my throat. I fisted my hands until I could feel the nails bite smartly into my skin. “If you can just put the knife away, we'll leave.”

“We're not leaving,” Tyler gritted out. I wanted to smack him; I didn’t want to be this man’s play toy or pincushion.

The man looked over at Tyler. "Boy, you must have a death wish."

"Maybe you should have gotten here sooner, so you could have gotten the table first. We. Are. Not. Leaving." Tyler enunciated the last four words slowly. He sat back in his chair and smiled at the guy.

The man looked at me, winked, and then punched Tyler in the face. I could hear the crunch, like someone stepping on glass, as Tyler's nose broke. Tyler and the chair fell backward from the weight of the punch. George stood and ran over to Tyler, but one of the man's buddies grabbed on to him, and the two of them went down. Mandy and Sarah threw their drinks, with the glasses, at the man who was holding on to George. Tyler got up, holding his nose, blood pouring down. I could feel the blood leave my face. I was never able to be around other people's blood. More blood gushed out as Tyler took his hand away, and I gagged at the sight of it. I had to look away, but I couldn't. He wiped his hands on his pants before he threw a punch at the guy. I moved my head just in time to avoid being hit by Tyler. The man leaped over me and into Tyler, tackling him to the floor. George was now fighting with the man on the floor while Mandy and Sarah were both in headlocks by a different guy. They were scratching at his arms, but it was no use. The guy wasn't budging. It would have been very comical if it had been a different situation and I hadn't been involved.

I slowly made my way off the seat at the same time Tyler pushed the man into me. We both fell, the man landing on top of me, knocking the wind out of me and my forehead smacked into the ground, stars bursting into my vision. The man was so heavy I could barely breathe. He was still on my back when Tyler came up and started punching him. I could feel the man returning Tyler's punches because his elbows kept jamming into my back. I tried to cough to get some air into my lungs, but it didn't work. The man's head slammed into my back, and I screamed. It felt like someone had just hit me with a large hammer. Tears sprang in my eyes, threatening to fall.

My hands clawed the cold concrete floor, trying to grip and move myself from under them, but I couldn't budge. Tears blurred my vision as I reached out to grab the leg of the chair next to me, hoping I could topple it on top of the guys, but my fingers only grazed it. I tried again to move with everything I had, but nothing. Darkness was starting to cloud my vision. This whole not being able to breathe thing was becoming a problem. One minute, darkness was coming closer, and the next, the weight was off of my back and I was being lifted into the air. My eyes connected with Gregory's, his eyes burning with anger while mine were burning with tears. He gently put me down on shaky legs, away from the fight.

"Thanks," I whispered.

Gregory nodded his head and went back over to the fight. A couple of other guys helped Gregory break apart the fight. Gregory pointed to Tyler. "Get your friends and leave." Tyler just nodded. "And don't ever come back,"

Gregory said. He shoved Tyler toward the door. George, Mandy, and Sarah followed Gregory and Tyler.

I started to follow when a soft hand pulled on my arm. Looking over my shoulder, the old man—who had served us—was holding a handkerchief out toward me. "Here you go, dear. You have blood down the side of your neck."

"Thank you," I said. I took the handkerchief and walked out of the bar, catching up with the others. As I tried to clean up the blood, I couldn't tell if I had a wound or if it was one of the guys' blood. Nobody talked as Gregory led us up the street. Tyler was holding his nose, George was holding his arm, and Mandy and Sarah had their arms entwined, whimpering. It took me a few minutes to realize that Gregory was taking us straight to the gatehouse. I shivered, knowing I would have to face my parents. Looking down, I watched my feet as we walked; I didn't want to go home, but I also didn't want to go back where we came from.

"This is where I leave you," Gregory said. I looked up to see the gatehouse just a few feet up ahead. The others walked up to the gatehouse, but I stayed where I was. Gregory walked toward me and stopped and lowered his voice, "if you were smart, you wouldn't want to be friends with them. Especially the guy you kissed. He started that fight. He might not have thrown the first punch, but he egged them on. He put you in harm's way because of that. Think about that the next time he wants you to do something stupid." I looked up, but he was already walking away. Taking a deep breath, I made my over to the gatehouse. The soldiers were already asking everyone for their passes, and since none of us had them, we told them who are parents were and watched as they called each of them up. We waited in silence for half an hour. Tyler looked like he couldn't care less, and Mandy was still whimpering, saying something about her neck hurting. Sarah cried silently. George looked as scared as I was. Was he going home to a monster? Finally, the door flung open, revealing my father—every inch of his face etched in anger.

"Let's go, young lady." My father grabbed my arm and dragged me out the door. As we got to the car—the only car that was used outside of the army—my father all but threw me in the backseat and then followed. The car ride to the house was a very long and tense five minutes. Before the car was even stopped, my father opened the door, grabbed my arm, and pulled us both out. He rushed us up the steps, and when he opened the front door, he threw me in. I hurled onto the tile floor, smacking my jaw, pain radiating up my face. That didn't slow me down, though. My hands shot out to help slow the momentum, but I twisted and they slipped, causing me to face plant onto the floor.

"How dare you do this to me," my father yelled as he kicked me in my stomach. I cried out as his foot hit my ribs, hearing a deafening crack. "My own daughter sneaking out." He grabbed my hair and pulled me up, slapped me hard across the face with a closed hand, the sting spreading through my cheek, and sent me into the hallway table. The table and I both landed hard onto the ground. My face stung, and I was doing all I could to not let the tears fall in front of him. It would be that much worse if they did. "You make me sick," he seethed in my face. Standing back up, he kicked me one last time in the gut before walking away.

I wheezed. I couldn't breathe. I tried sucking in air, but sharp pains shot up my abdomen and chest. After what felt like hours, I slowly got myself into a sitting position. I was finally able to take a few more breaths while I tried to ignore the pain. A gentle, familiar hand softly took my arm. I looked up into Agathy's soft blue eyes. I tried to smile but failed. She helped me up off the floor. "It'll be okay." Looking down at the table, I started to bend down to pick it up, but Agathy stopped me. "Let me get it. You just go upstairs, take a hot shower, and go to bed." I nodded my head and gave her a small, appreciative smile.

I kept one hand on my ribs and the other on the wall as I walked up the stairs. Every time I moved, it felt like I was being stabbed over and over again in my stomach. As I reached the top of the stairs, my mother stood in her doorway with a drink in her hand. "You are such a stupid little girl." With that, she turned around and headed back into her bedroom. I slowly walked to my room and shut the door behind me. As I crawled into bed, I covered my whole body with the comforter and let the tears fall. I cried myself to sleep.

CHAPTER SIX

Light shined brightly as I woke with puffy and swollen eyes; my abdomen screamed at me as I sat slowly up in bed. I tried taking a deep breath, but my ribs cried out in protest, causing me to yelp; I wasn't sure if one or more of my ribs were broken or if they were just badly bruised. Squeezing my eyes tightly shut, I slowly made my way off the bed; pain zipped through my body. My feet hit the soft fabric of the carpet and my eyes slowly opened. I pushed myself gently off the bed and headed toward the bathroom. Since my bedroom was still semi-dark, I had to place my hand on the wall and let it guide me. My hand curled around the handle of the door and I opened it and massaged the wall until my fingers hit the light switch. As the lights blared on, I pressed my eyes closed. One at a time, I slowly opened each eye, squinting into the brightness.

When the light spots danced out of my eyes, I took in my appearance. My hair was a mess, sticking out in every which way. A large bruise covered my right cheekbone, with a thin cut playing peek-a-boo through the storm-blue color. My fingers gently skimmed over the bruise. Flinching back, I lowered my hand. I tried to smile, but the pain from the bruise brought my lips into a grimace. Even glaring at myself caused me to cringe in pain.

Slowly, I grabbed the end of my shirt and tugged it up and over my head. I gasped as I took in the picture of my body—I knew it would look bad, but not this bad. A large black and blue bruise covered my left side, and another bruise covered my lower stomach on my right side. I couldn't tell if they were all from my father or if I had gotten some of the bruises in the bar last night. Slowly, my fingertips trailed down my left side, sucking in a breath and doing the same on my right. Dropping my pants, I examined my legs—only a few sparse bruises, nothing major. I went over to the shower and turned on the water, then walked back over to the mirror and just stared at myself until my face disappeared in the steam. Finally—making my way over to the shower—I got in and winced as the showerhead pelted bullets of water on my bruised body.

After my body had turned bright pink, I dragged myself out of the shower and into clothes. Setting my hair up into a high, messy bun, I made my way downstairs; it took me a couple of sets to get used to the pain, but I tried ignoring it as best I could.

As I reached the bottom of the stairs, I could smell bread baking in the kitchen. Following my nose, I walked toward the kitchen, ignoring the empty space where the table used to be but was now broken. Charlie's voice bounced through the air as he yelled at the staff on the other side of the door. Quietly, I slipped through the door and stopped in my tracks and stared in stunned silence at the kitchen table. It was layered with food, all different types of fruits: ranging from strawberries to tomatoes, every type of bread you could think of, and tender meats ranging from pork to turkey. I could only stare at the masterpiece. Maybe I had died and gone to heaven. There had never been that much food before; I'd never eaten so many different foods. The staff was busy running around, carrying plates to different rooms and then grabbing other glassware.

"Mia," Agathy said.

I looked over at her. She was standing by the closed basement door. "Hey."

She looked me up and down, frowning. "Let's get you changed."

I looked down at my clothes. I was wearing black yoga pants and a white tank top. It was Sunday; I always dressed like this on Sundays. "Why?"

Agathy hurried past me, gently grabbing my arm on her way, and led me back upstairs, leaving my stomach growling downstairs. When we got to the room, Agathy shut the door and locked it. She rushed past me and into the closet while I stayed in my spot, staring quizzically at her back. She grabbed a black duffel bag and threw it on the bed, followed by a couple pairs of my black pants, black t-shirts, black socks, and (thankfully, something other than black) underwear and bras. She rushed out of the closet, holding on to my black boots, and set them next to the duffel bag on the bed. Why she would put dirty shoes on the bed, I didn't know. Why she was throwing every black thing I owned into the duffel bag, I didn't know. Maybe she'd lost her marbles? She went back into the closet; I could hear hangers swinging into each other.

"Umm, Agathy?" I asked. I didn't move from my spot, just in case I had to run out of there.

"Yes, my dear?" she said. Walking out of the closet, she had another duffel bag and backpack along with my black wool coat and more clothes.

"What are you doing?" Was I being kicked out? Was she kidnapping me? Was it a bad thing that I hoped she was kidnapping me?

"Don't worry about me, dear." She threw clothes at me, I ducked, and the clothes littered to the floor. "Just change into those clothes. I should have everything finished soon."

"I don't understand," I said looking at the clothes she'd thrown at me. A pair of black pants, and a long-sleeved, silky black shirt.

"Just go change," she said. "I'll explain everything when the time is right." With that, she went back into my closet and began rummaging around in there. I looked back at the clothes and sighed. Picking up the pieces—wincing as I bent over—I made my way to the bathroom to get dressed.

Agathy worked fast. I mean really fast. I was only in the bathroom for a few minutes, and when I came out, both duffel bags were full and sealed up, the same with the backpack. She rushed past me into the bathroom and shut the door behind her. I kept my gaze on the closed bathroom door. What the hell was she doing? When the door opened, Agathy stepped out with another bag, and I could see my bathroom supplies in it. She went over and slipped it into one of the duffel bags.

"Am I going on a trip?" That I didn't know about?

Agathy just ignored me and went for my purse. Dumping everything out of the bag: my wallet, a book, and a bunch of candy wrappers, she replaced it with only my wallet and book. As she opened up my nightstand, she took out a few books and slipped them in along with my wallet. With my purse in her hand, she rushed into my closet; I just stared stupidly at the wrappers on the bed. My stomach growled angrily. Agathy came back out and set my purse down next to the bags. When she finally looked at me, she had a kind smile formed on her lips, but her eyes were calculating.

"What's going on?" I asked. I didn't know how I was supposed to react to her bizarre behavior.

"I need you to do me a favor," she said. "You need to go to the school and get your hidden box."

My jaw dropped. "But the school is closed." And possibly locked.

She nodded her head and walked over to me, handing me a key. "This will unlock the back entrance to the school. Go and get the box and come straight back."

I didn't understand why she was acting this way. "Why? What's going on?"

"I'll tell you as soon as you get back, I promise. But right now you need to go and get it. We need to be prepared before nightfall."

"What's happening at nightfall?"

"Just go. Use the back door to sneak out. I will make sure no one knows you're gone. But hurry, and do not stop for anything or anyone. Here." She handed me my wool jacket, gloves, and a hat. "Wear these. It's cold out. But like I said, do not stop for anyone. Go straight there and come straight back."

I hesitantly slipped my jacket on, Agathy helping—and by helping I mean shoving it onto my arms—along with the hat and gloves. She all but threw me out of the bedroom, and I had to run down the stairs to keep up with her. As she opened up the back door, cold wind blasting in our faces, she shoved me out before shutting the door behind me. Debating whether I should just go back into the house and ignore her request (or was it a demand?) or do what she told me to do, I sighed and walked toward the alleyway. I opened up the metal door and shut it behind me, looking at the house for a long minute. With my hands in my pocket and my eyes on the ground, I walked down the alley.

It took me an extra five minutes then it usually would for me to get to school. I decided to stick to the alley, going out of my way to stay hidden; I kept my head down the entire time, that way if someone noticed me they wouldn't exactly be sure it was me. When I arrived at the school, I ducked and tried to be as inconspicuous as possible. It wasn't until I was safely in the school that I brought my head up. It took me ten insufferable minutes to get the damn locker to open, and when it finally did, I wanted to cry out in relief. I moved everything out of the bottom shelf and slid my hand all the way to the back until I felt the small box. I jammed the wooden box into my coat pocket and shut my locker door. As I turned to leave, I slammed into a wall of chest and bounced back. Hands gripped my upper arms to keep me from falling backward. I looked up and my eyes collided with his green ones.

"What are you doing here?" I whispered. I looked around and let out a sigh of relief. No one else seemed to be lurking with us. As I looked back up at him, I recoiled. His eyes burned with anger and he clenched his teeth.

"What the hell happened to your face?" I could feel his anger vibrate off his body, and it seemed to soak into mine, causing me to get angry. It wasn't until I tried to narrow my eyes at him that I winced. I forgot my face looked like I'd just come from batting practice.

"I fell?" It came out more like a question than an answer.

"Are you asking me or yourself that question?" he said.

I rolled my eyes at him (which hurt) and pulled out of his grip. "What are you doing here?"

"Don't change the subject," he said. He closed his hands into fists.

"You don't change the subject. I asked you first." Very mature, I know.

"I watched you sneak in here and wanted to see what you were up to," he said. I looked at him in surprise. I really didn't think he was going to tell me. "Now, tell me what happened to your face."

"Umm, yeah, no," I said, walking past him. It would completely humiliate me to tell him my father did it. Good thing he couldn't see under my shirt.

Gregory walked up next to me, grabbing my arm to stop me. "You did not look like that when I left you. Was it that guy you were with last night? Did he do something to you after I left?"

Guy? What guy? "Wha—" Oh, Tyler. "Listen, you don't have to worry about my now colorful face. I'm fine." It looked like Gregory wanted to snap my body in two. It would suck, but if he used his hands, I wouldn't be too upset about it. He had nice hands. I looked at them, and I could feel a burn crawling up my face. "Well, I have to go," I said. His hands. I really had to think about his hands? He doesn't like me. He told me point blank last night that no one wanted to be my friend. Why would I care what his hands were like? I shook my head.

"Where?" he asked. I didn't look up. I could still feel the burn on my face, and I knew my face was playing "match the color" with a strawberry.

"Home." I looked down at my shoes. When did I put shoes on? I remembered putting the coat and hat on, but the shoes?

"Hey," he said. He grabbed a hold of my arm and stopped me. He tipped my chin up with his finger until our eyes connected. "Are you okay?"

"I don't remember putting shoes on," I blurted out, and I instantly wanted to punch myself in the face.

He raised an eyebrow. "What?"

"Nothing," I said. "Listen, I have to go home. I need to get back before anyone notices I'm gone."

Confusion lit up his feature. "Why?"

"Umm." *Should I say something or just stay quiet?* "I'm not really sure. Agathy told me to get something from the locker and then come straight back home. She wouldn't tell me why." I rushed out.

"Who's Agathy?"

"My maid," I said. "She's kind of acting bizarre."

"What do you mean?"

"Well, she seems panicked. It's hard to explain. And—" I stopped. I couldn't tell him what I thought she was doing. I knew I shouldn't be telling him anything. He might have saved my life last night, but he was still the world's biggest ass.

"And?" he prompted.

"And nothing. Listen, I have to get back." I walked outside and waited until Gregory was out before I locked up the school.

I looked up at Gregory. His head was tilted up, looking at the gray snow clouds in the sky. "Welp, I better be going," I said after a few minutes of watching him watch the sky.

Gregory looked at me, and I shivered at the intensity of his stare. "I want to know who did that to your face."

I smiled. "Don't worry about it. You do you, and I'll do me." He frowned at me, but I ignored it and continued toward my house.

"Princess." My spine tightened at that name. "About last night."

I turned around to face him and waved him off. "Listen, don't worry about it. It has all been forgotten. Why don't you go on home to your friends, and I'll go… Oh, shoot, I don't have any friends, so maybe I'll just hang out by myself."

"You're acting like a child," he said through clenched teeth.

As I shrugged my shoulders, he glared but I ignored it as I turned around and raced home. My heart hurt every time I thought of the *You don't have friends because no one wants to be friends with you* line. My face hurt, my body ached, and a headache was starting at my temples. I needed to go back to bed. Well, maybe food first. And then bed.

CHAPTER SEVEN

As I gripped the door handle of the back door, I turned it as quietly and slowly as I could. I didn't know how Agathy was going to cover for me, but the least I could do was come back stealthily. Warm air pushed against my face as I crept inside the house, and I quietly shut and locked the door behind me. No one was around. I wanted to run up the stairs, but I knew it would be better if I went up as quietly as possible, so I took one step at a time. My heart pounded in my ears, beating faster than my legs could run. I cringed when each step I took created a loud squeak in the stairs; I didn't think I'd ever heard the stairs creak before. I looked down at the steps and glared, and then looked up; I had five steps to go. Chewing on my lip, I contemplated my plan: running the last bit of the stairs would probably make too much noise but might just be for the best. I took a deep breath and ran, and didn't let it out until I was safely in my room with my door shut firmly behind me. My bed was empty: the duffel bags, my purse, and my boots were gone. *Hmm.* Either Agathy needed me out of the house so she could steal my stuff, or I imagined the entire scene this morning and was now going completely nuts.

"Mia." I jumped and stifled a scream as Agathy came out of my bathroom. I was pretty sure if she were any sneakier, I might have had to change my pants.

"You scared me," I accused, my hand planted on my chest. My heart thumped hard against it.

Agathy gave me a small smile. "Did you get it?"

I pulled out the box and handed it over to her. I watched as she took the roll of money out of the box and went over to the side of my bed. She bent down, and when she stood back up, she was holding my purse. As she opened it, she pulled my wallet out and slid the money into it; she placed the wallet back and closed the purse, setting it on the bed. "Good, good."

I peered at her. "I still don't understand what's going on." Placing my hands on my hips, I tried to stare her down; I wanted answers.

"I have everything packed and ready for you to go," she said as she smoothed down my already smooth comforter.

"Where am I going?" I said slowly, making sure even a deaf person could understand the words.

"Somewhere safe," she said. "Things are getting out of hand, and people are getting angry. They're coming, and they won't stop until everyone is dead."

"I'm sorry, what?" What was she talking about? Who were coming? Who did they want dead? Was it the rebels? Did she know about them?

She waved her hand in front of her. "You won't understand. You're still too young to understand."

"Hey! I'm seventeen. I'll be eighteen in just a few months. I'm pretty sure I can comprehend anything you have to say to me."

Agathy sighed and started pacing back and forth. "People are angry with your father. Some are changing sides. There are people who are talking about getting rid of everyone who comes from the council, starting with Lorburn's Leader and family. They want a new ruler. And the man who started this all is such a cruel person. He will turn Lorburn upside down if he gets to rule. We'd be living in terror. No one would be safe. It's important to get you out of here before they arrive. Otherwise, you'll end up dead."

I stared at her. Silence sliced through the room. Maybe I couldn't comprehend anything she was saying. Could I go back and say I didn't want to hear any of it? "Why kill me?" It had to be the rebels.

Agathy gave me a sad smile. "Because once your father's dead, you're to rule Lorburn."

"And this man who wants to rule would have to kill me first?" Maybe getting me out of here was a good thing. "I can't leave my family behind."

Agathy scowled. "Mia, I have always felt like you were a daughter to me. I watched you grow up into the beautiful woman you are today. And I have had to watch your parents beat you one too many times. You need to think of yourself if you want to survive."

"Bu—" My bedroom door opened.

My father walked in. He looked me up and down and glowered. "Where are you going?"

I shut my dropped jaw, which had popped open when he'd walked through the door, and looked down. My coat, hat, and gloves were still on. "I was just going to sit out back for a little while. Play in the snow."

My father's jaw tightened. "Aren't you too old for that?"

"I will get her out of the coat, sir," Agathy said. She helped take off my coat, and I slid my hat and gloves off. Thankfully, I'd been in the house long enough for my fingers, ears, and nose to warm up so they no longer looked red. Well, at least I hoped they didn't look red.

"I want you downstairs. We have company." With that, my father gave me one last glare and left. Agathy had set my coat, hat, and gloves down onto the bed.

"Come on, come on. Let's get you downstairs." Agathy pulled me through my bedroom door and lead me downstairs.

"When am I supposed to leave?" I asked. I didn't see how it was possible for me to leave the house without anyone noticing.

"Shh," she said. "We'll talk about the rest later."

She led me into my father's office. There were at least twenty people in the room. Not only were my parents here, but so were Tyler, George, Mandy, Sarah, and their families, plus others I'd seen around before. Members of the council were there too. My father stood in front of his large mahogany desk, my mother standing next to him. Everyone else sat across from them, looking up at them. Only a few people, including Tyler, had turned when we'd walked in the door. I avoided eye contact with Tyler, I knew what my face looked like, and I didn't want to see his reaction. Agathy gripped my arm, and we both went to the last chair in the back. Giving me one last squeeze, Agathy left and closed the door behind her. When I looked up at my father, he did not look like a very happy person at the moment. Then again, he rarely ever looked like a very happy person. He caught my eye and glared before moving his attention and rearranging his facial features when he faced everyone else. His face was devoid of emotion.

"I have a few announcements." His eyes raked across the room. "They will affect everyone in this room."

Everyone in the room exchanged nervous glances; this sort of thing had never happened before. If there was an announcement, my father would just send out letters, never personally invite people to his home. Tyler caught my eye, and I could see his eyes graze over me, shock flashing in them. Casting my eyes away, I lowered my head and watched my hands as they fiddled with my shirt; I could feel the burn of humiliation creep up my face.

"The first announcement," my father said. "There is a war coming."

Everyone gasped at the word war. We hadn't had a war in centuries. Wars were not well known. We learned about the long-ago wars in school, but we had never experienced any in our own lifetimes. Since then, things had changed, leadership had changed, rules had changed.

"What kind of war?" a deep voice asked.

"Someone who hates the way we run Lorburn has started his own army," my father spit out. "People who hate us have decided to join his army to fight against us. We have soldiers everywhere, but it seems that these rebels have more."

"Who is the leader?" another voice asked. I looked over to the man next to me, where the voice came from. He looked familiar; he had short blond hair and sea-blue eyes and looked only a few years older than me. I knew I'd seen him before, but I couldn't put my finger on where.

"Kieran Roderick," my father said.

"That can't be," one of the ladies said, others agreeing with her.

I looked up at my father. He looked grim. They all knew this man. But how? How could they know the leader of this new army?

"How can you be sure it's Kieran?" the man sitting next to me asked.

"We have Intel that has pointed to Kieran," my father said. "Which now brings me to the next announcement. Obviously Kieran will want to break Lorburn apart and become its next Leader, which is why it is important to have my successor begin learning how to lead."

My head perked up at that. I was the one who would inherit Lorburn when my father passed away. My father's face was carefully blank as I gazed up at him. His eyes moved around the room and locked on a pair in the front row: Tyler's. Looking back and forth between my father and Tyler, I put two and two together; blood drained from my face. *But haven't you always liked Tyler?*

"My daughter Mia will be marrying Tyler Slattery. I have already talked to his family, and they all agree this will be the best for Lorburn," my father continued, but I didn't hear anything other than white noise. I should have been happy that he would pick Tyler, someone who I'd had a crush on for a very long time. If he had announced this yesterday, I would have been ecstatic. But I wasn't happy. Maybe it was the fact that Tyler would rule Lorburn that made me unhappy. Or maybe it was the fact that my father gave me no warning before the meeting. Or maybe it was because I didn't get to pick the person I would marry. But the only words that repeated in my head were *He put you in harm's way.* As much as I liked Tyler, I couldn't help but remember that Gregory was right: Tyler picked a fight with someone so much bigger than him, and I ended up getting in the way. Would he do the same thing if we were married? Would he put himself above me and always protect himself?

I could hear people talking, but I couldn't pinpoint actual words. I liked Tyler, but I couldn't help but be worried about my future with him. Maybe we could grow to love each other. *Maybe we can't.* I felt a soft tap on my shoulder. I looked over, my eyes connecting to my neighbor's.

"Are you okay?" he whispered.

"How do I know you?" I should have answered him, but there was something so familiar about him. I knew him.

He smirked. "We met a few years ago. You were only thirteen or fourteen at the time, but you loved my scarf."

I narrowed my eyes, trying to remember a scarf. I shook my head. Nothing popped up about a scarf. "I'm sorry, I don't remember."

Disappointment flashed in his eyes for only a second, but then his smirk grew. "That's okay. I'm Alex."

The name didn't ring a bell. "Nice to meet you."

"So, are you okay?"

I bit my lip and looked down at my lap. Was I okay? I wasn't sure. I looked back up at him to find him studying me. I nodded my head. "Yeah."

"Okay," he said. He gave me one last glance, his gaze lingering on my bruised cheek, and then turned his attention up front. I turned forward, my eyes roaming the room until they connected to a very disgruntled pair of eyes: Mandy. She looked like she was ready to chop me up and feed me to the poor. I glanced away. She would definitely hate me forever, but I honestly didn't care.

If there was an attack coming, like Agathy seemed to think there was, how could Tyler and I get married? I didn't turn eighteen for a few more months. Because of the law, I couldn't marry until I was at least eighteen. You usually have to wait until twenty, but under certain circumstances, it could be moved to eighteen. So was Agathy just really worried for something that might happen years from now? But if that was the case, why was she packing my stuff now?

"Mia?" Tyler's voice broke through my thoughts. I looked up, some people started to leave while others chatted with each other.

"Hey," I said. I didn't know what else to say. Was he angry that we were matched together? Was he disappointed that he got me instead of Mandy?

"Can we go talk somewhere private?"

I looked over his shoulder to find my father watching us, a smug smile on his face. "Why don't we go into the library? No one really goes in there."

Tyler smiled. "That sounds great."

I got up from my chair and exited the room without saying a word to my father. As I shut the door to the library, I took a deep breath and let it out. Turning from the door, I watched as Tyler walked from bookshelf to bookshelf, admiring the books.

"Your family has a lot of books," he commented while he picked one up at random.

The last time I was in here was with Aileen, she had been looking for something, and I wondered if she had really hidden something in her long ago. "They're really not my type," I said.

"What kind do you like?" Tyler put the book down and sat in one of the deep brown leather armchairs while I stayed standing next to the door.

"The older kinds, from a different time period," I said. "The ones about mysteries, fantasies, and romances."

"Typical girl," he said, smiling.

I narrowed my eyes at him. "How do you figure?"

"All girls are into romances," he said, crossing his arms.

"But I also like fantasies and mysteries. You know the books about solving murders or the books about fairies."

He crinkled his brow. "Fairies? Murders?"

"Have you never been to the city's library?"

He laughed a nice, soft laugh. "No, I haven't."

I wasn't sure I understood what was funny about that. "Okay then."

"Okay what?"

"Until you read one of those books, you can't say I'm a typical girl." I chewed on my lip.

He raised his hands in front of him. "Okay, okay." His eyes raked over my face, his smile dropping. "I'm sorry about last night."

I looked away from him and sat down against the door. "It's not your fault."

"Yes it is," he said. "If I hadn't pushed you into going, you would have never gotten hurt at that bar."

"What?"

He brought his hand up and motioned toward my face. "I didn't realize you were hit until I saw your face tonight. I'm sorry."

I wanted to argue and tell him that it was my father, but what would have been the point? He probably wouldn't have believed me. Plus, it was nice that he apologized. "It's fine."

"All of them are bunch of criminals." He crossed his arms.

"Who?"

"The poor. They're all criminals, and I think they should all be punished to show an example."

"They are not all criminals. There are some bad people there just like there are some bad people here."

"Were you not in the room?" He pointed toward the door. "They have created an army to try and take over. How can that not be wrong?"

"I didn't say it was right. All I said was that there are still some good people out there."

"Like who?"

"Well, I—"

My words were cut off by a loud crash followed by screaming. I looked at Tyler, who had a look of panic slapped across his face. I stood up, creaked open the door, and peered out around it. Smoke was coming from down the hall, as people were running by and screaming. It wasn't until I heard the guns go off that it dawned on me that this was what Agathy had been afraid of. Shutting the door, I turned around and faced a petrified looking Tyler.

"Something's wrong," I said. I had to clear my throat a couple of times. "I think we need to find a place to hide in here."

"NO!" he said. "We need to get out of here."

"And go where? Out there where we can hear screaming and gunfire? I don't think so." I needed to find Agathy.

When I stepped closer toward Tyler, a loud blast went off behind me and I flew forward; my head slammed into the floor, my vision darkening out. Plaster from the wall behind me came fluttering down on top of me. My ears were ringing and I couldn't hear anything but the ringing. My body ached, and I desperately wanted to get up and move, but something pinned my legs down. I coughed a couple of times to get the dust out of my mouth while my vision started to clear, but dark stars still floated about.

"Mia?" I heard Tyler yell out. I could hear him coughing. I tried to turn my head toward him, but something was on top of me.

"Help," I coughed out. My ears were still ringing, but I was slowly starting to hear more and more: people were screaming and guns were going off. I tried to move, but my body wouldn't budge. I wanted to scream out, but I didn't want to get the wrong person.

"Oh my God," I heard someone say. "Are you alright?"

"I'm fine," Tyler said, "but I don't think she is." Must have been talking about me. *How nice of him.*

I felt a hand on my forehead. "Mia?"

"Agathy?" I could cry but decided against it. "I'm stuck."

"Hold on, I'll get it off of you."

"What's on me?"

"A bookcase," she said.

Of course a bookcase would fall on me. It wasn't like my body had enough bruises on it to begin with.

"Charlie, help me," I heard Agathy yell. As the bookcase slowly made its way off of me, pain I hadn't felt before began to swim throughout my body. When my legs were cleared, I slowly stood up, the black stars officially gone. I turned toward Tyler and my jaw dropped; he was still sitting in the damn chair with nothing on him. He could have helped me. *The bastard.*

"We need to go," Agathy said. I looked toward her. She looked pale and frightened. I looked over her shoulder to Charlie, who mirrored Agathy. I nodded my head and followed them out the door.

"Hey! Where are you going?" I heard Tyler yell from the other room.

"Get somewhere safe," Charlie yelled back to Tyler, not slowing down his stride.

I tried to keep up with Agathy and Charlie. I wanted to yell at them to slow down, but I knew I couldn't. Every move I made caused me to wince in pain and by the time we were in the basement under the kitchen, I had bitten roughly into my lip to keep myself from yelling out; I could taste the metallic liquid of my blood dripping into my mouth. Agathy and Charlie were moving a large mahogany cupboard by the time I made it up to them.

"What are you guys doing?" I could hear the panic in my voice. Now wasn't the time to start rearranging furniture.

"There is a secret passageway," Agathy said. I looked at them dumbfounded, waiting for her to explain more, but she didn't. I could hear people screaming and boots stomping above us. I started to squeeze my fist in and out. We needed to hide. After a few more frustrating minutes,

Charlie and Agathy had the cupboard completely removed. A door was now in view, and Agathy opened it and peeked through.

She stuck her head back out. "Mia, I want you to follow this passage. Here's a flashlight." She shoved a small metal flashlight into my hand. "You won't have any other light than that. When you get to the very end, put your hood up and go to the Mounting Lion. It's an inn about two blocks from the exit of the tunnel. You will take a left from the tunnel and keep straight. Don't talk to anyone until you get to the inn. When you get there, ask for Alithea. She will help you from there."

"Aren't you coming with me?" I asked, my body starting to shake.

"No, I can't."

"Why not?" I didn't want to leave her behind.

"I have to keep them from getting you." She walked over to one of the darkened corners and went behind a large wooden box. When she came back around, she had my duffel bags, backpack, jacket, and purse. She walked over, handed me my jacket—which I put on—helped me put my backpack on, set the duffel bags on both of my shoulders, then finally slid my purse on. Agathy walked me to the entrance of the door and practically shoved me through. "Be safe." Our eyes locked as she shut the door, the light going with it. I could hear the cupboard being shoved back into place.

I turned on my flashlight and turned around. It smelled like rusted metal in here. I started walking forward, trying to keep the flashlight in front of me. My hand shook so bad it caused the light to bounce around. I was terrified. All I could think about was putting one foot in front of the other and moving forward. There would be time later to think about what might have happened to my parents.

CHAPTER EIGHT

I wasn't sure how long I had been walking down here. I couldn't hear any noises from up above, so I wasn't sure if there was still a fight going on. As I walked, I tried to keep my mind from thinking about what might have happened to my parents and all those people in the house, and if Tyler had found a safe place to hide. Putting one foot in front of the other, I also didn't want to think of whether my parents had gotten out alive or if they'd been unlucky. Watching the light bounce off the walls, I couldn't help think of my current predicament: I didn't know what would happen next and I didn't know who Alithea was or how she was going to help me.

My feet shuffled across the dirt and grime on the floor; I was getting tired, and it didn't help that the duffel bags were heavy. My shoulders and neck started to hurt from the strain, my legs begged me to stop walking, but I had to keep moving forward.

It was so dark in here that I had fallen five or six times. My feet kept hitting raised stones and I didn't have enough time to catch myself. The last time I fell, I banged up my left knee and it throbbed every time I walked. I just wanted to sit down and drink something, but I didn't have anything to eat or drink. I considered stopping and going through the bags, but I figured once I stopped I'd have a hard time starting up again. Plus I figured everything in the bags were clothes; I mean, I did watch her pack them this morning.

My eyelids were getting heavy, and I was just about tempted to drop my body to the ground and sleep when a light appeared ahead of me: a small, circular light. *Please, please, please let that be the exit.* I pushed myself to keep moving, and it took me fifteen more minutes before I came to the source of the light. Light drizzled down from a metal gate above me; a ladder was attached to the wall and led up to the grate. I guessed I had to climb it. *Great.* I heaved myself up the ladder and pushed at the grate, my arms protesting. I looped one of my legs around one of the rings of the ladder so I wouldn't fall, but the grate wouldn't budge. I tried to keep the panic down that was starting to rise in my chest and moved up to the closest step and straddled it. I lifted my arms up and pushed with all my might. After five minutes of pushing, the grate finally lifted a tiny bit, and I used the rest of my strength to push it all the way over to the side. I grabbed on to the ladder and just stood there for a few minutes, catching my breath. Fresh air blew its way down and caressed my face, motivating me to move. Unhooking my leg, I grabbed the next ring, something sticky coating my hand and squirmed my way up the rest of the ladder. Snow covered the ground, so by the time I dragged my body out of the hole I was drenched. It was starting to get dark out, the sun starting to fall; I'd been down there longer than I thought. I picked myself up off the ground and looked around. I was in an alley.

It took me a few minutes of rest to remember the directions Agathy had given me when I remembered I slipped my hood up and started making my way toward the inn. People were milling about, so I pushed my hands in my pockets and kept my eyes down. A loud bang went off to my left, I jumped and chills danced violently down my spine. Spinning over, I could see smoke billowing around the walls. Screaming filled the air, and I couldn't tell if it was coming from the other side or if it was coming from this side. People started rushing by me, panic visible on their faces.

I picked up my pace along with them; I needed to get to that inn. One second I was walking, and the next a hand grabbed my arm and pulled me up against the wall. The body covered mine, the head bending so close that I could see tiny white flakes in his green eyes.

"Are you still stalking me?" I blurted out.

Gregory narrowed his eyes at me. "No. I just happened to be here and watched you approach."

Right. "I have to go." I nodded my head to the side to indicate my leaving, but he wouldn't move.

"It's not safe for you here," he said.

"It's not safe for me there, either," I said, pointing behind me. "I have to go."

"Where are you going?"

"Why?"

He tightened his grip. "I can help."

I tried getting my arm out of his grasp but failed. "I don't need help."

He laughed a humorless laugh. "Yes, you do. Do you even know where you're going?"

"Yes, she gave me directions."

"Who gave you directions?"

Crap. "Um…no one?"

Gregory rolled his eyes. "Is this what your maid had planned?"

Just as I was about to answer, another loud blast went off right behind us, throwing us to the ground. Gregory positioned himself on top of me to help shield me from the falling debris. I tried to ignore his huge body on me, but my cheeks flamed at the thought of how nice this would feel under different circumstances. *Get it together, Mia. Get it together. You're literally in a life-and-death situation, and all you can think about is how nice it would be to have his body on you?*

"Are you okay?" he whispered in my ear, my body shivered in response.

I had to swallow a few times before I could answer. "Yeah." *I only hurt all over, and your added (gorgeous) weight isn't helping.*

I felt him nod his head, and then he slowly stood up. Just as I was getting up, I was swung into the air and onto my feet. I looked over at Gregory with a raised brow, but he just shrugged. I could have gotten up by myself; I would argue my point when we didn't have to dodge guns and bombs.

"Where are you headed?" He dusted off his pants while he kept a lookout behind us.

"To the Mountain Lion Inn," I said. "Do you know where it is?"

"I'll take you." He grabbed my hand and pulled me in the direction I had been heading in. He moved us fast through the streets. If it weren't for the fact that he had a hold of my hand, I would have lost him. The duffel bags weighed me down, and it didn't help that I'd walked all day in the tunnel. I hadn't eaten or drunk anything, and my energy level had its warning blinker on.

"Can you slow down?"

"Not if we want to be blown up."

"I'm pretty sure they wouldn't bomb over here." I was sure they were just sticking to the other side. You know, a kill-all-the-rich sort of thing.

"I think you're wrong," he said.

"I don't think I am." My breaths came out faster and faster. I started to feel a little dizzy, but we would be at the inn soon. I just had to keep my focus on the end plan and ignore the way the world tilted.

"They've been attacking your side all morning, but around noon they started to come to this side," he said.

I looked around. Everyone still looked the same, except they did look a little anxious. "It doesn't look like it."

He shook his head. "Trust me, they have."

I rolled my eyes there was no point in arguing with him. I just wanted to sleep. My body was protesting. I looked down at my feet to find my white sneakers covered in dirt. I looked back up in time to catch myself from slamming into Gregory's back. My hands pushed against his shoulders to stop my momentum and I could feel his muscles contract at my touch. It was tempting to squeeze his shoulders, but I thought better of it, so I slowly unhinged my hands. "Why did you stop?"

He moved his arm and pointed ahead. The building in front of us was on fire: people were screaming, some were crying, some were looting, while others just stood watching as the flames licked the building.

So he was right; they were attacking both sides. I cleared my throat. "I guess you're right."

He looked over at me. "I know. I'm always right."

I rolled my eyes. "So why did we stop? I need to get to the inn before I pass out." My head started feeling heavy, as blood started to slowly drain from my face. The world around me kept tilting and my knees were starting to buckle.

He looked me over from head to toe and then back again. Concern flashed across his face. I must have looked as bad as I felt. "This is the inn."

"Are you sure it's the right inn?"

"Yes. Why were you coming here?"

"Are you super duper positive this is the right one? You could be wrong." He had to be wrong. How else was I supposed to find this woman?

He narrowed his eyes. "I've lived in this sector all my life. I'm sure I would know exactly which building is which."

I narrowed my eyes at him. "Maybe, maybe not."

He dragged a hand through his hair. He looked like he was ready to yell at me, which caused me to start laughing. I bent over on my knees and laughed; I could feel tears pounce in my eyes from laughing so hard. I wasn't sure what was funny. Maybe I was too tired. Maybe I was dead and this was just a dream. Or maybe I was so scared that the only thing I could do was laugh. When I was done laughing, I stood up, swiped away the tears, and looked at Gregory. He was looking at me like I'd just grown three new heads.

"Did you hit your head?" he asked. I could feel the agitation rolling off of him.

I tried not to laugh. "I think so. Who knows?"

He shook his head. He looked over at the building and then back at me. He did this a couple more times before he made up his mind. “Why were you coming here?”

I wasn't helping myself by keeping my mouth shut. “Agathy told me it was very important for me to get here and get to someone, and that they would keep me safe.” Except now I had no idea what to do. And very little energy to do it.

“Why is it important? I know people are fleeing from your side, but why did your maid have you escape?”

He didn’t know who I was. *He didn’t know who I was because I never gave him a name for him to figure it out. One point to Mia. Zero points to Gregory for being a loser.* For some reason, I assumed everyone knew who I was. But I had been wrong. I looked over at the burning inn. “People were attacking my house, and there were lots of screaming. Agathy said they would come for me.”

“Who would be coming for you?”

“I’m not exactly sure.” I’m sure it was the rebels who were after me, but I wasn’t going to say it out loud. “I was supposed to find someone named Alithea, and she was supposed to help me.”

His hand softly cupped my chin and forced my face to look up into his. “Why would people be coming for you?”

I shrugged my shoulders. “Probably because of my parents.”

He kept his hand on my face. It felt nice. Like hypnotizing nice. "Why?"

I took a deep breath in and then let it out. "I'm Mia Cowan. My parents are Andrew and Melinda Cowan." I could see understanding dawn on his face. "My father is in control of Lorburn and…if something happens to my parents, I end up ruling, so those people would be after me." Gregory just looked at me for a good solid minute. Then he let go of my face, grabbed my hand, and we were off. "Where are we going?"

"We're going to find this Alithea and get you out of here."

"Umm…do you know who she is?" And why was he now so eager to help?

"Nope."

My shoulders slumped. Couldn't one thing go right today? Maybe she would hold up a sign and it would say "Mia, I'm here to rescue you," but I doubted it. That would be too easy. We walked all over the inn area and asked around. I didn't think it was wise to do it, but Gregory didn't care. Blasts were starting to get closer and closer, and Gunfire was everywhere. We finally gave up the search when we saw men coming toward the inn with guns. Gregory led the way down an alley. I kept tripping over my feet, but Gregory helped me keep going. At one point, Gregory had me give him both duffels so I wouldn't be weighed down anymore. I still had my backpack and purse, but it wasn't hard to walk anymore. We took off running at one point when we heard screaming coming from a block away.

After a half hour of running, he took me into a rundown building. Shutting the door, he locked us in and he led the way to the very back and through another door, which he locked behind us. I looked around the small room. A bed sat in the corner, with a lamp next to it, and on the opposite side was a door that led to a bathroom. Clothes were piled on the floor next to the bathroom and papers littered the floor next to the bed, other than that there was nothing else in the room.

"Is this your place?" I asked.

"Yeah," he answered. He walked past me and turned on the lamp, illuminating the room.

"So…umm…what do we do now?" I kept looking at the bed and then to him. My mind kept coming up with fun ideas, but I kept shushing it. Now wasn't the time, and technically I was with Tyler. Unless he was dead, which would be a bummer. *Maybe when I have food and water in me, I'll feel something for what happened to Tyler.*

"We hide out." He went over to the bathroom and turned on the light, brightening up the room more. "There isn't much room, but it's better to be in here than out there."

That I could agree with. "Shouldn't we find Alithea?" I slid my backpack to the floor, along with my purse, and then slipped my jacket off and dropping it on the floor. I looked around the floor and decided it was good enough and sat down. My stomach grumbled in the quiet.

"It's getting dark. We can go in the morning." He sat down on his bed, setting his elbows on his knees and his head in his hands.

"Why are you helping me?"

He looked over at me. "You need help."

I rolled my eyes. "If you get caught helping me, you could, I don't know…die, and it would be my fault. I appreciate your help, but I don't know why you're doing it."

He just shrugged his shoulders. "Would you rather be on your own, trying to save your own life?" I just shrugged my shoulders. "That's what I thought. You have no one else to turn to. I'm the only one you can trust for right now. If people are looking for you, it won't be too long before they put out a reward for anyone who can find you. And around here anyone would jump a chance to get money. I won't do that."

Wow, there was like a whole other side to Gregory. He seemed genuinely nice. "I didn't know you had a nice side."

He scowled. "I don't. Maybe if you stopped getting yourself into trouble, I wouldn't have to keep helping your grouchy ass."

I rolled my eyes. "Yeah, because the bombings and guns are all my fault." He looked ready to say something, but I cut him off. "Listen, I'm starving. Is there any way we can get food?"

He looked like he wanted to say something but just shook his head. He bent over the side of the bed and sat back up. He threw me a paper bag, identical to the one he was holding. I opened it up and smiled: a sandwich, chips, an apple, and a bottle of water were stored in it. Pulling out the sandwich, I took a deep bite and moaned in happiness.

"Where did you get this?"

He looked over me and smiled. "It was in your bag."

I should have been angry that he'd already gone through my bag, but I was too hungry and tired. We ate in silence. We could barely hear the gunfire anymore. We would be safe for the night: I hoped. Gregory finished before me and went into the bathroom, closing the door behind him. I rolled my empty bag into a circle and leaned my head against the wall. Now that I was full, my eyelids seemed extremely heavy. I could hear the door open as Gregory emerged from the bathroom.

"Take the bed," he said.

I looked up at him. "I'm fine right here. It's your place. You should take the bed."

He let out an exaggerated breath. "Take the damn bed, or I'll come over there, throw you over my shoulder, toss you on the bed, and make sure you can't leave it."

"Fine," I gritted out. I liked the second option much better, but I would never tell him that. What happened to me hating him? Then again, he had saved my life twice, so maybe I was okay with not hating him. I stood up from my spot, my body pleading with me to just sit back down and walked over to the bed, where I plopped down. I slipped off my shoes and curled up in the bed. It was comfortable. He'd be lucky to get me out of bed in the morning. I closed my eyes as sleep invaded my brain. "Thank you."

"You're welcome." His voice came from next to me.

I felt the bed dip and him settling in next to me. My eyes snapped open, and I was face-to-face with Gregory. "What are you doing?"

He smiled. "Going to sleep."

"The floor is that way." I pointed behind him.

His smile grew. "I never said I was sleeping on the floor." I made a move to get out, but he stopped me. "Neither one of us will get a good night's sleep if we're on the floor. And I have a feeling tomorrow will be a long day for both of us. So just suck it up. It's not like I haven't slept with anyone before."

I narrowed my eyes at him. "Well, I haven't."

"Just relax and pretend I'm not here."

I turned over to face the wall. "How can I pretend you're not here when your mountain of a body is next to me?"

Gregory laughed a very masculine laugh. A smile started to form on my mouth before I could stop it. *Damn him.* "Stop laughing and go to sleep. I can't sleep if the mountain shakes the bed."

"I bet you would love it if the mountain shook the bed," he whispered in my ear. My eyes bulged out as I heard him laugh more and move away from me. My face burned and turned the color of a tomato. I was no longer sleepy.

I stared at the wall for about an hour before I heard Gregory's breathing even out. I turned over and looked at him. He looked peaceful and younger in his sleep. He was such an odd person. I smiled, thinking of his laugh. He had a nice laugh. I closed my eyes, smelling him in, and drifted off to sleep.

CHAPTER NINE

Slowly opening my eyes, I looked around; there wasn't much to see in the pitch dark. As I tried to sit up, something moved around my waist and pulled me back, my back colliding into something hard. That moved. Trying to hold my panic down, I looked around frantically but it was impossible to see. So I closed my eyes and tried to remember the day before: the attack, the running, Gregory, the inn on fire, Gregory's place. My eyes popped open. The thing moving back and forth against my back was a chest, to be more specific, Gregory's chest. I had two options: one, I could slip out of his embrace—somehow—and make it clear this was very inappropriate under these circumstances, or two, I could pretend to go back to sleep and curl up and absorb his heat.

I froze as I felt him move closer behind me. His warm breath skated across the back of my neck; goose bumps popped up and attacked my body. I knew I should really, really get out of this situation—he had been a jerk most of the time I'd known him—but at the same time, he had saved my life. *How much do you actually know him, though?* I shrugged my shoulders in response to my question and instantly regretted it as his arm pulled me closer. How much closer could I actually get? I didn't want to know. *Liar.* I scowled at myself.

"Why do you keep moving?" Gregory mumbled into my hair, causing more goose bumps to let loose.

"I got ants in my pants."

Gregory laughed. "I could help you get rid of them."

I pushed his arm away and crawled out of his embrace, trying to keep my heart from thumping out of my chest. Did he just really say that? "Only if you want your hand chopped off."

"Aw, you're no fun," he said. I slid out of the bed and hit the wall. Face first. I bounced back, and the backs of my knees hit the bed, which pushed me forward and I tumbled to the floor. I could hear his laughter all the way down here.

"Stop laughing," I grumbled. I crawled on hands and knees until I hit the door to the bathroom. As I slowly stood up, I moved my hand around the wall until I hit the switch. Light illuminated from the bathroom and I had to cover my eyes as the bright light penetrated them. Slowly, I opened one eye at time until I could take the lights. I turned around to see Gregory with an arm across his eyes and smirked. "What time is it? There are no windows. Is it morning? Is it night? When should we go out looking for Alithea? Do you think I'm still in danger?" The questions poured out of me.

"Do you always ask questions this early in the morning?"

"Yes." I asked questions all of the time. Just because it was morning didn't mean I wouldn't ask them. I looked around the small room, grabbed my duffel bag that was sitting next to the wall, and brought it in with me as I closed the door behind me.

"It's six," Gregory yelled from the other side of the door.

"Why did I get up so early?"

"Does it look like I live in your body to give you information about what it does and why?"

I ignored his question and unzipped the bag, pulling out a pair of black pants and shirt. Slipping out of my current pants, I changed them with the new pair and then rolled up the dirty ones. After I took off my shirt, I looked down at my body; my bruises were getting uglier, with a mixture of green in the mix of blue. My fingers trailed across the sore spots, back and forth, and thankfully, they didn't hurt as much as yesterday, but they were still sore. I picked up the new shirt and had just put it over my head when I heard the door open. Hurriedly, I tried getting my shirt back on, but it got stuck on my ponytail I'd had up since last night; My arms were dangling above my head, my hands trying to grab the shirt.

"Need any help?" I could hear the amusement in Gregory's voice.

I scowled. "Nope, I can get it," I should have locked the door. I felt the heat of him before I felt his hands on the shirt, untangling it from my head. He helped me get it over my head and stepped back, his eyes roaming over my body, and his body stiffening as he got to me stomach. Quickly, I covered myself with the shirt as best as I could but I knew it was too late. "If you don't mind, go take a hike."

"Your body has bruises on it," he said.

"Umm…can I say you are still asleep and this is all a dream?"

"The bruises on your body are from the same person who gave you the bruises on your face, aren't they?" His hands clenched into fists at his sides.

What could I say? "It's nothing." I turned around to the sink and turned on the water. Bending down, I searched through the duffel bag until I found a smaller bag; grabbing it I pulled it open and took out my toothbrush and toothpaste. I lathered it up and started brushing, ignoring the lasers hitting my back.

"It isn't nothing," he said. "Why are you protecting this person?"

Because he was still my father. I spit out the toothpaste and rinsed out my mouth and set the items back in my bag and took out a brush. "It would be pointless. He's probably dead." I tried to keep my voice steady. I didn't want to think about my parents and what might have happened to them, so I ignored it as I brushed through my hair and put it back into the ponytail. When I turned around, he was still staring at me with a horrifying expression on his face. Tears suddenly popped into my eyes, but I didn't avert them. "I'm running for my life. I have no idea who is after me. Or, I at least have an idea. I have no idea if I will survive. I have no idea if I can even trust anyone. My parents are most likely dead, and I'm the next target. I have no other family. I don't even know what to do next. Yes, I have bruises covering my body, but as I see it, that doesn't matter at the moment. What matters is whether I can find a way to survive or not. So please don't ask me again why I have bruises covering my body. You don't know anything about me. And I don't owe you an explanation of my life or how I look." Thankfully, the tears never fell from my face; they had started to dry up. One thing was for sure: I didn't want to cry through any of this. I needed to be tough. I didn't know if I was in shock or denial. All I knew was I was tired of him asking questions about the bruises. Even if he'd only asked once before this.

He kept his eyes on me, his hands still fisted at his sides. A tick started up in his jaw as we stood staring at each other not saying anything. Finally, he turned and went back into the other room, and I took a deep breath before I followed him out.

Gregory leaned over the side of the bed, I couldn't see because of his large frame, before he stood back up—clothes in his hands—and walked back into the bathroom; slamming the door behind him. I walked over to the bed and set the duffel bag down; I zipped everything up and grabbed the other duffel bag and backpack. I pulled open my purse and dumped out the contents: two books, a knife, and one wallet fell out. I opened up my wallet and peeked through; the money I had brought back from the school was in it, along with my ID, and more money was added to it. Skimming through the bills, I was amazed at the amount of money sitting in my wallet—I had enough money to live comfortably for at least six months. How did she get this much money? I closed that wallet and set it back in the purse, along with the books and knife. The bathroom door opened up, and I turned around. Gregory's hair was wet, and he was pulling down the rest of his shirt, covering his magnificent washboard abs. Which was a shame. I looked up at his face; he still seemed angry, but I didn't care because he could get over it.

"So, what's the plan?"

He looked like he wanted to say something but just shook his head. He walked by me and to the pile of crap on the floor and started going through it. He was silent for so long that I started to get nervous. Biting my lip, I watched as he went through papers and berated myself for assuming he would help me. "I…ah." *Smooth, Mia, real smooth.*

From his crouch on the floor, he looked up at me. "The inn burned down. I think we should go back there and see if anyone is around. If Alithea is looking for you, I bet she'd go back and wait."

I felt hopeful at the "we" part. "So you're going to help me?" I hated how my voice came out wobbly.

He went back to the pile of crap. "I think the first thing we should do is eat," Gregory said, ignoring my question. He stood up and slipped something into his pocket.

"Wouldn't it be better to find Alithea first?" I asked.

"No." He held up his hand to stop me from talking. "We need food for energy. I don't have any here. This morning might be the only chance for you to eat." I noticed the lack of 'we' that time.

"I'm fine. I've gone without food before for days. I think I can handle going without food for now."

He narrowed his eyes. "You have money to spend on all types of food, but you don't eat? What the hell?"

Well, when you're not allowed to eat, it doesn't matter the amount of money you have. "Don't worry about it. I'm fine. I don't need food," I said. I threw a smile on, trying to reassure him, which instantly failed.

"Well, I'm hungry, so let's go." He grabbed both duffel bags and slung them on one arm. I slipped the backpack onto my shoulders and slid my purse across my chest. Gregory walked to the door, opened it, and walked through. I followed quickly, not wanting to get lost in the building.

As we made it out of the building, the sun was beating down. It must have snowed last night because fresh snow covered the ground. Gregory led the way down the road, and I tried keeping as close to him as I could. We rounded a couple more decaying buildings until we walked up to a small rundown shop. It looked much like the bar from the other night, but instead of smelling like alcohol and trash, it smelled like eggs and bacon. He took us to a small table in the very back so that no one would see us. Pulling out a chair for me, I sat down and he walked over to the opposite side and sat down, where he was able to face the entrance.

Gregory picked up his menu as I looked around the small shop; the walls were made of brick, and many of them were falling apart. The floor was wood, and the tables were made of blue plastic. People were coming in and out, talking in whispers. I was surprised to see the establishment open after what happened yesterday.

“Here.” Gregory was holding out a menu for me.

“I'm fine,” I said, not taking the menu. I knew I had a lot of money to use on food, but I didn't know how long I would be on the road, and the money could be used elsewhere. “Why is this place running? I figured with what happened yesterday people would have scattered."

“I think they stopped firing on citizens when they realized many of them would join in. So it's back to business they go. And just take the damn thing,” he said, shoving the menu in my face.

I just shook my head. “Nope. You can eat, and I'll just wait.”

He shrugged and dropped the menu, but I could tell he was pissed. My stomach betrayed me by growling at the smell of food. Gregory rolled his eyes but thankfully didn't say anything. I was hungry, but I could go without for now.

"What can I get you two?" a redheaded waitress asked, with a notepad and pencil ready to jot down our orders.

"I want two hot chocolates, two orders of French toast, two orders of eggs, and two orders of white toast." Gregory handed over the menu. My mouth dropped open. How could he eat that much?

"Nothing for me," I said.

The waitress took both menus and walked away. Looking at him closely, I watched as he crossed his arms and kept his attention on what I assumed was the door. He was on edge. Hell, I was on edge. I bit my lip as I stared at his face; it was a nice face to look at. I was still looking at him when his eyes caught mine. He raised an eyebrow. I tried to raise mine back but failed epically.

"How old are you?" He looked to be somewhere in his twenties, but I couldn't be too sure.

"Twenty-three." He kept looking back and forth between my face and whatever was behind me. "What about you?"

"Seventeen," I said. His eyes bulged, and he rubbed his face. I hastily added, "I'll be eighteen in three months." He scratched his head and had an uncomfortable look on his face.

"What are you thinking?" I asked.

"Nothing. You just don't look seventeen." He kept his eyes focused behind me.

I groaned. "Please don't tell me I look younger."

He cleared his throat. "No, you definitely don't look younger. So that's why you were at the bar the other night. You weren't old enough to go to the one on your side, so you thought it would be fun to sneak over here."

"Well, it wasn't my idea. Trust me, I wouldn't have gone if I'd known what was going to happen." I moved my hand up and down the table.

"Learned your lesson, didn't you?"

I rolled my eyes at him as the waitress showed up. She started putting the plates on Gregory's side when he stopped her.

Gregory pointed over to me. "One of each goes to her."

"Gregory, I told y—" I started, but he put his hand up to stop me from talking. I glared at him.

After the waitress put the last plate down, Gregory started eating. I just stared at my plate. The food smelled delicious. My stomach growled painfully. "If you're not going to eat it, you're just wasting it," he said.

"I told you I was fine. I'm not hungry." I glared at him. I didn't know why I was being stubborn. I was starving now that food was in front of me.

"Your stomach says otherwise," he said. "Just eat the food."

I glared at him once more and then started to eat. The French toast was delicious. The eggs were mouthwatering, but the bacon was the best; the meat sent bursts of flavor into my mouth. Once I'd cleaned the plates, I looked up to see Gregory staring at me. "What?"

"I told you, you were hungry," he said. A smirk started to take over his mouth.

I narrowed my eyes at him. "I would have been fine if I hadn't eaten it."

"Watching you eat is fascinating."

"What? Why?" I asked, confusion taking over.

"Well, the one time we had lunch you ate the pizza like it was a gift from God. You did the same with the breakfast."

"I like food," I said defensively.

He threw his hands in front of him. "I wasn't saying it to upset you."

I rolled my eyes. "Whatever."

"What?" Confusion now crept into his face.

"Nothing," I said. I sat a napkin down on the table.

Gregory narrowed his eyes and searched my face. Just as he was about to say something, the waitress came by and gave Gregory a piece of paper and collected the empty plates. Gregory took a black wallet out of his pants and took out some money. I reached for my purse, but Gregory shook his head. He handed the money and paper to the waitress and stood up, and I hastily followed him toward the exit of the shop.

"I heard they're looking for some girl, can't seem to find her," I heard as I passed a table of two men eating. My feet stopped involuntarily and my ears perked up to catch more of the conversation. Both men had their heads bent down while they ate and whispered, oblivious to where I was standing. I wondered if they would notice if my head joined theirs.

"What girl?" the other whispered back.

"I dunno, some rich girl, but there is a price on her head, so whoever finds her gets a reward."

"What kind of reward?"

"A thousand dollars," the other said excitedly.

"How are we supposed to know who we're looking for?"

"They're supposed to be handing out pictures in an hour. I want to find her. D'you know how much I could get with a thousand dollars?"

I hurried away from their table, my mind reeling. People were now going to start actively looking for me unless there was another girl out there these people were looking for, which I doubted. As I hurried forward to catch up to Gregory, I grabbed his hand to stop him. Turning around he took one look at my face and pulled me into the closest abandoned alley; which wasn't very far since many of the alley's were abandoned.

"What's wrong?" he asked. He looked me over, checking to see if I was hurt.

"My face is going to be on papers!" I rushed out. I tried to keep the panic from crawling up my throat, but I could feel the claws digging in.

"What are you talking about?" His brows pinched together.

"We have to find Alithea." I tried to sort through my head for what I had to do. "Find a way to get out of here before it's too late."

"Wait, what are you talking about?" Confusion and concern masked his face.

"Otherwise they'll find me and do God knows what."

Gregory cupped my face with his hands, bringing my attention to him. "What in the hell are you talking about?"

"I just overheard two men talking about the rebels. They're looking for me. There is a reward on my head—a thousand-dollar reward mind you—and in about an hour they will have pictures of me and will be handing them out to everyone."

"Shit," he said, letting go of my face. He started to pace back and forth while rubbing the back of his neck. "We need to get to the inn now."

Well, duh, I thought, but I knew better than to say it out loud.

He grabbed my hand, and we walked as fast as we could to get to the inn. It only took us about twenty minutes, but it felt like hours. I tried to keep my head down, but what I really wanted to do was look around and see if people already got the pictures. I took out my ponytail and let my hair fall in my face to help cover it. We stopped across the street from the inn and I bounced on the balls of my feet as I looked around.

"What does she look like?" he asked.

We were looking at was left of the building. "I don't know. Agathy told me to find Alithea."

"How are you supposed to find her if you don't know what she looks like?"

I never thought of that. *Shit.* "I don't know. She knew I was coming, so I thought maybe she would look out for me."

"Well, we can't stand around here all day. People will start looking for you," he said.

"Maybe we could ask someone?" It came out as more of a question than a statement.

"It could be risky," he said. Gregory was still holding my hand as he moved us closer to the building.

"What other choice do we have?"

"I don't like it. If Alithea were here, she would be hanging around or something. We have maybe a half hour before your picture is given to everyone. Let's just walk around the building for a few minutes. I say if we don't find her in fifteen minutes, we leave. Deal?"

I nibbled on my bottom lip. I knew it was important to find Alithea but was it important enough? We could get caught, and I would be screwed. And Gregory would be too, most likely. But what could we do if no one came up to us? We couldn't exactly hide away at his place and hope it would never get searched. I looked up at him to see his eyebrows pinched together. "Deal."

We walked in front of the building, peering in to see if anyone would be cleaning up or looking for stuff. We walked all the way around the building: twice. People were loitering around, but no one came up to us to talk. Gregory kept a hold of my hand the whole time, either to make sure I kept up with him or to make sure he wouldn't lose me I didn't know which.

As we turned to head back to the safety of his building, something caught my eye. A person was peering around the opposite wall of the inn and as my eyes hit theirs, they waved me over. I pulled on Gregory's hand to stop him.

"There's someone back there." I pointed to the alley where the person had just been standing, but the spot was now empty.

"How do you know?"

"I just saw them. They waved me over. It could have been Alithea," I said. I could hear the hope in my voice.

"Or they started handing out the pictures and someone wants to turn you in."

I stared up at him. I hadn't thought of that, but something in my gut told me that wasn't true. "I don't think so. We should check it out."

He looked down at me, probably contemplating whether or not to go. He closed his eyes for a brief second and then opened them. "Fine, but if I tell you to run, you run back to my place."

"Okay!" I said. I wouldn't tell him I had no idea how to get back to his place on my own. We slowly made our way over to the alley, and as we rounded the corner, a figure was standing all in black, their hood up, looking at us.

"Alithea?" I asked. It was worth a shot to ask.

The person lowered her hood, and long black hair flung loose. She nodded her head. "Mia, I've been looking for you all night."

"Why did Agathy tell me to meet you?" I asked.

"I'm here to help you. It's no longer safe for you to be here. Rebels have taken over. We were warned only a few days before. My mother set up as much as she could to get you out, knowing they'd want you."

"Who?" Gregory and I asked at the same time.

She looked at Gregory, inspecting him. "I'm not sure he should be here, can't trust him."

"I could say the same thing about you," Gregory said.

"I trust him," I said. "Who's your mother?"

"My mother is Agathy," she answered. Sadness ripped through her words. "She didn't make it out alive last night."

It felt like someone had punched me in the chest. Tears pricked my eyes. Agathy had always treated me with kindness, and I'd always loved her like she was my real mother. I pinched my eyes closed, keeping the tears at bay. "I'm sorry."

"She was a great woman," Alithea said. I opened up my eyes. Alithea's eyes were shining. "She cared for you too, like you were one of her own." I nodded.

"Why are they after her?" Gregory asked.

"They hate those who have more than the rest, and they want them all to suffer. Yesterday they attacked the rich to get to the Cowan's' house. To be able to overturn the system, you need to get rid of the Leader, which, of course, includes their whole family since the Leaders inherit Lorburn. I'm not sure what has happened to your parents, Mia, but there are men looking for you. You're to rule Lorburn if your parents are dead, so it's best to get you away from here."

"Where will I go?" I asked. Dread swam like a shark in my knotted stomach.

Alithea handed over an envelope. "My mother wanted me to give this to you. It has two train tickets. We leave tonight, and we're to head to Inonia. Now, you," she said, looking at Gregory. "Will you be able to keep her safe until tonight?"

"Yeah," Gregory said, nodding his head.

"Good, now Mia needs to be there at nine forty-five tonight. I will meet you there. It would be best to get off the street until then." She was looking around making sure no one was around.

"Shouldn't you hold on to a ticket?" I asked.

She closed her hand over mine. "No, just in case something happens." She let go of my hand. "I will see you tonight." She put her hood back up and walked down the alley. I just stared after her.

"We should get back to my place," Gregory said. He grabbed my hand and led me away from the alley. I kept my head down and let my hair fall around my face; I couldn't help but ignore the thoughts that were roaming in my head. One thought, in particular, was that there wasn't a ticket for Gregory. I really didn't want to do this without him. We were both silent and in our own heads as we entered back into the safety of his place.

CHAPTER TEN

It was nightfall, and I was anxious to get to the train station. After Gregory and I got back to his place, he left to gather any information about what was happening outside. This gave me time to organize my bags a little better. I had unloaded both duffel bags, rolled my clothes as tiny as I could, and placed the contents back in. I was able to fit all of my clothes and bathroom necessities in one bag, which would help me tremendously because I didn't want to have to lug around two heavy bags, plus a backpack and purse. With the other duffel bag, I went through Gregory's clothes and started packing, rolling his clothes up the same way. I was going to make him come with me, whether he liked it or not.

After meeting Alithea, I was skeptic about her and I didn't want to put my trust in a woman who claimed Agathy was her mother. This was the first time I heard about Agathy having any children, she never talked much about her home but I was positive Agathy would have mentioned having children at one time, and she never did. I didn't know much about Gregory, but I'd known him longer, and so far he had saved my life. Twice.

As I zipped up the last duffel bag, I sighed. At least we would both be clothed this whole trip. I set the bags down on the floor, followed by my backpack and purse, and I sat cross-legged on the bed, waiting.

I had been waiting on the bed for two hours before I got up and started pacing back and forth. Gregory seemed to be taking forever, which made me nervous. What if he'd been caught? What if he'd decided to just leave me here? What if he'd met up with that skank I saw him with the other night? I shook my head. I was just being paranoid. What would it matter if he met up with the skank? It wasn't any of my business. Why was I even caring whether he was meeting up with her when my life was literally on the line? I could see my small soft hands fitting perfectly into his large calloused hands. I frowned. If he'd spent this whole time with the slut, I would beat him senseless. Didn't matter if he could snap my body in two. He could be risking my life with that sk—

The door opened, breaking through my thoughts, and Gregory walked in, closing the door behind him; he looked haggard. I felt bad for the thoughts that had just been going through my head, but I quickly set them aside. "Any news?"

Gregory sat down on the bed. "There are rumors that you've been seen with a male, but no one knows for certain. Except for..."

"Except for?" I prodded after he'd been quiet for a few seconds.

"I went back to the restaurant to talk to the waitress. She wasn't there, but the owner told me where I could find her. It wasn't very easy—he gave shit directions. Anyway, I found her place and could see her talking to some guys in uniform. I got as close as I could without being detected. I could only hear bits and pieces, but they know about us."

"Crap." At least with this news, I hopefully wouldn't have to fight with Gregory or bribe him to come.

"Fortunately, she doesn't know who I am. Unfortunately, she gave a very detailed description of both of us. They told her if we come back again tomorrow morning to let them know immediately." Gregory looked down at his watch and then looked back up at me. "We leave in five minutes."

I picked up the duffel bag that had his clothes in it and threw it at him. "Here."

He looked at me, his eyebrow cocked. "What?"

"I was able to fit all of my clothes in one bag, so I packed some of your clothes in that bag." I crossed my arms over my chest, ready for the fight. When we'd come back earlier, we'd never talked about whether or not he was coming. I'd wanted to, but he'd left right away.

"And why are my clothes in the bag?" I could see his hand tightening on the strap.

"Because you're coming with us." I stared him down. There was no way he was going to win this.

"Listen, Mia, I'm not coming with you." With that, he stood up and walked into the bathroom, shutting the door behind him. My mouth fell open, but I quickly closed it and went after him. Opening the door, I crossed my arms and stared daggers into his back, hoping he could feel the pointy ends.

"You *are* coming with me." I started to tap my foot.

"I'm not," he said as he splashed water on his face.

"Yes, you are."

"No, I'm not.

"Oh my God, how old are you?" I was now officially angry. "Why are you being such an ass? You're coming with me whether you like it or not." I turned around and walked toward the bed. As I reached it, I turned back in time to see Gregory looming over me. Startled, I jumped and nearly toppled onto the bed.

"You do not get to boss me around here," he said, spitting out every word. "I don't give a shit what family you're from. I make my own choices. I do *not* answer to demands."

I balled my shaking hands into fists, hoping he wouldn't notice them. "I need your help."

"So you think bossing me around makes me want to help you?" He stepped away from me, his body tense. A vein started to pulse on his forehead and he grinded his teeth.

I slowly stood up, keeping my hands in front of me to show I was harmless. "If I'd have asked, you'd still have said no."

"So?" he bit out.

"I need your help. I don't know how to protect myself. I don't even know how to survive on my own. I don't know this Alithea person. How can I trust that she's on my side? How can I trust she's really Agathy's daughter? For all I know, this could be a setup. I don't even know anyone but you who would be on my side. I'm all alone in this. Both my parents could be dead, which would mean that I'm the Leader of Lorburn. Which means people are trying to kill me. So, would you please help me? Until I can get on my own two feet. I'll pay you for your help," I added in at the last second. Maybe payment would change his mind.

He kept his angry eyes on me and stepped forward, where I instantly stepped back, putting my arms up in front of me to protect it. My breathing was coming in and out fast. I was waiting for it: The hit. I practically jumped when I felt his hand on my arm, slowly moving it from my face. As Gregory lowered both of my arms, his face no longer showed anger, but I couldn't quite tell what it showed.

"I'm not going to hurt you," he said. He let go of my arms, and I nodded my head. Tears formed in my eyes. I tried to hold them back, but one slipped through the gate, followed by thousands more. I put my hands up to my face to try and hide. I sat down on the bed and just cried. I could hear Gregory breathe in and out for a good solid minute before I felt his arms wrapping around me. I didn't know why I was crying, I had been so strong up until now. I cried until I had no more tears to rain out of my eyes. Gregory held me the entire time, even after the tears were long gone. I didn't mind. His arms and body were warm and soft. I had never been held like this before; Agathy's hug definitely had not been like this hug.

As much as I wanted to stay cocooned in his arms, I knew I couldn't. We had to leave for the train, so I slowly moved my body away from his and toward the bags on the floor. "We should get going." I could feel his gaze on my back but ignored it. I slipped the backpack on. "And I would like us to pretend that never happened."

"Agreed. I think I might have caught something just from your tears." I rolled my eyes and ignored him. "Here." Gregory dropped a large black hoodie on top of my duffel. "Put it on over the backpack. Keep the hood up and put your jacket on over it. I want us to be as inconspicuous as possible."

I nodded and did what I was told. I slipped on my jacket and put the hood up. I grabbed my duffel bag and slid it up my arm. Next went my purse. As I turned around, Gregory was dressed all in black too and holding the other duffel bag. I raised an eyebrow.

He shrugged his shoulders. "As long as you're paying for service, I'm your man."

I shook my head and tamped down the smile threatening to form on my face. "How much?"

"We can figure it out on the train." He walked toward the door. "But we need to leave now."

I followed Gregory through the abandoned building, and out into the night. It was dark out, but Gregory had us walk into the deep shadows of the buildings so we wouldn't be bothered or followed. Gregory moved at a fast pace, while I, on the other hand, had to walk twice as fast just to keep up with his long strides. By the time we arrived at the train station—ten minutes later—I had to catch my breath. My lungs burned in protest and my calves ached. I reluctantly followed him up the stairs and sat down as I noticed the bench next to the building. I sat there wheezing and trying to catch my breath. I hated exercise, and I hated more that I was terribly out of shape.

There wasn't much to the building; it was one story, had a door in the back where the workers went in, and a small window in the front to buy tickets. Another small wooden bench sat against the building, right next to the window. Trains were the only way people could travel between regions.

Gregory shifted and started to walk around. I just wanted to sit and rest but knew I had to look for Alithea. I stood up, my legs protesting as they started to cramp up and moved around. Gregory walked toward the stairs that led to the path up the hill to Gildonia. I shuffled in the other direction toward the railway, looking back and forth, trying to see if I could catch sight of Alithea.

"We will be leaving in five minutes," a man yelled from the train.

I looked over at Gregory. We'd been here for only a few minutes, and Alithea was about ten minutes late. Had she gotten here and not found us? Did she leave to go looking for us? I started walking up and down the train again, looking for her. My pace quickened and my heart started racing as panic bloomed in my chest. She had to be here. The train started making noise as it turned on, and I rushed back to Gregory to see him running toward me.

"She's not here," I said. Tension started to crawl up my throat.

"I need to get a ticket," Gregory said, looking over his shoulder. "Get on the train. I'll meet you there." He grabbed my shoulders and pushed me toward the train.

"You can use Alithea's ticket," I said.

He looked behind his shoulder again and looked back at me. I tried to see what he kept looking at, but I couldn't since he towered over me. He raked a hand through his hair, and his eyes darted all over the place. "You looked everywhere for her?"

"Yes." I started to bounce on my toes.

"Fine, let's get on." He shoved me onto the train and he just made it through the doors before they closed. "What compartment are we in?"

I rifled through my purse, looking for the tickets. When I pulled them out, Gregory snatched them out of my hands—causing me to glare at him—and walked toward the very back of the train. I followed and kept looking in each compartment on the way down to see if maybe Alithea was already in one. As we made it to the compartment, Gregory shut the door behind us. The compartment was small with a chair on either side and a small window. Immediately to the left of the compartment door was another door. I opened it up and a tiny lavatory appeared, big enough for one at a time. I tried to imagine Gregory's tall frame going in there but couldn't. He would have had to duck while he went. I closed the door and walked over to the chairs, which were made of brown leather and each had a share of holes in them. As I sat down on the chair to the right of the window, Gregory sat opposite me and looked out.

It was dark out, and our reflections shone back at us. I looked at Gregory through the glass; his face was impossible to read and he seemed to be concentrating on something, but I wasn't sure. That could be the face of man just trying to think. I smirked, and he glared at me. I tilted my head and wondered if he could read minds. *If you can read my mind, you look really sexy with all that stubble on your face.* He turned his glare to the window. Nope, he couldn't read minds. He looked exhausted though I knew he wouldn't admit it, but I was happy he'd agreed to come with me, even if I had to pay him.

"Thank you," I said. He turned to look at me. He was quiet for a few minutes, and I squirmed in my seat.

"They knew you were going to be at the train station," he said.

"Who?" I asked. My eyebrows crinkled in confusion.

"The rebels."

"How? We were careful when we left your place."

"I saw a bunch of odd-looking military Jeeps, not like the ones the army drives, back at the station. Only a few guys were near them, so I figured they were on the train looking for you. When we got to the entrance of the train, I watched a bunch of them get off at the rear exit."

"That's why you shoved me in," I said.

"Yeah," he said. "I don't know how they found out you were going to be here. Maybe they caught Alithea and she gave you up."

I narrowed my eyes at him. "I don't believe that."

"You don't even know her. You said it yourself earlier. She could've wanted the reward and decided to turn you in."

"Why would she have gone out of her way to give me tickets?"

Gregory just shrugged his shoulders. "Believe what you want, but I think sh—"

The compartment door opened, making both Gregory and me to jump up from our seats. "Tickets, please," the elderly man in front of us said. He was wearing a light-blue t-shirt and tan corduroy pants. His hair was white and thinning, and he had smiling brown eyes. Gregory handed over the tickets, assessing the ticket collector. The elderly man ripped off the bottom piece and handed it back to Gregory. "We will be getting to Inonia in eight hours. Please relax and enjoy the ride." With that he left, shutting the door behind him.

Gregory pocketed the tickets and walked toward the door. He took off his leather jacket and shut off the light. I could see the silhouette of his body as he walked back toward his chair. He propped the jacket up against the window and lay his head on it. "We should probably get some rest. Who knows what will be waiting for us." He closed his eyes.

"What did you want for payment?" I blurted out.

A smile formed on his lips. "I'm not sure yet, but once I know, I'll let you know."

The bastard probably already knew what he wanted, but he was going to be a stubborn ass in the meantime. I rolled my eyes and tried to make myself comfortable. I kept my jacket on—no pointing trying to take everything off. It would be too much of a pain. I leaned my head up against the cold window and closed my eyes. I had no idea what to expect when we got to Inonia. Were people still going to be after me? Would I even find safety? The train jostled our bodies as it made its way to our destination. It took me quite a while to get my mind to shut off. When I was finally able to do that, I fell asleep.

CHAPTER ELEVEN

"What do you think?" Gregory asked, peering into my eyes. We lay on our sides, facing each other. His hands cupped my face, his thumbs caressing my jaw.

"I don't know…I'd have to ask my parents," I said. I slid my arms around his waist, pulling him closer to me. His body heat kept me warm.

His eyes darkened at the mention of my parents. "We are not going to tell them."

I raised an eyebrow. "Why not?"

"I don't like them—especially not how they treat you. You deserve better," he said.

I let go of his waist and slid one hand up to his face. I moved my hand back and forth, smoothing out the anger wrinkles. "But won't they worry if I just leave without telling them where I would be going?" I leaned closer to his face, our noses touching.

"Let them worry," he said. He rubbed his nose against mine. I stared into the depths of his eyes, hypnotized by what I saw. I closed my eyes as I felt his lips hovering over mine. I could feel his hot breath on my mouth, and I leaned up a little bit closer, hoping to finally kiss

him. Just as our lips almost touched, the bed shook. My eyes popped open at the same time Gregory moved his head back and looked at me quizzically. "What was that?"

The bed shook harder. I grabbed a fistful of sheets. "I don't know. Where are you going?" I asked. Gregory was disappearing from my eyes.

"Hold on to me!" he said. I tried to grab on to him, but my hands just kept slipping through. It didn't make sense. I watched him disappear as fear entered my body. I was alone. He'd left me. "Mia!" I could hear his voice calling for me, but I couldn't see him. "Mia, wake up. You need to wake up."

I opened my eyes, blinking rapidly as Gregory's face swam in and out in front of me. Heat brushed against my cheek as the dream popped back into focus. Why would I ever dream of us? Like…that? It…it was…it would never, ever, ever happen.

The train was still rustling us around but seemed to be going at a slower rate. "What's hap—" I started to say when he clamped his large hand over my mouth. He put his finger to his lips and shushed me. He removed his hand after I nodded my head.

"We have visitors," he whispered. He moved away from me and walked to the door to our compartment; I watched him closely, noticing he'd put his jacket back on. Nervous energy radiated off of him, his hands rubbing the back of his neck.

It brought me right back to that dream. God, I hoped I hadn't yelled or said something out loud. Agathy used to tell me that I talked in my sleep. Nothing would have been more embarrassing than if he had heard me talking in my sleep. I swallowed and clamped my hands together. I had questions I wanted to ask, like *What's going on? How long have you been up? Did I speak in my sleep about you kissing me?* I put my head in my hands and shook my head. By the time I was finished berating myself for dreaming such a dream, I looked back up at Gregory, who was looking back at me. I raised an eyebrow. He tilted his head. I wasn't sure I understood how we were going to talk through body language; I was clueless at what he was trying to say. "You can talk as long as you whisper."

Duh. I flushed even further. I'm pretty sure my face resembled a tomato by this point. I cleared my throat. "What kind of visitors?" I crossed my fingers that it would be the kind of visitors who sang.

"The same kind who were looking for you back in Gildonia." My heart sank, and my stomach dropped. We were now stuck on a train with nowhere to hide.

"How did they get on board?" I asked. I rushed out of my seat and over to him.

"Some of them must have stayed on and decided to do a thorough search of the train, and now they're headed this way," he said. He opened up the door slightly, peering through it.

"How do you know?" I asked, trying to peer through the small crack, but I had no way because of Gregory's large, muscled, annoying body. The body I had dreamed about. *The view now would be much better if he weren't wearing anything.* I shook my head. I could not think about something like that. What was wrong with me? Our lives were in danger, and the only thing I could think of was his naked body? Had I hit my head recently? *Yes.*

Gregory slowly shut the door and turned toward me. He cocked an eyebrow, as I tried to keep my face neutral. I did not want him thinking I was thinking of the wrong thing to think. "I woke up and went looking for a food cart, and that's when I heard one of them. Said they were looking for a girl and that she might be here."

"Oh." My stomach growled. I wanted to ask, "Did you get any food?" but instead asked, "What do we do?"

Gregory looked around the compartment before he turned back toward the door. He slowly opened it and glimpsed outside. After a few seconds but what felt like eternity, he closed the door and turned his attention back to me. "They're a couple of compartments down. People are out loitering in the hallway, watching them. The train has started to slow down, so I think we should sneak out of the compartment before they get any closer and move toward the back." He marched over and grabbed the duffel bags; I stayed where I was.

"Why would we go to the very back?" I tried to follow his plan, but I could see big holes in it.

"The back of the train has this small platform and can fit a person or two on at a time." He slid both of the bags up his arms and walked back over to where I was standing.

I raised my eyebrows. "So we're just going to stay on the platform and hope no one looks?" Because that would work. Not.

"No," he said, looking at me. "We're going to jump off."

My jaw dropped. Was he crazy? "Are you crazy?"

My body froze at the serious look on his face. "We need to get you off the train before they find out you were on it. The train has slowed down quite a bit, so when we jump—yes, it will hurt, but no it won't kill us—we'll be able to walk away from it. It's still nightfall, and with the dark clothes we're wearing, we should be pretty covered."

"But what happens if they notice us when we walk out of the compartment? Or when we're walking in the hallway toward the deck? Won't they follow us? Take the chance to jump off after us?" I said. Images of broken body parts kept floating through my head. I had enough bruises on my body. I didn't really want to add broken bones to that list.

"Well, when the ticket collector was in the hall, I stole this." He held up a set of keys, and I looked at him quizzically. "They lock and unlock all of the doors. So no matter what, I plan on locking the door behind us on the platform. By the time they get it unlocked, we'll have already jumped, and the train will have brought them too far ahead of us."

"Oh." I hated this plan. "When do we go?" *Please say never. Please say this is a joke. Please let this just be a dream.*

Gregory smiled. I frowned. "Now."

Gregory softly opened the door again and he motioned for me to go first and as I walked by him he stopped me. He slid the hood up over my head, his fingertips brushing against my neck as he finished. As his fingertips slid down my neck, I swallowed nervously and watched as he stepped back. He slipped his hood on and beckoned for me to move. We shifted our way to the middle of the hallway; I looked right and saw a gathering of people hanging around in the hall, watching the commotion halfway down the train. I tried to see, but my height wouldn't allow me to. Gregory quietly shut the door and turned me to go left. Even more people were standing around watching. Gregory led us down toward the deck and I held on to the bottom of his hoodie so I wouldn't lose him.

It was difficult making our way through the crowd, and it made it even harder when the train jostled around. "We're almost there," I heard Gregory say a few moments later. I watched as he took out the keys from his pocket, and I almost rejoiced when the door came into view until men started yelling from behind us.

"Get them!" a deep voice bellowed. I kept telling myself not to look back, but I looked back. People were jumping out of the way, for the men in uniforms were running toward us. I glanced up at Gregory, whose eyes narrowed. He muttered curses under his breath, grabbed my hand, and started pushing people out of our way. A thunderous bang went off, and I could hear a ping of metal hitting metal. I ducked as another bang went off.

"They're shooting at us," I yelled as Gregory moved us to the door. People were now screaming all around us, trying to get back into their compartments. We slipped through the door, the cold air biting our faces. Gregory let go of my hand while he messed with the keys. He kept trying different keys in the lock. I looked up at him, horrified. "You don't know which key would lock it? Why don't you know?" I said hysterically. I looked through the glass of the small window. The men were approaching much faster than I liked. I could feel my pulse spike and I wrung my hands together.

"What was I supposed to do? Ask the ticket collector which key to use when I stole them from him?" he asked, his words dripping with sarcasm.

"There are about a hundred different keys on that thing," I yelled through the wind.

"Then shut up so I can concentrate," he said through gritted teeth.

This was how I was going to die, because of Gregory's stupid plan. If I lived through this, he would no longer make the plans. His plans were brainless. Dimwitted. Unintelligent. And obviously not thought out enough. I peered through the window again and wanted to scream.

The men were almost there. They had just reached our compartment, and it would only take them a few more seconds until they got out here to us. I squeezed my eyes shut, chanting in my head, *Please lock the door, please lock the door, please lock the door!*

"Got it!" Gregory yelled out. My eyes popped open and my heart started to slow down a little. Gregory stalked to the left side of the deck, and I followed him. He opened up the gate that kept the platform protected. "You're going to jump first."

I narrowed my eyes at him. "It was your plan. Shouldn't you jump first?"

Gregory scrubbed a hand over his face. "I need to make sure you jump, so you need to jump first. We don't have all night."

I swallowed and looked at the ground rushing past us. Pounding and yelling were coming from the other side of the door, and I knew we were out of time. Green grass covered the rushing ground; hopefully, there were no rocks or sharp items hidden in it. I looked up at Gregory. "Alright."

Gregory positioned me to the ledge of the platform. "The train isn't going too fast to really hurt us when we jump," he said in my ear, causing goose bumps to travel down my body. Now was not the time for those. "When you jump, just make sure you protect your head. I'll be right behind you."

I nodded my head, and before I could think my way out of it, I jumped. The wind whipped around me as I flew through the air. I was in awe about how remarkable it was, but it didn't last very long. One minute I was up in the air, and the next I crashed into the earth landing on hard on my right side, the ground knocking the wind out of me. My shoulder slammed roughly into the ground, pain zipping through my arm, and my hipbone smashed painfully in to a rock, and it felt like someone used a hammer on me to nail something in. Tears splashed from eyes. I couldn't scream. I wanted to scream. I couldn't catch my breath. It took me minutes, or maybe it was hours, before I could take a full deep breath in and let it out. I finally forced myself to sit up and cried out in pain. My shoulder and hip were the worst. It took me a few moments to get my breathing back under control while tears flowed freely down my face. Using my left hand, I inspected my hip to see if anything was broken—and after a good amount of prodding, I determined it wasn't broken, just awfully bruised. I then poked at my shoulder and whimpered. My shoulder wasn't broken, but it was dislocated. The only reason I was able to tell was because it wasn't the first time my shoulder had been dislocated. I needed to put it back into place but couldn't do it on my own.

I could hear grunts and looked over to see Gregory walking—more like limping—over to me. I stayed seated as I waited for him. Yeah, he was officially off the planning-making committee. "How are you?" he asked, his eyes raking over my body.

"Oh, you know, my right hipbone is seriously bruised, along with a dislocated shoulder. I'm sure I have bruises everywhere else too." I was pissed at him. I was pissed at the men who were after us, if it wasn't for them we wouldn't have had to make the stupid plan.

He rolled his eyes at me, but his lips twitched in amusement. "Your right hipbone and right shoulder?"

I wanted to smack him, but I also didn't want to move a muscle. Everything hurt. "Yeah. I need my duffel bag." Gregory dropped my duffel but kept the weird, amused look on his face. I unzipped the bag and grabbed a shirt to wipe my face and use as a sling.

"Did you twirl in the air?"

I looked up, holding on to the clean shirt. "I'm sorry?"

"Did you twirl in the air?" His eyes were now flashing with amusement. Any second I was ready to tackle him to the ground and kick his lights out. Or I would have if I hadn't been banged up and barely able to move without hurting.

"Why would I twirl in the air?" I wiped off the dried tears and dirt from my face.

"We jumped from the left of the train, and the way you jumped from the train you should have landed on your left."

"Oh." I didn't understand what the big deal was about. "Is it a big deal?"

"No," he said. I could hear the laughter in his voice. I was ready to punt him. "It just would have made my day if I saw you twirl in the air." Yup, I definitely wanted to hurt him.

I narrowed my eyes at him. Gregory had a smile on his face. Made me want to harm him even more. As I stared at his lips, I couldn't help but notice his awfully nice mouth; making me want to do damage. "The next time we have to jump off a train, I'll make sure you see me twirl in the air." I rolled my eyes and began making my shirt into a sling. I could hear his laughter, but I ignored it.

"What are you doing?" he asked after he was finished laughing. He crouched down next to me.

"I need to make a sling for my arm." I looked over at him. "You'll need to help me put my shoulder back into place."

"I don't know how," he said, the humor gone from his voice.

"I do," I said. I tore the shirt into one long piece.

"Right, because all you rich people go to school and learn these things," he said bitterly.

I kept my eyes on my shirt. "No, because I've had my shoulders dislocated a few times, and Agathy had helped teach me how to put it back into place."

I could feel his body stiffen next to me. "And how does one get their shoulder dislocated a few times?"

I kept my eyes on my shirt. "When someone who has a father who's yanked her arm too rough and too fast." I could feel the anger rippling off his body, which meant he probably put my bruised face and what I just said together.

"Mi—" he started to talk, but I interrupted him before he could start. I didn't want to go down that road.

"Look, I need your help. My shoulder hurts. So please, just help me," I said.

He was quiet for so long I finally looked up at him. He was angry. I raised an eyebrow. It looked like he wanted to say something, but he just shook his head. "Okay. What do I do?"

"I need you to lift my right arm away from my side," I began as I lay down on the ground. Gregory sat next to me and lifted my right arm away from my side, and I gritted my teeth. "Now lift it up close to my head and act like it's reaching for my other shoulder, and do it fast," I said. I could hear him take a deep breath and let it go. I bit my lip to keep myself from crying out. I'd done this before; I could do it again. He lifted my arm toward the other shoulder. I squeezed my eyes shut, and he moved fast, putting it back into place. I screamed from the pain and relief. A few tears escaped my closed eyes and fell slowly down my face.

"What now?" he asked softly.

I opened my eyes to see him watching me. He moved his hands toward my face, and his rough, calloused fingers swiped at my tears. "I need you to tie the sling around my arm." After he helped me with the sling, he helped me up from the ground. "Are you hurt? I saw you limping." I asked, hating myself for just asking now.

"I hurt my ankle, but it's getting better." He zipped the duffel back shut and stood up. "We should get going."

I nodded my head. "Where are we?"

"We were about two hours out from Inonia when we jumped from the train. So by walking distance, we're about a day or two out." He started moving forward next to the tracks. I followed him. This was going to be a long and painful walk.

CHAPTER TWELVE

We walked yesterday in silence, each caught up in our own thoughts. My thoughts kept going back to the men who were after me. It wasn't fair, but there was nothing I could do about it. It also kept floating images of my parents: both hurt and healthy. Were they still alive? Were they scared? Did they miss me? And more important, if they were dead and these rebels were defeated, could I run the Lorburn? Did I have it in me to be a Leader? That was the scariest part: running Lorburn. I was only seventeen. I wasn't old enough to run Lorburn. Once, I tried to run for a leader position in the Book Club at school, and I ended up with negative votes. There should have been no way I got negative votes; negative votes shouldn't have been possible. And that was for a book club. Lorburn was a *whole* different situation, and I needed time to prepare. Even though my father chose Tyler to be his successor—after we were married—over me, I felt a little peace knowing I didn't have to hold the weight of the Lorburn on my shoulders. I wasn't strong enough for what the people needed. They needed someone who could naturally lead them, and that wasn't me. I'd be the moron who kept stuttering and pronouncing words wrong when talking at a conference. I'd end up getting a panic attack and just rocking back and forth on the floor in the corner, crying. Could that have seemed a bit dramatic? Maybe. But could it also have been the truth? More than likely. I was weak. My father knew it, I knew it, and even Gregory knew it. But I had other things to worry about at the moment. Like walking toward a region that might be overrun with rebels ready to kill me. And I was beyond exhausted. Last night we'd ended up stopping and sleeping in shifts. I'd been restless: I'd wanted a bed, food, and water. We'd both decided to start walking early, so we started before the sun even kissed the sky.

The wind started picking up, cold air slapping across my face. I lowered my head as far into my jacket as I could, but I made sure I could still see the rolling dirt hills ahead. That's all that was there in the middle of nowhere. Dirt, dirt, and more dirt. I officially missed the snow. It was cold out, but it wasn't the cold that bothered me. It was the wind that kept picking up the dirt and flinging it into our eyes. I gave up on trying to use my hood as protection midway through yesterday. The wind kept swishing it back, and with only one arm able to move, I gave up fixing it after the tenth annoying time. So I was fairly certain dirt was caked in my ears because I no longer could hear sounds without a muffle to it. The only trees we came upon were so pathetic I wanted to cut them down to take them out of their misery. They had no leaves, and all the branches drooped to the ground. I think the trees wanted to lie down. The farther we walked, the worse the smell of manure became. I wasn't sure if we were getting closer to Inonia or a cow farm.

I looked over at Gregory. He had both hands deep inside his pants pockets, and he kept his focus on what was in front of us. He was walking faster, his ankle feeling better. My legs were much shorter than his, which meant I had to double my steps. I pointed this out yesterday, but he just rolled his eyes and continued on with his pace. I thought about complaining until he slowed down but then realized I didn't have the energy to complain. My legs were sore from all the walking we did yesterday and so far today—not to mention the trip out of my house the day before. My arm throbbed each time I moved it on accident, and to top it off I'd woken with a migraine, and it seemed to slowly get worse, possibly because of the lack of food and water.

I wanted to stop walking and crawl into a bed and stuff my face with food. And possibly find a hot bath to soak in. But I knew it was very unlikely any of that would happen anytime soon. Looking down at my feet, I counted each shuffled step I took. Maybe that could occupy my time. *One. Two. Three. I want to hang myself from a tree. Four. Five. Six. Gregory can be suck a prick. Seven. Eight. Nine. Ten. I want to kill all the men.* Or at least those who destroyed my life.

"We should be there soon," Gregory said, breaking through my murderous thoughts. I looked up at him. He was standing ten feet in front of me, and had a smirk forming on his lips and I had a feeling I was going to want to punch him. There was only one reason he was smirking like that, and it probably had something to do with me.

"Okay," I said, breathless and narrowing my eyes at the smirk that was turning into a full -blown smile. As I caught up to him, I had to crane my head all the way back. "Is there something amusing you?"

"Nope," he said. "It's just that you should see your hair right now."

I narrowed my eyes and moved my moveable arm up to my hair. My hair was no longer in its ponytail; I could feel my hair everywhere and the knots in it. It was as stiff as a tumbleweed. Great. Just great. I tried to smooth it out, but my fingers were too cold to cooperate.

"Here," he said. His hands moved to my hair, his fingers gently untangling the knots. I knew I shouldn't have him touching me like this, even if it was just my hair, but I couldn't say anything. Biting my lip, I tried to keep in the moan that was dying to break free because of the way his hands worked my scalp. His eyes peeked at my lips, and I licked them nervously as he leaned in closer. I could feel the warmth of his breath as his grazed my ear. "All done." He let go of my hair and straightened back up.

Grabbing my hair with my free arm, I tucked in back into a ponytail, all the while keeping my eyes off of him. As I wiped my hand down the front of my pants, my head snapped up as I heard him laughing. He had a nice laugh, but I was too busy to notice because I was trying to decide the best way to kill him.

I moved past him and started walking. That had been a waste of time. My face felt much hotter because of that little humiliation. Why had I thought he was going to kiss me? Why would I even have let him kiss me? I wasn't attracted to him. And plus, I was "engaged" to Tyler. I could hear Gregory's stupid laughter and his boots catching up next to me, but I kept my attention away from him.

"So, tell me about yourself," he said. Thankfully, he was done laughing.

"Why?" I asked. "So you can laugh at me more?"

"I wasn't laughing at you," he said. I turned to look at him and raised an eyebrow. "Okay, I was laughing, but you should have seen yourself. Your hair was everywhere. You have two red circles on your cheeks—from the cold—and your eyes were so large I thought I was looking at a doll."

"You're a jackass," I said, turning forward again. "I don't know what kind of dolls you've seen, but I've never seen a doll whose hair was blown out." Gregory had this special way of annoying and pissing me off at the same time.

"How am I jackass?" he asked defensively.

"You just insulted and laughed at me. That's how you're a jackass." I would've tried to walk faster, but I only had so much energy, and the tank was almost running on fumes. His hand grabbed my good arm and pulled me to a stop. He turned me around, and I glared up at him.

"I didn't insult you," he said. He frowned, his eyes searching my face. "I didn't mean to hurt your feelings. I'm sorry."

I gulped. Tears sprang to my eyes and I couldn't stop them; they came out of nowhere like a freight train. The more they started to gather in my eyes, the more embarrassed I got. I could feel them hovering on my eyelids. Gulping a few times to try and get myself to calm down—*I'm not going to cry. I'm not going to cry. I'm not going to cry*—I took a deep breath and slowly let it out. Thankfully, the tears started to dry up, never hitting my cheek. "It's fine. I'm used to being picked on. It's just with everything going on, I was just hoping…I don't know. We should get going." I started to turn, but Gregory wouldn't let me.

"You were just hoping what?"

"I don't know, that you'd treat me with decency. I know I'm not the greatest-looking girl out there, but hearing someone laugh at the way you look hurts, especially when you grew up listening to it from everyone. I've had to hear my mother tell me that I was the ugly child over and over again. It was like her favorite sport when she was drunk. *Mia, you will never be as beautiful as your sister. Mia, why can't you make me proud? Mia, no one will fall in love with you. Mia, when you have children, they will look like trolls*. And I don't want to have trolls for children. Do you know how horrifying it is to have nightmares of trolls coming out of your body instead of humans? I've had to listen to girls make fun of the way I look and constantly put me down. It hurts. And of course I can't say anything. If I ever said anything, it would just cause more problems at home." I looked away and backed out of his grasp. I hadn't meant to word vomit. Why had I opened my mouth? My mouth usually got me into trouble or created awkward situations. I blamed it on my lack of energy. Whenever I ate next, I'd tell him that I was just delusional and he shouldn't listen to anything I said.

"I'm sorry," Gregory said. I nodded my head. "And you're wrong, you know?"

"How am I wrong?"

He smiled. "Because you are stunning." He flashed his pearly whites as I glared.

"You're so stupid," I mumbled as I started walking forward. Gregory laughed and caught up to me.

"So tell me about yourself."

"What do you mean?" I asked.

"Tell me about your childhood," he said, looking over at me. I just shrugged my shoulders. "Do you not remember your childhood?"

"I do, I just don't want to talk about it," I said.

"Why not?"

"Let's just say it wasn't the best," I said. I didn't want to divulge too much of my childhood to him. "What about yours?"

Gregory smiled. "Fine, I'll go first. My childhood was fantastic. I have three younger brothers: Michael, Johnny, and Caleb. My family moved to Minonia two years ago. I've been working with the construction crew since I was sixteen. It's a good job. I get to work with my hands, which I enjoy doing." He winked at the last part. I rolled my eyes in response. "I found my own place a few years ago. No one ever went into that building before or after I moved in, so I never had to worry about people stealing my stuff. Though I still had a hiding spot for the important stuff. I have some friends I hang out with and get a beer with. You know, the usual."

"Why didn't you move with your family?" I asked.

"My father and I had a falling out," he said.

"Oh," I said. I wasn't sure what else to say.

"Since I shared, now it's your turn."

"I never agreed to that." He crooked an eyebrow at me, and I shook my head. "Okay, fine. I've known Agathy all of my life. She's taken care of me since I was very little." I smiled remembering Agathy. "This one year, on my birthday—I think I had just turned five—she woke me up really early and gave me a small birthday cake before anyone else was up. We shared the cake—it was chocolate and strawberry. The frosting was the best part though. We ate the whole thing, then she let me go back to sleep. It was a secret between the two of us."

"She sounds great," Gregory said.

"She is—I mean was," I said. A frown tugged on my lips.

"Hey, she would be proud of you," he said.

I looked up at him, my eyebrow raised. "Why?"

"Because you've made it."

"With your help," I said. I hated to say it, but I knew I would have never made it this far without him.

"She would have been proud that you trusted someone you didn't know to help you."

"You think so?" I asked.

"Yeah." He bumped his shoulder into me, a smile on his face.

I winced. "Wrong shoulder." He just smiled and continued walking. I rolled my eyes at his annoyingly cheerful attitude that had come out of nowhere. Maybe he'd been abducted and something else possessed his body. It was possible. He had smiled twice in less than ten minutes. Maybe I could get along better with this possessed Gregory.

We walked for a few minutes in silence. I hoped he was right about Agathy; that she would be proud of me. I'd always wanted to make her proud. She'd been there for me since day one and helped me recover from the terror I grew up with. I glimpsed over at Gregory. He had his hands back in his pockets, and the smile was still attached to his face. I wanted to know more about him. "My sister passed away when I was twelve," I said, breaking the silence.

Gregory looked over at me. "I'm sorry. How did she die?"

I flinched at the word. "She got really sick one night. I heard her throwing up in the bathroom." I could remember that night like it was yesterday. "She was covered in sweat, and her hands were clenched around the toilet seat. Agathy was trying to get her to eat some toast, but every time she nibbled on something she would throw it back up. I tried to help, but Agathy kicked me out of the bathroom. After a few minutes, I opened the door and sneaked a look. I saw my sister throw up a lot of dark, red liquid—blood.

"I miss her terribly. She was my best friend. We only had each other. We used to fall asleep together after we made up crazy ghost stories. I was terrified of the dark—kind of still am—and she always turned a flashlight on in the room so I wouldn't be scared. We used to play hide-and-seek in the house and steal cookies from the kitchen while running from the staff. She was my rock."

"I'm sorry, Mia," Gregory said. I watched as he moved his hand toward mine, but at the last minute he shoved it back into his jeans pocket. "How did your parents take it?"

"They were angry," I said. I could remember the exact expressions on their faces. "They wouldn't let me go to the funeral. Said I was too young. I was angry with them. I just didn't understand why they didn't want me to attend my own sister's funeral."

I'd been so angry when they told me I wasn't allowed to go. I'd screamed at them and tried to run past them to the front door; I'd planned on running away and finding a family that would take me in and love me. Of course I hadn't run fast enough, my father had grabbed my arm, dislocating it for the second time in my life, and thrown me into my room. He'd then decided to discipline me while my mother had just watched with a drink in her hand. It had taken me over a week to be able to move. Agathy had helped me with showers and walking around. He had broken three ribs and my ankle. Bruises had covered my body, and they hadn't even called the doctor. Agathy had called a private doctor to look at me one night when my parents were out. They'd never known how much Agathy helped.

"Your parents are awful people," Gregory said, breaking through my memories. Shrugging my shoulders, I continued walking, I didn't want to talk about my parents. I didn't want him to know just how weak of a person I was. That I couldn't even stand up for myself in my own house. "Did you ever tell anyone?"

I looked up at him. "What do you mean?"

"Did you ever tell anyone about the bruises?"

I looked away, but I could feel his eyes on me. "Don't know what you're talking about."

Gregory stopped and grabbed my arm, preventing me from walking. "I'm not stupid. I saw the bruises on your side and face. The bruise is still waving off your cheek. I know you know I know. I also know those bruises didn't come from those 'friends' you were with at the bar the other night. So, why didn't you tell anyone?" He quoted the word friends with his fingers. *Oh, look, the notch on my anger meter just went up.*

I pulled my arm from his grasp and started walking. "I'm not talking about this." I didn't want him to know how bad it was. I should have kept my mouth shut and never told him about my sister.

"They killed your sister, didn't they?" he asked.

I stopped walking and spun around. "What? No, of course not! She was very sick. She'd been sick her whole life." I couldn't believe he would have the balls to say that. My parents might have had hatred toward us, but they would never take it that far. I knew deep down that my parents loved us. They just had a very shitty way of showing it.

"Right," he said sarcastically. "Did they tell you that, or did you just come up with that on your own?"

I gaped at him. "You don't know what you're talking about. We're not talking about me, my life, my family, or anything else anymore," I said.

"Then why did you bring up your sister?" he asked.

"Because you asked me to share something about myself with you, and I stupidly did it. If I had known you were going to be a gigantic ass and judge my parents, then I wouldn't have said anything," I shouted.

"No, I don't think that's it." He started walking toward me. "I think you brought it up so you could finally let go of the burden of the secret of how horrifying your parents truly are."

"Now you're just being stupid," I said angrily. *There went another notch.* I turned around and started to walk away from him.

"Way to be mature," he said from behind me.

"Whatever," I mumbled. Crossing my good arm across my chest, I stubbornly marched ahead. Eventually, Gregory passed me—mumbling something about how stubborn I was—and kept a few paces between us. I didn't know where exactly we were, so I was fine with him taking the lead. Neither one of us spoke to each other. It was going to be a very long trip.

CHAPTER THIRTEEN

I didn't know how long we'd been walking; I was exhausted and the pressure in my head started pounding in my eyes, I needed to rest and eat. My legs kept cramping up, and my feet were screaming in protest. Neither one of us had spoken since our last conversation, even if I wanted to talk, I didn't think I would be able to. My throat was painfully dry and it was no longer cold out. The sun beat down on us and sweat drenched through my clothes. At one point, I had to tie my leather jacket around my waist so I could cool myself down. A few times, my feet slipped on some rocks and I fell to the ground. The first time I did, Gregory tried to help me up, but I ignored his outstretched hand and crawled my way back up. The last few times though, he kept on walking. My hand was cut up from the rocks, my good arm always shooting out to break my fall. It started to sting terribly the last time I fell, and I had to brush out dirt and rocks and stickers; that was when it started to bleed. So I decided to put my jacket back on, that way I had the protection of the long sleeve.

It was windy, but only hot air puffed in my face. I didn't even remember the last time I'd eaten or drunk anything. My mouth was parched, and my lips were chapped. My bottom lip had split open, letting blood trickle into my mouth. I was covered in dirt. At one point, we'd had to fight through a windstorm, and we'd come out looking awful. I wanted to go back to when it was cold, but it was just getting hotter and hotter the farther we went.

I wanted to shower. I wanted to eat. I wanted to sleep. I just didn't know which one I wanted most. My head hung down as I watched my feet shuffle through the dirt, which I started doing the last time I fell. Watching my feet was the best chance I had to keep myself from falling. My left arm dangled loosely by my side while my right arm was hanging in its sling. I had no energy to actually pick up my feet, so I listened as they shuffled against the ground.

When I wasn't listening to my feet move, my mind flashed pictures of my home. I wanted to be home so badly. I had always told myself that anywhere but home would be paradise. Well, I had been wrong. So terribly wrong. I was running for my life with a guy who got on my nerves and I got on his nerves—he was probably regretting agreeing to come along with me. We had our moments when we got along, but how could we survive when we wanted to wring each other's necks half the time? Maybe we would be better off splitting up when we hit Inonia, I would still pay him for taking me this far. Maybe he could show me some fighting moves before he left so I would have a way of defending myself.

My chest tightened just thinking about that. I didn't want to do this alone; I didn't even know what I was doing.

I was just running, but at some point I'd have to stop; I'd have to fight. And it would be better to have someone by my side than to do it by myself. It bothered me that I needed to rely on someone else, and it bothered me that I'd actually miss our bickering back and forth. But what bothered me the most was that I was so preoccupied with Gregory that I hadn't even considered what my parents were going through, and I wasn't quite sure if I cared enough to know if they were alive or dead. How ungrateful of a child was I? Shouldn't I have wanted to figure out if I would ever see them again? Would I ever want to see them again? The questions kept repeating on a cycle in my head. Those questions didn't bother me nearly as much as the one that kept popping up: was it wrong to hope they were dead? I missed my home terribly, yes, but I didn't know if I missed them. I missed Agathy greatly, and my heart ached painfully every time I thought of her. But when I thought of both of my parents, I honestly didn't feel anything. It was like a void. Did that make me a terrible person? Was I just in denial? Shock?

"Mia," Gregory yelled from up ahead.

I looked up. Gregory was a great deal of distance away, and I hadn't realized I had gotten so far behind. "What?" I croaked. I coughed, my mouth too dry to yell. He'd have to wait until I caught up to him.

Gregory stood there, watching me as I slowly walked toward him. My legs wanted to give out. Every time I took a shaky step, I knew I would be going down. But I didn't.

Thankfully, I made it to him before collapsing. "What?" I asked, covering my eyes from the setting sun.

His gaze searched my face, his brow wrinkling. He frowned as worry flashed across his. "I didn't realize you were this bad."

I didn't even have the energy to get offended by that comment. "Huh?"

"We only have a few more minutes left to walk. We're almost there. See—" he turned and pointed forward "—those buildings over there? That's where we're headed. We're almost to Inonia." I couldn't tell if he was trying to reassure himself or me.

I wanted to jump up and down, but I had no energy. "Okay."

"When we get there, we have to try to blend in," he said as he started walking. I followed grudgingly, trying to motivate myself to keep walking. I was almost there; I could do it. First stop would be to find somewhere to sleep, eat, and bathe. I would say goodbye to Gregory and find my way to safety.

I almost cried out in relief when we finally came within reach of a giant glass building, but I figured that would draw unwanted attention toward us.

"We need to find a place to stay," Gregory said. He molded into the corner of the building and looked around it while I looked at the ground and talked myself out of sitting.

"I was thinking," I rasped out. "We should go our separate ways."

Gregory glanced at me; his face tightened as he narrowed his eyes. "Why?"

"Well, *obviously* we don't get along and don't enjoy each other's presence, so it would make sense for us to go our separate ways," I said, looking into his furtive face. "And to show you how nice I am, I'll give you half the money I have as a thank-you."

Gregory rolled his eyes and turned his attention back around the corner. "I don't want half of the money, and we're not splitting up. Those men we narrowly escaped on the train will be here and are most likely out looking for you as we speak. I'm surprised they didn't have men search from here to where we jumped out. Plus they already know you're with a male, and I wouldn't be surprised if they knew who I was. Like it or not, it's best if we stick together. Also, you couldn't survive on your own."

I wanted to smack him. "But why would you want to stick with me?"

"Because if I don't, you'll end up dead." He turned to look back around the corner.

If I hadn't been so tired, I would have kicked him from that insult. But instead, I pushed that insult into a little box at the back of my mind, so when I was more awake, I could yell at him. "I can take care of myself."

He turned to look down at me with a raised eyebrow. "Right."

I narrowed my eyes at the back of his head since he'd turned back around. I glanced back down toward the ground. I really wanted to sit. Or maybe sleep. Or maybe ea—

"Things look clear," Gregory said.

"Okay, now what?" I asked. I winced at the pain of swallowing; my throat felt shredded.

Gregory looked at me, his eyes roaming my body. "We're going to find a place to stay, get showered, eat, and then sleep."

"How about sleep first?" I asked, just as my stomach growled in its emptiness.

"Let's find a place first," he said, taking my hand. I peeked down at our combined hands but ignored the lone butterfly fluttering in my stomach. We walked down the street, staying in the shadows of the buildings and I hoped we would arrive wherever Gregory was taking us soon. My energy level was blaring, as the fumes were almost gone.

Gregory finally stopped us in front of a derelict building, and I swayed on my feet. In large, bright blood-red colors, a sign read "Dissolution Inn." I glimpsed over at Gregory with a quizzical look. He just shrugged his shoulders and walked inside, pulling me along with him. As we walked in, I wanted to walk right back out and find something much nicer. The walls were covered in crumbling flower wallpaper, the carpet might have been white at one time but was now a revolting brown—hopefully it was only mud that was stuck to those carpets—and the one and only couch, which sat across from the front desk, was missing a cushion and had massive holes with ashen stuffing spilling out. A dead potted plant sat next to the desk, the leaves all dried up. The desk itself was worn down with scrapes and gouges all over the front, and the man standing on the other side of the desk topped the whole place off—he was grimier than the room. His glasses were smudged so badly that I was surprised he could even see out of them. I really wanted to reach up and grab them so I could clean them for him. His short blond hair was sticking up all over the place like he had just had a conversation with a lightning bolt minutes before we'd walked in.

"Wha' can I get ya?" he asked with a deep voice. It was almost comical to hear a deep voice coming from someone that skinny. If I hadn't been scared I would get some sort of disease by just breathing in the air, I would have laughed.

"Just need a room," Gregory said as he positioned himself in front of me. I couldn't tell if he had done that to protect me from the seeing the desk clerk—too late—or the desk clerk from seeing me. If it was the latter, we would have to have a little talk about his caveman personality. I didn't need to be protected.

"Jus'one?" he asked. He tried to peer around Gregory to look at me.

"Just one," Gregory said.

"It'll be a hundred a night," the desk clerk said.

Gregory started to take out some money from his wallet and handed it over. I looked up at Gregory. "Gregory, I should ha—"

Gregory turned toward me and scowled. I crossed my uninjured arm, which was not as intimidating as it would have been if I'd had two uninjured arms, and glared. I wanted to pay and I had the money for it. I looked up at the desk clerk to see him watching me with a gleam in his eyes. My body shuddered from the creepy stare and I glared back at Gregory and kept my mouth shut. Gregory paid for the rooms, and the guy pointed us in the direction of the room we were staying in. The moment we were locked inside our room, I rounded on Gregory.

"Why didn't you let me pay?" I asked.

"What were you going to do exactly? Open up your wallet that holds more money than he's ever seen and wait to see if we get robbed in the morning?" he said. He walked toward the bed and turned on the lamp.

My mouth dropped opened as horror seeped inside my body. The lobby of the inn had nothing on the room we were staying in. The room was disgusting: the bed was covered in dust and milky brown stains—it was moldy, and a rotten smell was coming off of it—the floor was covered with crumbling paper. The smell of pee filled the room and I gagged a few times, swallowing bile that crept up my throat. I didn't even want to know what the bathroom looked like if this is what the room was like. I was so tired, but I would have rather slept outside than in here. Gregory walked around the room like he was used to this; he probably was.

"You should probably take a shower," Gregory said.

"You can have it first," I said, still looking around. "I'm still getting used to the room." I didn't want to touch anything. I could possibly die just sleeping in this room.

"Alright." He walked to the bathroom and shut the door behind him, the shower turning on a few moments later.

Maybe I could convince him to change places. Couldn't we find something nicer? Cleaner? There had to be something a little better than this. We would just have to keep looking around. If I had to crawl around just to find a better place, I would. There would be no way we were staying here. We could catch something. With the way the bed looked, I could get pregnant just sitting on it, with my clothes still on. I wrinkled my nose as chills ran up my spine and I covered it with my hand, but it did little to block out the smell. It was nasty.

I was still standing in the same place when the bathroom door opened and steam floated out, followed by Gregory. My eyes traveled to him without my permission. He was wearing nothing but a clean white towel around his waist, and I watched at the way the muscles in his chest and abdomen contracted as he made his way over to the bed.

Wiping my mouth, checking to make sure no actual drool fell out, I'd watch him move. This was the first time I'd seen a guy this naked before. There was absolutely no fat on him, he was all muscle. He was God's gift to women.

"The bathroom is all yours," he said, his head still bent over the duffel bag.

Jumping at his voice, I cursed myself for staring, and moved. The bathroom was the only decent thing in the place. It wasn't a hundred percent clean, but at least the bathroom smelled liked lemon and the towels smelled fresh. *Thank God.* I turned the water on and had my sling off before I realized I hadn't brought anything to change into. Dropping the homemade sling on the sink and leaving the water on, I went out to grab some clothes. Now wearing pants, Gregory was still shuffling around the duffel bag, without a shirt. He looked up when I walked in.

"I need clothes," I mumbled lamely as I fumbled through my duffel bag and grabbed whatever was on top. I raced back into the bathroom, undressed quickly—carefully holding my arm—and took pleasure in the hot water pounding on my head and back. The water helped ease my headache, but it still was raging on like a storm. By the time I turned off the shower, the whole bathroom was completely fogged up. I took my time getting dressed in clean clothes. Trying to put the sling back on, I had difficulties tying the knot. So I kept my right arm upright and walked out into the room. Gregory had gotten rid of the dusty comforter from the bed and was sitting down on the sheets, and, unfortunately, had a shirt on.

"Can you help me put the sling back on?" I asked, holding out the fabric. Gregory stood up and took it from my hand. Carefully putting the cloth through my arm, he tied it up at the top. The whole time I stared at his face, he had this cute, determined look on his face when he was tying it. *Which I will never admit to anyone.* When he was done, he moved around me and to the door.

"I'm going to go grab some food." He slid his leather jacket back on. "Lock this door as soon as I leave and don't answer it. I have a key, so I'll be able to get back in. If you hear anyone outside the door, lock yourself in the bathroom. Got it?"

I stared at him. "Will anyone be coming here?"

"Hopefully not," he said. "I'm hoping no one noticed us earlier." He opened the door and walked out, and I followed to lock it behind him. I took up his spot on the bed and waited, straining to hear anyone or anything. My heartbeat pounded in my head, making my headache worse and hearing anything else difficult. I used the time to brush through the knots that were still tangled in my hair. By the time I got all the knots out, my head hurt ten times worse.

Every muscle in my body tightened as noise shuffled by outside of the door. The door handle moved, and I jumped off the bed, making sure I'd be able to make it to the bathroom. The door creaked open and Gregory pushed through. My body sagged against the bed in relief. He was carrying a couple of brown bags, which were emitting some of the most delicious smells. I moved toward him and snatched one of the bags out of his hand. The smell was unbelievable and I moaned out in joy, my stomach growling with me.

"Hungry?" he asked. I could hear the amusement in his voice.

"Starved," I said. I dug into the bag, taking out chips and stuffing them into my mouth: the food was mouthwatering. We sat on the bed and ate in silence, both sucking down the food as fast as we could. When I finished off the food and water, I placed the trash back into the bag and lay down on the bed. My headache was gone, but my eyelids were starting to be too heavy to keep open. I watched as Gregory placed both duffel bags in between us. I crooked an eyebrow.

He shrugged his shoulders. "That way we won't get in each other's space."

"Got it," I mumbled as my eyes closed.

"Go to sleep," Gregory murmured somewhere next to me.

I ignored him as the dream world slipped me away from reality.

CHAPTER FOURTEEN

Tingles of warm air caressed the back of my neck, so I leaned in closer toward the body heat behind me, the arm around my waist tightening. When I moved, my shirt raised a little bit, exposing my midriff, and I felt a calloused finger making tiny circles on my stomach, causing goose bumps to attack my body. I felt the muscled chest behind me breathe in and out, our breathing mirroring each other's. At one point, I swear I felt a pair of lips press against my neck. I was comfortable; too comfortable.

I didn't want to wake up from this cozy dream and go back to my reality. I wanted to stay in this person's arms and wanted to forget my life and forget the people who were after me. The fingers stopped playing circles on my stomach, and the large palm dragged across my stomach until it reached the other side, pulling me in even closer until my body mashed with his. My eyes popped open. The room was still dark, but some light shined through the cracks of the curtains. I peeked down at my waist—*yup, it was definitely not a dream*—a large arm was wrapped around my waist, and my body was plastered to a very muscular one behind me. A very muscular body I shouldn't have been up against. I tried to swallow, but there seemed to be something stuck in my throat. I was positive we'd fallen asleep with both duffel bags in between us. What had happened to them?

The vital question remained: how would I get myself out of his arms? *But do I really want to?* I'd slept much better last night than I had my whole life. It had to have been because I was over exhausted—nothing to do with the large Neanderthal behind me. I shouldn't have been cuddled up with some guy because I was technically "engaged" to Tyler. That was if he was still alive. My heart panged at the thought of Tyler; I hadn't thought of him since the library. I wondered if he was okay and hoped he'd made it out. There was no need to be mad at him about what had happened; he'd apologized. Instead of running away to make sure I lived, I should have been planning a future with him. Thinking of Tyler made me wonder if there would ever be a time when I could go back home, to pick up where I had left off. My father had made an excellent choice by choosing Tyler to be my husband; he was a natural-born leader, and I'd had a crush on him for a long time. We could be happy. *Yet I'd have to be okay with becoming friends with Mandy and Sarah.* The upside though was if Tyler was to become the Leader, I would be able to do what I wanted, and I wanted to teach, to help others.

Fingers gripped into my flesh, erasing all thoughts of Tyler out of my mind. My heart raced and my skin tingled as Gregory started slowly moving his hand back and forth—caressing my stomach—his fingers slowly moving up and down. A gasp escaped before I could stop it and

Gregory's hand stopped at once, I could feel his body stiffen behind me. He moved his hand up and away from me, and I felt the bed dip as he rolled over and off of it. I watched his silhouette as he strode to the bathroom, and had to squint at the blinding light Gregory turned on until he closed the bathroom door behind him. A few seconds later, the shower turned on. I already missed the warmth of his body. *No, no I don't.*

Shaking my head, I heaved myself out of the bed. Scrounging on the floor, I found the missing duffel bags on Gregory's side; sometime in the night he must have moved them. I grabbed mine and took out the items I needed for the day. I was dressed and brushing my hair when he finally emerge out of the bathroom. His dark, chocolate-brown hair was dripping water onto his shirt.

"Good morning," I said. "Why did you take another shower? You took one last night."

He scratched the back of his neck and mumbled something about needing a cold shower. I raised a brow but didn't comment. He went to the side of the bed, sat down, and started putting on his black boots. "We should get something to eat. And try to find anything useful while we're at it."

I nodded. "That sounds good. Listen, Gregory, I wan—"

"We should get going," he said, cutting me off. Getting up from the bed, Gregory walked toward the door. I closed my eyes and counted to ten to calm the irritation rising within me. I opened them and glared at his back but quickly smoothed my features when he turned toward me.

"Should we bring anything?"

"Leave the duffel bags, but bring your purse and backpack just in case we can't come back to the room," he said.

I grabbed my bags and followed Gregory out the door. We walked in silence on the way to breakfast. Few people were out, and each person we saw seemed to be in some type of hurry.

I followed Gregory into a small decaying building: tables and chairs took up most of the floor space. Toward the back, a door swung opened and closed after someone with a tray of food went through. Gregory asked one of the waitresses for a small private booth near the back, and we followed her to the back and sat down. After we looked through the small menu and ordered our food and drinks, the waitress took our menus away and walked to the back room. An awkward silence fell between Gregory and me. He was looking everywhere but at me.

"Gregory, is something wrong?" I asked. I snaked the loose hairs behind my ears.

He gave me a calculated look. "No. There aren't many people here yet."

"What time is it?" I looked around. There were only four other people in the place. I'd been too preoccupied by the smell of food to notice it as we walked in. The place was practically empty.

"Around seven," he said.

"Where is everyone?"

"I don't know. Maybe work."

"People work this early?" I hated going to school this early.

He gave me an annoyed look. "Yes, *princess*, people work this early. Sometimes even earlier than this."

I glared at him. Back to the nicknames. "I didn't know. I still have a lot to learn. I'm still new at this."

"Hopefully not for long," he said, once again looking everywhere but at me.

I looked down at the frayed yellow placemat. My finger scratched against the placemat, as I tried to ignore the way I wanted to stab him with the fork that lay in front of my hand. It felt wrong to constantly think of ways to hurt him, but then he'd open his mouth and that feeling would go away. As I propped my elbow on the table, I cradled my head in my hand and wondered what could be up Gregory's ass today; was it a stick? A metal pole? Maybe I could ask him and start a fight; I really wanted to start a fight with someone.

Food entered my vision, and my stomach growled hungerily. Food was the only thing that made my happy—it would always make me happy. People talked about how they couldn't wait to meet their soul mate, but I already had one: food. I truly believed food was my soul mate. We ate in silence, which was nice. I stopped thinking of ways I wanted to fork him and thought more about wanting to get to know him. My mind liked to flip-flop when it came to how I felt about him. But maybe if I had known him better, I wouldn't have wanted to plot ways to hurt him when he opened his mouth. I barely knew anything about him and I wanted to know what his friends were like, what he thought of his job, if he had a girlfriend. Strictly for educational purposes. Not for any other reason. Also, I wanted to know what it was like to grow up in his family. What kind of future did he have? Would he ever get married? Was he a good leader? What would it be like to kiss him? My fork dropped to my plate as I choked on my food. Gregory cocked a brow but then returned to eating. I coughed a few times, tears pricking at the corners of my eyes, trying to unstick the food that was currently holding up residence in my throat. Gregory leaned over and thumped me hard on the back, which helped free the trapped food. Swallowing, I grabbed my water and chugged it down. After I was finished, I set the cup down and looked around; watching as a few more people filtered in the shop.

I glared at Gregory. "You didn't have to smack me that hard." He just shrugged his shoulders and continued eating. Conversations started to rise as more and more people trickled in. It appeared Gregory and I had come in at the right time, as the place started to fill up. An elderly couple sat down next to us, the wife smiling warmly at me.

Returning the smile, I turned my attention back to a sullen-looking Gregory. "What is wro—" My voice died down as I listened to the couple's conversation. My spine straightened and Gregory's face turned serious.

"Supposedly the daughter is missing," the older man said.

"Hopefully she got out before everything went down," the woman said. "Or she's already dead like her mother, so she won't have to face those men."

My heart stopped and then immediately picked back up at a run. My mother was dead. I could feel the blood drain from face and roar in my ears. I stared at the couple and ignored the burning holes Gregory's eyes were making; I couldn't turn my attention away from the older couple.

"I heard after they captured Leader Cowan, he tried to offer her life so he could live," the man said, shaking his head. "That whole place is gone. It's been taken over by—what did they call them? Oh, that's right. Rebels. They're trying to command the other regions, but, of course, the Ambassadors are fighting against them. I wonder what will happen now."

My hands shook. My chin trembled. I blinked back tears as they started to rush in; I didn't want to make a scene. *My own father offered me up?* I looked down at my placemat. *Why would he offer me up?* A tear broke loose and slowly slid down my face like a funeral march. A large hand grabbed mine and pulled me out of the chair. Gregory threw money on the table and pulled me out of the restaurant. We were halfway down the road toward the inn when I had to stop. I couldn't breathe. I tried gulping down air, but my lungs wouldn't work. The world tilted and my stomach churned. It felt like a hand had shoved through my chest and was twisting my heart. I couldn't breathe. I put my hands on my knees and tried to suck in some air. Nothing. Gregory squeezed my hand and pulled me into an empty alley.

"Breathe," he said. He put his hands on my shoulders.

"I...I can't." I gulped at the air. My heart was pounding like a freight train. The world tilted even further as the dizziness swooped in.

Gregory lifted my head and cradled my face. "Mia, breathe in."

"I...I can't," I said. Tears formed in my eyes, blurring my vision.

"Yes you can," he said. "Breathe in."

I shook my head, a tear breaking loose and marching solemnly down my cheek. Something flitted across Gregory's face before he drew my face to him, and our lips touched. His lips were soft and smooth as they moved against mine. Closing my eyes, my lips started moving along with his. He'd kissed me. He'd really kissed me. And it was nothing like the kiss I'd had with Tyler. This was so much better. This was a firework kiss. Lightness exploded in my body and overpowered the darkness. In that moment, I forgot about the conversation and my father, I forgot about my mother, I forgot I was running for my life. In that moment, I could only think of Gregory and what he tasted like: chocolate tangled with maple syrup. I grabbed hold of the collar of his jacket and hauled him closer, and kissed him back. Harder. Right now he was my air, and I needed it all. He pushed me up against the wall in the alley. We were body-to-body, lips-to-lips, yet I still felt we weren't close enough. A yell broke out and we tore apart. Slowly, I opened my eyes. Gregory and I sucked in air, trying to catch our breaths. He lay his forehead against mine, his eyes still closed. I wanted more. I wanted to drown in him.

"Umm..." He had to clear his throat a few times before he lifted his head off mine. "We should get back to the inn. Figure out what to do next."

I just nodded my head, because I couldn't find my voice to say anything. I shouldn't have kissed him. He shouldn't have kissed me. I definitely shouldn't have felt the way I had. Closing my eyes, I put our kiss in a box at the back of my mind with a lock and a key; I would go over that when I was alone and not running. Gregory started striding down the alley, but I just stood there. The conversation at breakfast came back to me. "How could he do that?" I asked.

Gregory stopped and turned toward me, confusion written on his face. "What?"

"How could my own father offer me up like some worthless animal, so he could live?" I started to get angry.

"Parents are supposed to protect their children, not offer them up for slaughter."

Gregory walked back toward me. "Mia, we should ge—"

"How could he be so cruel?" I asked. My hands shook, and my nostrils flared. My heart pounded painfully against my chest. "How could he let his wife drink so much to the point where she didn't care about her children? How could he feel justified in beating his child until she's limp on the ground? How could he cause so much grief for a child who is supposed to be having the time of her life? How could he ruin Lorburn?" I was so angry. Everything I went through, living in that house, hit me in full force. I should have never cowered to him—I should have given it back somehow. Escape should have been my only priority. And Gregory was right, my father might have actually killed my sister and instead of listening to Gregory, I got angry at him. He probably had killed my sister. My father was a monster. And there was no way in hell I would offer myself up for him.

Gregory stood in front of me but kept a good deal of distance between us. "He will get what he deserves, I promise."

I looked at his face. "I don't want to go back."

Confusion lit his face. "What do you mean?"

I shook my head. "I don't want to go back to Gildonia. I want to escape and start over. Go somewhere new. Hell, I even have enough money to start a new life." I could hear the hysteria in my voice. "I could learn how to plant food and maybe learn how to kill a cow. I could find a cabin and live there all alone. Read books and entertain myself until I die."

Gregory looked at me as if I had lost my mind. "You have this thing call responsibility. If anything happens to your father, you have to take your rightful place, which is leading Lorburn."

"I want to have my own life," I said. "I don't want responsibility." I knew I sounded juvenile, but I didn't care. I was not going to lead. *Nope. No way.*

Gregory ignored my comment and walked back toward the street. Reluctantly, I followed him, trying to think of ways to convince him to see it my way. We walked the rest of the way back to the inn in silence. I let him lead while I followed, deep in my thoughts of a new life. How would I get a new identity? Where could I live where no one would recognize me? I was watching my feet as we walked, so I didn't notice Gregory had stopped until I crashed into the back of him.

"Why did you stop?" I asked, coming around him. Looking ahead, an older man with six younger men, dressed in green and brown uniforms (uniforms I'd never seen before, the army wore blue) were standing in front of the inn. "I'm not sure this is a good sign." Gregory gave me a look that said, *You think?*

"Mia," the older man said. "You have no idea how pleased I am to see you."

I raised an eyebrow. "Do I know you?" He didn't look familiar.

He smiled. "I don't think we've ever met, but I know you." He walked up to us, his smile turning into a sneer. Chills ran down my back. "I'm Kieran Roderick."

I looked at him blankly. The name sounded oddly familiar, but I couldn't figure out where I had heard it. His hair was graying, and he had a round belly. The skin around his eyes was wrinkled, not even hiding the evil that roamed in them.

The man, Kieran, smiled a grimy smile. "I plan to be the new Leader of Lorburn."

Shit.

CHAPTER FIFTEEN

"What do you want?" Gregory gritted out. He positioned himself in front of me, either to protect me from Kieran or to hide me. Either way it didn't work.

"I would like to have a word with Mia," Kieran said. A pleasant smile was creeping across his face. *Pleasant my ass.* I narrowed my eyes at him.

"I don't think so," Gregory said. I nodded my head in agreement. Whether Kieran could see it or not, I didn't care. *Way to be tough when the actual worst thing to happen, happens.*

"I'm not going to hurt the girl," Kieran said. "I just want a word. We can even have it here." He motioned to the inn and walked in. The men stayed behind, their hands on their guns. Gregory watched as Kieran's back disappeared. "I don't like this."

"We should run," I suggested.

Gregory shook his head. "You'd end up getting shot."

"You think you wouldn't?" I asked incredulously. I wouldn't get shot. I would zigzag the whole way when I ran.

It would be kind of hard to hit someone who was not only moving but also all over the place.

"Of course I wouldn't." He smirked. "I can outrun you."

"But you're not faster than bullets," I pointed out.

"You've never seen me run, so how could you say that?" he asked.

My mouth gaped, and I put my hands on my hips. "There's no way anyone's faster than bullets. You would have to be inhuman, and will you look at that." I waved my hand around him. "You're completely, one hundred percent human."

"You really just have to be faster than the other person." Gregory shrugged his shoulders.

"You would seriously leave me behind and—" My words were interrupted by a clearing of a throat. Looking over, one of the men that stood next to Kieran was standing in front of us. I hadn't even heard him approach.

"Mr. Roderick would like to see you now," he said sternly.

Guess it wasn't the time for Gregory and me to get into an argument about leaving me behind so he could save his own ass. The man marched toward the inn and I followed reluctantly, Gregory right on my heels. The man stopped short of the entrance and stepped aside for me; I walked in and found Kieran sitting in a chair. Two men stood behind him in a military stance, holding their guns across their chests.

"Please, have a seat." Kieran gestured to the decaying sofa.

I looked at the couch and sat down, but not before I said a few prayers about not catching something from it. Gregory didn't budge from his position next to the door. *He probably wanted a chance to run if things went south.* The rest of the men followed us in and positioned themselves behind Kieran and Gregory, their hands securely on their weapons. I gulped as I looked at the large arsenal that could end my life in the blink of an eye.

"Mia, my darling, how are you doing?"

I shivered at his words, and not the good kind of shiver. It was the kind of shiver when you had to touch something slimy. I kept my mouth closed.

"Just get to the point," Gregory spoke for me.

"I'm just trying to be pleasant," Kieran said. A sardonic smile shifted on his face. "But of course, let's get down to business. As you know, my men have been looking for you, Mia, and they've had some difficulties. You're a slippery one, aren't you?" He laughed. "Anyway, do you know why they're looking for you?"

"To kill me," I said. His voice sent chills down my spine and my gut was screaming at me to run.

Kieran laughed. "Kill you? No wonder you have been running. I'm not trying to have my men kill you. What would be the point?"

"The point?" Gregory asked. I could hear the annoyance coming out fluidly. "You would get everything you wanted if she was dead."

"Of course I wouldn't," he said, waving off Gregory. "The Ambassadors would get in my way and become an annoyance if anything happened to Mia. I don't want that. I'd lose valuable men if I'd have to fight against them. I would still win, of course, but my army would be awfully depleted."

"Then what do you want?" I asked. This conversation needed to be over with quicker than it started; nothing good could come from it.

"Well, of course. Isn't it obvious?" Kieran asked. He was sitting up straight—perfect posture. He looked down his nose at us like we were beneath him. He cocked his head as a smirk appeared.

Trying not to grimace, I glanced over toward Gregory, who had his head tilted and lips pursed, confusion written all over his face.

"I ordered my men to find you and bring you to me." His smirk grew into a smile. "I plan on marrying you."

I laughed. I couldn't help myself, but I laughed. In hindsight, it wasn't the greatest thing to do, especially if the guy in front of you killed people for fun. It was just so unpleasant and disturbing that my mind thought it was hilarious. Of course, his face turning red as I laughed wasn't a good sign. I felt the couch bend as Gregory leaned over and covered my mouth with his hand. "Do you have a death wish?" he mumbled in my ear before he stood back up. He kept his hand over my mouth, but I had already sobered up at the mention of death.

Yet the idea of marrying him was so ridiculous. There would be no way in hell I would marry him.

"I'm sorry, what?" Gregory asked. I could tell he was trying to keep the disgust out of his voice, but he failed. It gave me comfort knowing I wasn't the only one disgusted by this turn of events.

"I plan on marrying Mia," Kieran said. The vein on his forehead started to tick.

No way in hell, buddy! "Why?" I asked. It came out muffled since Gregory still had his hand over my mouth.

"Well, you see," Kieran said. "You are a young, healthy, and beautiful young woman, but you have no experience leading Lorburn. You're immature and have no skills. You need someone to put you in your place. Someone who will show you what it's like to be an adult. Someone to show you how to deal with the uprisings and angry citizens. So you should marry someone who has the experience. Plus, you're at the right age to start bearing children and raise a family."

I could feel bile crawling up my throat. I looked away from him and at the dirty floor. Children with him? Yeah, no. I would rather jump off a train fifty-four-hundred-thousand times than have children with him. I would've answered, but Gregory's hand still interfered with my mouth.

"If you marry Mia, you become Leader of Lorburn," Gregory stated. Who cared about whether he would be Leader? I cared about the sickening fact that he wanted to mate with me. My eyes traveled up and down as I looked at Kieran; I cringed as a naked Kieran popped up in my head. He was definitely *not* God's gift to women.

Kieran clapped his hands together and smiled. "Now you understand."

I licked Gregory's hand and felt triumphant when he moved it and wiped it on his pants. I needed to speak. I looked at Gregory, who looked ready to fight. "What if I said no?" I said, turning my attention back to Kieran.

"You don't have a choice," Kieran said.

"Why not?" I was so tired of people telling me I didn't have a choice.

"Actually, you do have a choice," he said. "Either marry me or plan your funeral."

"What?" I jumped up from the couch. Gregory came around and pulled me behind him.

"How sweet," Kieran said. "Your boyfriend here can come with you. I could use a man like him in my army."

"He's not my boyfriend," I said at the same time Gregory spoke.

"There's no way in hell I would ever join," he said.

I had to think. If I didn't agree to the marriage, Kieran would most likely kill both Gregory and me on the spot. If I did agree, I would have to marry Kieran. He would run Lorburn—and ruin my life in the process. Either way my life would be ruined. "How would you run Lorburn?" I asked, stalling for time to think of a way out of this. I could feel Gregory stiffening.

Kieran beamed while my stomach dropped. "I would get rid of this nonsense of titles. No one would be rich. Everyone would be equal. There would no longer be sectors or regions. It would be one giant home for everyone. Every individual would get the same education and have a chance at the same jobs. You and I would rule, of course, but there would be no Ambassadors, no council, no unnecessary laws. Everyone would work for one cause and one cause only: to bring this Nation back to the beginning. I would tighten our army and make sure they roamed the streets and actually enforced the rules. And of course, there would be rules every person must live by. There will always be rules. So, if you decide you value your life, I'll share the rest of my plans with you one day."

Some of it actually sounded okay, but I didn't like how he wanted the army to roam the streets and enforce rules. How could I even trust what he was saying? *I don't.* "Do you think my friend here—" I patted Gregory's arm "—and I could talk privately?" I asked. A plan started to form in my head.

"No," Kieran said.

I tried hard not to glare. "You're asking me if I want to die or marry you. Don't you think that requires some thinking? Especially when the guy you're dating is just a couple feet away." I grabbed ahold of Gregory's hand. Gregory, of course, squeezed my hand until my knuckles rolled. "We've been through a lot, and if I'm going to be with you, I have to end this." I peered up at Gregory; a muscle in his jaw twitched. "And when you have to end a love like ours, you should do it privately." I hugged Gregory and hid my face in his chest, sniffling loudly. Gregory jerked his arms around me awkwardly. He stroked my arm with his fingers, and tingles erupted from each stroke.

Kieran cleared his throat. I leaned away from Gregory and rubbed my eyes, hoping they were red from my "crying." "Of course," Kieran said. "I'll just be right outside."

"No," I said. "Could we go to our room? It would feel more appropriate there." I could feel Gregory's eyes on me, but I couldn't look at him. So I kept my eyes on Kieran, hoping he would let me have this.

Kieran's gaze bounced back and forth between us. "Fine, you have an hour. We are heading back to Gildonia at nightfall."

"Thank you!" I said. Kieran nodded his head. I pulled Gregory with me down the hall and could feel his eyes burning holes into my back. As we entered the room, I locked the door I turned to find Gregory staring at me in disbelief.

"Are you fucking crazy? Do you have a death wish? What is wrong with you? Do you really want to marry him? You guys would have the ugliest children. Did you even think about the children? This is how you would have trolls for children. You realize that, right?" Gregory paced back and forth in the room.

His questions jumped back and forth between different topics. I tuned him out as I watched him run his fingers through his hair and curse. Somebody's mind was running a little slow. I smiled at him. "That's how I would get troll children?"

"This isn't a joke!" he yelled. "What is wrong with you? Why aren't you taking this seriously? I thought when you laughed in his face you might have hit your head at some point. And then I realized you were just stupid."

Anger started to boil in my chest. I said slowly, "I'm not stupid. You call me stupid one more time and you will find yourself with something sticking out of you. I didn't mean to laugh at him but come on, who would take that seriously? And seeing how my life is on the line, I did the only thing I could do other than cry, which was laugh." I cleared my throat. I was terrified, but I couldn't focus on that emotion. I would be paralyzed if I did. "Let's fight later.

For now, I have a plan." Walking over to the window, I peered through it. Kieran had sent men to stay in the hallway. I wasn't surprised. "We need to escape."

Gregory's eyes narrowed. "And how exactly are we going to do that? If you haven't noticed, he brought men with him, and I wouldn't put it past him to have more."

I ran past him and into the bathroom. There was a window there, and after pulling the curtain free, I could see an alley. "Come help me," I yelled.

Gregory walked into the bathroom. "What?" He looked up at me standing on the toilet while I tried to open up the window.

"I can't open it," I said, pinching my finger between the bottom of the window and edge. "Ouch."

"Move," Gregory said. I jumped from the window, my finger in my mouth, and Gregory took my spot. He opened the window in seconds. It wasn't fair. *How did he do that so fast?*

"I must have loosened it for you," I said.

"Right," he said. "So, what's this big plan of yours?"

"Okay," I said. "We sneak out of this window and go down the alley. From there, we head to the streets and find somewhere to hide until we can get out of Inonia."

"There is a slight problem with your plan," he said.

"No there isn't," I said. It would work perfectly. I knew it.

"I can't fit through the window," he said, crossing his arms across his chest.

I looked back up at the window and realized he was right. Crap. I would be lucky enough to get through it. "Okay, what can we do?" I asked. We needed a head start. This was supposed to be our head start.

Gregory walked past me and into the other room. I followed him. He stalked over to the window and peered out of it. After a few minutes, he closed the curtain. "Here's the new plan," he said as he walked over to the duffel bags. Picking them up, he walked back to the bathroom, and I followed him back into the bathroom. "You're going to go out the window," he said as he threw out the duffel bags. "Will you be able to carry both duffel bags and backpack while your arm is in a sling?" It was a little late now, seeing as he'd just thrown them out the window.

I wouldn't be able to run fast if I had to run. Hopefully it wouldn't come to that. "Yeah, I think so."

"Okay," he said. "You're going out the window, and you're going to head toward the train station. Do you think you can get there?"

Probably not. It must have shown on my face because Gregory shook his head and sighed. "Okay, this is where you're going," he said. "When you jump, you're going to go right and straight through the streets. Make sure you try to blend in with those walking around. Three blocks down you will take a left. After you turn, go straight for a few more blocks and you'll come to a deserted building. The building's only ten minutes from the train station, but it's empty. Go in there and hide, and wait until you hear from me. Make sure you keep hidden on the way there."

"What are you going to do?" I asked. "How do you know it's deserted?"

"I found it last night after you fell asleep. I went out to make sure we had an escape route—and it's a good thing I did. I'm going out the door and slipping out the back," he said. I nodded my head. We would save the talk about leaving me behind while I slept for another time. For now, we just needed to survive.

As I stood on top of the toilet, I looked out the window; it wasn't a very far jump, but with my shoulder I knew it was going to hurt. "Why can't we both sneak out the back?" I said looking back at him.

"It's just easier this way," was all he said.

"Right," I said. "If you don't show up, I will hunt you down and kill you? Got it?"

He shook his head, clearly amused. "Whatever," he said. "Just don't die."

Oh, how encouraging. I took a deep breath in and let it out. Awkwardly, I started to put my legs through the window. Gregory helped me, holding me by my underarms—my shoulder screamed in pain—and helped lower me to the ground. As I touched the ground, he let go. Sliding both duffel bags up my good shoulder, I hobbled away and could hear the window shut behind me. Making sure my feet weren't making too much noise, I shuffled down the road. When I got to the end of the alley, I pulled the hood of my jacket up and looked toward the front of the entrance. Kieran and his men were standing around a green Jeep I hadn't noticed before and talking. Next time I'd be more observant. Thankfully, the streets were packed with people, so I shouldn't have a hard time sneaking by.

Saying a quick prayer, I put my head down and walked quietly across. People bumped into me. It was getting harder to keep my head down, so instead I just stared straight ahead. It was difficult to walk, as I had to shuffle my way around others. *I have to keep going straight for how long?* I tried to remember what Gregory said.

It wasn't until I walked the first block that I heard the yelling. Chancing a look behind, I could still see the inn and I could see Kieran yelling at his men. They must have figured out we'd escaped. Damn! I was hoping we would have had more time. Just as I thought that, Kieran looked my way. Our gazes connected. For a few seconds, we just stared at one another until someone bumped into me, breaking our connection. When I pushed forward and started running, the duffel bags bounced against my side. Kieran's voice floated toward me, as I heard him yelling at his men. With people walking in all different directions and the weight of the duffel bags, it was hard to pick up my pace. A shot rang off behind me, and people started screaming. I moved faster and shoved people out of my way, mumbling sorry but not staying long enough to hear a reply. Another shot banged out, and more screaming came from behind me. As I took a sneak peek behind me, I could feel the blood draining from my face. Three of Kieran's soldiers were gaining on me. I couldn't outrun them. I looked around frantically as I ran; I needed to hide. As I ran past an opened door, another shot went off, and I was pulled in through the door. I was pushed behind someone as they shut the door. I looked up into the face of an elderly woman.

"This way," she croaked, grabbing my good arm and pulling me toward the back.

"What are you doing?" I asked. I tried to pull out of her grip, but she was too strong.

"I'm saving your life." She stopped as we made it to the back. She put her crooked finger against her lip. "You should be able to escape back here."

"Why are you helping me?" I asked.

"You need the help," was all she said.

She opened up the door and I slid out. "Thank you," I whispered. She just nodded her head and ushered me on. I moved silently, hearing the metal door of the shop close. Keeping to the shadows, I listened closely to the shouting on the opposite sides of the buildings. By the time the building came into view, I let out a breath of relief. It was hard to tell where I was going, but I had finally made it. I walked up to the building and surveyed the area: it was empty. When I pulled the door open, I winced at the loud scratching sound. I stopped immediately and flashed my eyes about to see if anyone would come running toward the noise. After a few minutes of quiet, I slowly opened the door a little bit more and slid right in. Closing the door as quietly as I could, I stood in the silence of the pitched black building. I couldn't see a damn thing.

“Gregory?” I whispered, hoping he was already there. After a few minutes of silence though, I knew my answer. Minutes later my eyes finally adjusted to the dark, and I walked my way further into the building. My hands trailed against the cold metal wall, until coming up against a wooden door. I felt my way down the wood until my hand caught the cold, round door handle. Turning the handle, the door opened quietly and I made my way in. My head hit a string that was hanging down and I pulled it, and light illuminated the room—a small closet. Old moldy mops were on one side with a bunch of buckets, while there were brooms on the back wall.

Closing the door behind me, I made room next to the wall for me to sit and turned off the light. The floor was freezing, so I unzipped my jacket and placed it underneath me. I sat there, straining my ears to hear Gregory or anyone coming into the building. There was only stillness. I pulled my knees up and set my chin on them. A creak sounded outside of the door, and I stopped breathing. I knew if it was Gregory he would say something, call my name. For what felt like hours, I sat there frozen before finally letting my body relax when I couldn't hear anything. I started to nod off; the running had taken so much out of me.

I must have fallen asleep, because when I heard a loud crash, I woke suddenly and smacked my head against the wall behind me, causing me to bite down on my tongue. The pain vibrated through my head, and I could taste the metallic of the blood from my tongue. I stayed completely still, not knowing exactly which direction the crash had come from, but it sounded like it had come from inside the building. Slowly, I moved my hand toward my backpack and put both straps on my uninjured arm. Just in case I had to get away fast, I would at least have the backpack. I stayed crouched, ready to flee for what felt like an hour, but nothing came from the noise. I settled myself back against the wall and rubbed the back of my head. My head was killing me now. I closed my eyes. Gregory was supposed to be here by now. What if I had been asleep when he'd gotten here and I'd never answered when he'd called out for me? Would he go looking for me? What if he hadn't made it out of the inn? I felt sick at that thought. No, he had to have made it. A loud screeching came from the other room and I stayed completely still. The sound echoed through the building again, and I clamped my hands over my mouth from yelling out. Someone was here. My heart thumped in my chest painfully and it hit harder when I could hear creaks from the person walking in. *Please let it be Gregory, please let it be Gregory.*

"Mia?" his voice whispered through the room.

I exhaled my breath and smiled. I crawled to the door and opened it. "Gregory?"

"You're here," he said. I could see him coming closer to me. I stood up and pulled on the string. I blinked across the brightness as I watched Gregory walk toward me. As he got in front of me, I noticed a large ugly cut lining his forehead, making its way from his eyebrow to his ear.

"You're hurt," I said, reaching up to touch it. He grabbed my hand and pulled it back down, his face a mask of emotions.

"I saw them run after you," he said. "I tried to lead them off. After you disappeared, they focused on me, and I had to run all over the region to lose them. I didn't want to be followed, so I hid out for a few hours."

I was happy to see him, but I'd never admit it. I bit the side of my thumb as I watched Gregory shut the door and sit down in front of it. "We should probably clean up your cut." Blood was still scattering out of it. Gregory wiped his head and looked at the little bit of blood on his hands.

"It's fine," Gregory said as he leaned his head back against the door and closed his eyes. I unzipped a duffel and took out one of my clean shirts.

"Here." I threw the shirt at him. "Use that to hold against your head so it stops the bleeding."

Gregory threw the shirt back to me. "It's fine."

I bit my lip out of frustration. "If you won't do it, I'll come over there and do it myself."

"IT'S. FINE," Gregory said, slowly and loudly.

I breathed in and out. My body shook. I didn't know why I was getting so angry with him, but I needed him to take this seriously. "You're bleeding. If you don't stop the bleeding, you will die, and frankly I don't want to have to dig a grave."

Gregory tilted his head at me. Annoyance cleared from his face and understanding dawned. Gregory stood up and came toward me. I flinched as he grabbed me and pulled me into a hug. I didn't know what was going on. My arms moved of their own accord to hold on to him. "I'm okay," he murmured into my ear. My body began to shake terribly as I buried my head into his chest. His hand rubbed up and down my back. Gregory sat down without letting me go. I burrowed into him as I felt the first wave of tears hit. He just held on to me as I cried into his chest.

Once the tears all dried up, I pulled out of his embrace. I didn't know what had come over me. Why did I cry? I was too tired to think. I used a duffel bag as a pillow as I lay down and turned my back to Gregory. Closing my eyes, I could feel sleep taking over and the last thing I heard was Gregory saying, "I'm sorry." I didn't know what he was sorry for, but I needed to hear him say it. My heart needed it, which confused the hell out of me. What was going on?

CHAPTER SIXTEEN

I woke up sprawled out on the floor, Gregory's jacket covering me. Rubbing the sleep out of my eyes, I slowly sat up and clutched Gregory's jacket closer to me—leaning in and inhaling his smell; it was woodsy mixed with smoke. I smiled and just sat there for a few minutes, smelling the jacket in. *Go find the owner of the Jacket and just smell him in.* Yeah right, like that wouldn't be weird or anything. *And sniffing his jacket while he's gone isn't weird?* I shook my head. I shouldn't have been smelling anything of his.

As I stood up on shaky legs, I walked out the opened closet door, and found Gregory standing next to one of the boarded-up windows, one hand on his hip while the other one raked through his hair. His shirt clung snugly to his body and I watched hypnotized as his arm move back and forth, back and forth. I could think of something else his hand could do. I blinked up and looked away. *What the hell?* I gulped a few times trying to get my bearings.

"Morning," I said as I walked over to him. "What are you looking at?"

He kept his gaze on the boarded-up window in front of us. "Nothing, I'm just thinking."

"About?" I prodded.

"What our next plan is going to be," he said.

"I didn't think we had an original plan. I thought it was more of a run-for-your-life kind of plan."

He was quiet for a few minutes before answering. "Kieran's looking for you. He probably figures we'd go to the Ambassador of Inonia for help, or catch a train out of here. But if we don't do one of those two things, we will be stuck in this building. And I doubt Kieran wouldn't start a search party."

"Okay?" I said. "So what are we going to do?"

"Our best bet is to go somewhere else, throw them off our scent."

That was fine with me. But where would we go and when would we leave? "So when do we leave?"

Gregory finally looked over at me. "I need to find out the trains' schedule and figure out which one's the best to take. By the way, I got some food." He pointed to a large paper bag sitting on the ground. "You need to make sure you eat. I'm hoping we can leave tonight. But in order to do that, I need to figure out what Kieran's planning on doing. That way we won't get caught while we try to escape. Get some more rest while you're at it. You'll need your energy for tonight."

I walked over to the paper bag and sat down. I took out a bagel and started munching on it. "I want to help," I said between bites.

"It would be better to keep you here, hidden away," he said, watching me eat. "We don't need you to get caught before we have a chance to escape. Unless you've changed your mind and are willing to marry him."

I looked up from my bagel and glared at him. "Ew."

He smirked. "Too old?"

"Among other things," I mumbled between bites. Gregory laughed. I peeked up through my lashes toward him and glared.

Gregory finally finished his stupid laughing, and we both sat in silence. When I finished up the bagel, he just stood there, staring off into space.

"I don't know what our next move will be, other than finding safety." I watched as he chewed his lip. "What I think you should be doing is stepping up as acting Leader." He turned toward me and leaned up against the wall. "You wouldn't have to run and dodge bullets. You would have an army behind you." He crossed his arms and ankles. He looked casual while he nonchalantly commented on my cowardly skills. "We're not going to be able to hide forever. So, you'll need to make up your mind about what you want to do," he said.

I crumpled up the paper bag and dusted the crumbs off my pants. "I want to start a new life." At least that was the truth.

"If your father is dead, you're next in line to rule," he said with all seriousness.

"I don't want to rule," I said.

"Why not?"

"I don't want to be anything like my father," I said. "And Kieran has a point. I have no idea what I would be doing. I have no experience. I liked his ideas of changing things, except I don't trust him. I do want everyone to be equal, but that will never happen. People will always want what others have. I want change, but I'm only seventeen. People won't listen to me. They'll see a silly little girl trying to boss them around. And how am I supposed to take care of everyone in Lorburn if I can barely take care of myself? The citizens would truly be better off with a different Leader."

Shrugging his shoulders, he never took his eyes off of me. "You're bossy, stubborn, and care about others. I think you'd be an okay Leader."

I glowered at him. "Really, just an okay one? Plus I don't want to be one." This conversation needed to end.

"So you want to run away from your responsibilities?" he asked.

"I'm not running away from my responsibilities," I gritted out. "They're still my dad's responsibilities."

"Your dad's most likely dead, and if he isn't, he will be," Gregory said bluntly.

"No he isn't." I stood up. "If he were dead, we would know. Kieran seems the type to announce it to everyone. Why are even talking about this?" Heat crawled up my neck as my anger started rising. Pacing back and forth, I clenched and unclenched my fists.

"Because you want to run away and hide like a coward," he said angrily.

I turned toward him and marched up to him, my finger jabbing into his chest. "A coward? Are you kidding me? I'm not a coward. I'm surviving. I've just decided to put myself first for once. All of my life, I've been told what to do, what to wear, and what to say. This is the first time I have had a chance to escape and save myself. Yeah, the situation sucks, but it's the only chance I got." I could barely breathe I was so angry.

"You are a coward! What about all those innocent lives that Kieran and the rebels go through? Do you not care about them? Do you not want to help them? Everyone's here for a reason. You were born into a family that leads, and you want to take that for granted. You're so busy looking out for yourself you don't even notice anyone around you and their suffering. Since the first day I met you, it was always about 'me, me, me.' Why don't you grow up and stop being so selfish." He stood glaring at me, his chest rose up and down as fast as my heart beat against mine.

Tears pricked the corners of my eyes, but I wouldn't cry. "You're an asshole. You know that? Maybe if you...you...you," I stammered.

"I...I...I...what?" he mimicked. "Do you think I'm having the time of my life running from the rebels? Do you think I wanted to leave Gildonia? But you don't care what I think because you had my clothes packed without even asking. You demanded. That's all you do, and when something doesn't go your way, you get upset and act like a toddler." Gregory walked over and punched the wall. As the clank of metal pierced through the air, I flinched back involuntary. "For once in your goddamn life, think of someone other than yourself. Step up and take your rightful place."

Each word hit me like a brick, and I closed and opened my hands over and over; I wanted to hit him, make his life miserable, but I also wanted to cry which I wouldn't give in to. "You can't tell me how to live. You don't even know me. You really think you know me just after a few days? You know nothing. This is my decision. I'm not going to rule. And if you hate my decision and think I'm *so* selfish, then you don't have to come with me. You can go home. Go back to that life you thought you loved. Which we both know you didn't. You hated it." My breathing escalated, my chest rising and falling with each quick breath.

"It's a stupid fucking decision." He walked toward the door, swinging it open. "I'm going to check the train schedules." He slammed the door behind him, and my mouth dropped open. How could he be pissed at the decision I wanted to make? How could he make so much noise? What if someone had heard the door slamming like that? Rushing over to the closet, I stepped in and closed the door behind me; sinking to the floor, I crawled over to the spot I had been in last night. I shouldn't have cared what he thought. It was not a stupid decision. What about my happiness? Why did I have to be responsible for the Nation when I didn't want it?

I could still smell his scent from his jacket. I picked it up and tossed it across the small room. As I grabbed my jacket, I slipped it on and pinched my legs up close to my body, hugging them with my good arm. I didn't want the life I was born into; I wanted a life where I could be happy and have some fun. And if that meant I had to be on the run, then that would be fine with me. When it came to marriage, I should be able to choose who I want to spend the rest of my life with, no one should choose for me. Being on the run was the first time I'd felt alive. It was the first time I'd wanted to fight to wake up in the morning. Shouldn't you live a life you want to fight for?

Eventually, I dozed off after many hours of brooding, and I woke up to the sound of scratching coming from the main room. I rubbed my eyes and stood up, holding on to the wall so I wouldn't fall over. My stomach grumbled loudly and I was lightheaded, so I stood there for a few minutes until the black spots faded from my vision. Finally, when I was able to move, I opened the door slightly and peeked through. As Gregory walked toward the closet holding some bags, I silently opened up the door to let him in.

"I brought some food," he said, "and some supplies."

My stomach growled at his response, this time more loudly. He handed me a paper bag and I went back to my spot, near the mops and buckets, and sat down. Taking the items out of the bag—two sandwiches, two apples, and two waters—I took my portion and then slid the rest across to where Gregory was now sitting down, leaning up against the wall. Biting into the apple, I almost moaned in delight at the sweet taste, I could feel the juice sliding down my chin, but I was too hungry to worry about wiping it away. We ate in painful silence. Neither one of us was going to apologize. We were both too stubborn.

After I finished the food, I took my sleeve and wiped away whatever was left on my face before taking a deep gulp of water and sitting back up against the wall. I looked everywhere but at Gregory. I was still pissed at him, but I wanted to know what he had found out. Finally, I locked eyes with him and raised my brow expectantly. He just shrugged his shoulders.

I rolled my eyes. "So, what did you find out?" I had a feeling if I didn't say anything, we would be sitting in silence for the rest of the day into evening; I wasn't sure what day it was, or if it was night or day.

"A train leaves first thing in the morning for Centonia. I figured we'll head out tonight once it gets dark and find a place to hide closer to the station. That way all we have to do is hop on a train."

We. That one word started a flame of hope in my chest. So he wasn't mad enough at me to abandon me. "Why not just go in the morning?"

"It would be easier to just go tonight." He started to go through the other bags. There was something he wasn't telling me.

I rubbed my right arm, wishing I could get it out of the sling already. "So what aren't you telling me?"

"Kieran's having his men search every building," Gregory said. "I'd rather be hiding out closer to the station than be found here."

I nodded my head and pointed to the other bags. "What are those?"

"Supplies." He grabbed one of the duffel bags. "Once we get on the train, we should change your appearance."

"What? Why?" I asked.

"Because it would be easier to get through other regions without getting caught if you didn't look—" he waved his hand toward me "—like you. Especially if you want to run away from everything."

Ignoring his jab, I asked, "How am I supposed to change my appearance?"

"I got something to change your hair and new clothes." He started pushing everything into the duffel bag.

"What do you mean change my hair?"

"Cut and change the color."

I grabbed my long hair. I didn't want to cut it or change the color; I loved my hair. He had to be crazy. *Yup, crazy.* My eyes just stayed on the duffel bag as Gregory loaded it with the items he'd brought. Even after he was finished and the bag was zipped back up, I just stared at it.

Gregory and I sat in the closet for hours in uncomfortable silence. He was attaching knives to the top of his shoes and securing them with a Velcro-type rope. I sat watching him arm himself up. I wonder what he would say if I asked if I could have weapon. *"Sorry, Mia, but you're too delicate to touch one of these." "You couldn't handle something this sharp." "You won't take responsibility if you hurt someone." "Your lips look yummy."* I didn't know where that last one came from, but I knew he would never say anything like that.

Once it was nightfall, we headed out of the building, keeping to the shadows. Gregory carried both duffel bags while I kept my backpack. I had shoved my purse in it earlier so I wouldn't have to worry about anything but the backpack. As we got closer to the station, Gregory took more and more difficult routes. I was so tired of running. I would gladly chop off my legs so I wouldn't have to run, but that would have hurt, and I hated pain more than running. By the time we got to the hiding place, I was annoyed. It was a tiny cave. I missed the closet. At least the closet would have been a little bit warmer.

Gregory and I sat in the tiny cave in silence all night. The only thing I enjoyed about the tiny cave was the sunrise. It was beautiful: red, orange, and yellow painted the sky, and I felt at peace looking at the different colors. Once I settled into my new life, I planned on watching the sun rise each morning. Gregory, of course, ruined the moment by opening his mouth and telling me it was time to head to the train station. I was exhausted and I wanted to sleep, so naturally, I slowly stood up and followed Gregory. I had just let out a breath of relief as we hit the train station when I felt a tap on my shoulder. I stopped and looked behind me. Shit.

"Gregory," I said. Turning around and looking at him, Gregory was staring at the guy who was behind me and mumbling something, but I knew it wasn't good.

"Mia?" the man said. He was dressed all in blue.

I squinted my eyes at him. "No."

He tilted his head. "I'm sorry?"

"I meant to say I'm not Mia." I smiled politely and turned back around. I took a step, but Gregory blocked my way. Unease trickled down my spine. "What are you doing?"

"This is Mia," Gregory said to the man behind me.

My mouth dropped open. "Gregory." I snapped my fingers in his face, but he grabbed them and pushed them down. "What are you doing?"

Gregory stared at me for a full minute before talking. "Trust me." His face was completely expressionless.

The man behind me spoke before I could yell at Gregory. "Mia, you're safe now. Mr. Wibert has had men looking everywhere for you."

"Why?" I was on defense, but I didn't move my angry gaze from Gregory.

"He wants to see you," Gregory said. "We need to go."

I stared in disbelief as Gregory followed the man in blue. What the? "Wait!" I yelled after him. "Where are you going?"

"To Leader Wibert's house," the man spoke for Gregory. Gregory walked over to the military Jeep that was idling next to the station. I gaped at him. Why did he figure I would just follow him? Trust him?

"What are you doing?" I yelled as I ran up to Gregory.

"You need to do what's right," Gregory said. He gave me that look again, but I didn't understand it.

When I stopped walking, I dug my feet into the ground. Gregory stopped but wouldn't turn around. "Gregory?" I looked from Gregory's back to the man in the blue now standing by the Jeep, watching us. I walked around Gregory and positioned myself so that I could see Gregory's face. "Gregory?" Gregory raised a brow at me. Then it finally dawned on me. "You did this." He didn't answer. I looked at the Jeep and shook my head. "You're such an asshole."

I could feel tears prick at the back of my eyes, so I looked down at the ground to try and calm myself down. I wouldn't cry in front of anyone, including the big jerk standing in front of me. As I took a deep breath and let it out, the tears finally subsided. When I looked back up and into Gregory's face, his face was blank. I bit my tongue and shoved Gregory as hard as I could. He only moved an inch, but it made me feel better. Turning around, I marched over to the stupid Jeep that the stupid man was standing in front of. Stupid Gregory.

"Mia, you might want to act your age," Gregory yelled behind me. I ignored him and kept walking. I was a couple of feet away from the truck when a large hand yanked my good arm back, stopping my progress. "Listen to me." *Now he wanted to talk?*

The man looked like he wanted to intervene, but I held my hand up to stop him. "Can we have a moment?" I asked. The man looked at me, then at Gregory, then back at me, and nodded his head. Anger rippled down my body as he had to get permission from Gregory first. The man went into the Jeep and shut the door. I turned around and faced Gregory. Thankfully, Gregory let go of my arm. "What?"

"You need to trust me. Use your head," he said.

I narrowed my eyes at him. "Trust you? You're handing me over to Aedan. How the hell am I supposed to trust you? So when exactly did you set this up? When you were out getting bullshit supplies? Was that all an act? Is it safe to know I won't have to be changing my hair color? Do you even have a soul in that body of yours? Or is it made up of one big pile of shit?" I was so angry I missed the emotion that flashed across his face. He had sold me out. "So what are they giving you, an award for bringing in the most wanted?"

Irritation bloomed from his face. "Is your tantrum over? Or do you need more time?" He covered my mouth before I could yell back. "I know your tiny brain is working overtime trying to think of all the insults you want to spout out at me, but maybe on the ride over you can take the time to understand why I did this. Maybe I'll even get a thank-you out of this. Kieran isn't the only one looking for you. You have allies. You need allies. Sometimes, you have to do something unpleasant to reap the rewards." He motioned his head toward the men in the Jeep. "You're going to get in that Jeep with me. You just have to trust me. I wouldn't put you in harm's way. I have a plan. Trust me."

"Why didn't you tell me?" I was so angry. I felt betrayed.

"You wouldn't have agreed to go. You would have been stubborn and refused to leave the building. You could have gotten us caught."

"I don't trust you," I gritted out.

"You need to!" he yelled in my face. "You would have done the exact same thing if you had been in my shoes." He lowered his voice so no one could hear. "You hate me. I got it loud and clear. You can hate me all you want, but this has to happen. You have to meet your allies. Everything could fall apart if you don't stop acting like a bitch."

A bitch? He thought I was acting like a bitch? I clenched and unclenched my hands for a few seconds. I took a deep breath, let it out, and slapped Gregory as hard as I could across the face, my palm stinging with the impact. "Go to hell. Why does everything have to fall on my shoulders? Why me?"

Gregory stared at me through livid eyes. "Did you ever think everything is not about you?" With that he walked right past me and into the vehicle. I took a few minutes to collect myself and flinched inwardly as I looked at my red palm and turned around and followed Gregory.

CHAPTER SEVENTEEN

Tension was so thick in the Jeep you would have to cut it with a sword. I sat up front with the man who'd talked to me earlier, while Gregory sat in the back with another soldier. Gregory's knees dug into the back of my seat, and I couldn't tell if it was because of the amount of room in the back was too small or if he was doing it on purpose. I was still fuming—it would be a cold day in hell when I forgave Gregory.

"So, how are you?" the driver asked.

I shrugged my shoulders, tensing at the pain in my right shoulder. "Fine, I guess. I've only been running for my life since Kieran and his men attacked Gildonia." I wasn't sure why I was talking. I'd been determined to not say a word, but I hated silence. It made me uncomfortable and gave me too much time to plan Gregory's murder.

"I can't believe they did that," the man said. "Your father's still alive. They're keeping him hostage. I don't know much else, but I'm sure Mr. Wibert will fill you in on anything you've missed."

I just nodded my head and looked down at my hand; it was still red, but at least it didn't hurt anymore. The moment I'd sat down, I'd regretted hitting Gregory. As much as I wanted to do harm to Gregory, I'd never actually meant to hit him. I was so angry because he was right. Everything wasn't about me and I was being selfish wanting to save myself over others. Didn't that show I wouldn't be a good Leader? I wanted to apologize, but I didn't want to do it in front of these guys. I wanted it to be private so I could berate him some more before I relented and told him I'd found the light.

We went through the gates with no problems and it was amazing to see the vast difference between both sides of the gate. Buildings were crumbling and the road was littered where we had been hiding out. Here, the buildings were glistening in the sun and the roads were spotless. On the other side, men and women were hanging around dumpsters, looking for something to eat or something to wear, while on this side, men and women walked in expensive clothes. It made me sick.

When the Jeep finally stopped, I looked out the window. If I hadn't been used to seeing houses like this, my jaw would have dropped, but I'd once lived in a place like this. The house was a three-story brick mansion with four large white columns in the front. Reluctantly, I got out of the Jeep and followed the men up the steps. I turned my head and found Gregory still standing next to the vehicle, staring up at the building in disgust. Sighing, I turned back around. The door opened up just as we got there, and we stepped through and into the enormous foyer. The walls were all a pale blue color, the high ceilings white.

"I'll be right back," the man said. He walked all the way down to the end of the hallway and disappeared around the corner. The other soldier stayed with us; I was a little disappointed, was hoping I'd have been able talk to Gregory. As I moved my right shoulder back and forth, I winced from the pain; I hoped to be out of the sling soon. With my good hand, I smoothed down my shirt and started tapping my foot. The soldier looked over at me and narrowed his eyes. I stopped tapping my foot, straightened my back, and tried to keep the panic down. I wanted to fidget so I could focus on anything other than the fact I was going to see Aedan. This overwhelming urge to grab Gregory's hand and drag us out of there took over, and it took everything in me to not move.

I looked up at the plain white ceilings, thinking they should have used more color when I heard the footsteps coming down the hall. I looked over and could see the soldier and Aedan walking toward me, with a younger man following.

"Mia!" Aedan said, opening up his arms. I took a step back. I didn't want him touching me. As I stepped back, I ran into something solid and moving. Turning around, I looked up at Gregory, his facial features shifting slightly at my look, but I turned back around before I could inspect it too much. I didn't have enough time to move before Aedan pulled me into an embrace. After a few seconds, he finally let me go. "Mia, how are you doing?"

"O-okay," I stammered. I tucked a loose piece of hair behind my ear: nervous habit.

"I'm glad to see you alive," he said with a tight smile. "This is my son, Jake." He motioned to the younger man behind him.

"Nice to meet you." Jake stuck out his hand, and I tentatively shook it. Jake held my hand a little too long, and I could hear Gregory grumble behind me. I let go of his hand and let mine drop at my side.

"We're glad to see you alive," Mr. Wibert said. "We've heard many rumors you were dead, but I'm glad that's not the case. Now why don't you go get a shower and clean clothes on, and we can discuss the situation over lunch."

I nodded my head. "Thank you."

An elderly woman walked over and took the duffel bags from Gregory and started walking up the stairs. I grabbed Gregory's hand and started pulling him with me. We had things to discuss.

"Mia, why don't you leave the young man down here," Aedan said. "We'll get him his own accommodations."

I looked up at Gregory, hoping he would say something like, *She doesn't go anywhere without me*, but he just nodded his head and let go of my hand. I glared at Gregory then followed the elderly woman up the stairs. She took me into a room with a giant king-size bed and set the duffel bags down next to bed before exiting the room, shutting the door behind her. *I wonder if she's allowed to speak.* I looked around the virtually empty room; a king-size bed and a mahogany dresser were the only items in there. As I shuffled over to the door on the left, I opened it and switched on the light, and the bathroom was illuminated. I went over to the duffel bag, opened it up, and started searching. The bedroom door opened, and I turned around in time to see a gray-haired man walking in with a small black bag.

"I was told you needed some medical care." The man walked over and set his bag down on the bed, opening it up. "How long has your arm been in a sling?"

He started taking syringes, white packages, and needles out of his bag. "How long?" I asked stupidly.

"Yes, how long?"

How long had it been? Three days? "I'm not really sure. The days seemed to blend in together."

He smiled. "Running for your life can do that. What happened?"

"I jumped out of a train and landed on my shoulder," I said. "I dislocated it. Gregory helped put it back in place."

"Ah, your friend from downstairs," he said. "Let's get the sling off." He walked over and helped me with the sling.

"What's your name?"

He smiled up at me. "Al. Now please take off your shirt so I can see your shoulder properly."

"Is that necessary?" I asked, not wanting to undress in front of him, even if it was just my shirt.

"Yes," he said. "If we want it to heal completely I'll need to see the area."

I nodded and hesitantly lifted my shirt off. It took a few minutes because I kept having problems with lifting it over my head. Eventually, Al ended up helping. Every time I touched my shoulder or his hand brushed against it, I winced. After the shirt was off, Al started poking all around my shoulder and I had to bite down on my lip to keep from whimpering. After a while, he took out one of the longest needles I had ever seen and started toward me. I stepped out of his reach. "What are you doing?"

He looked at me curiously. "This will heal it all up. Your shoulder will feel stiff for a few hours, but it will be completely healed and the pain will be gone."

"How?" I asked. I didn't trust him. Who knew what could actually be in that needle.

"Haven't you ever been sick and needed a shot to make you feel better?" He tilted his head and pinched his eyebrows together.

"My dad never let me see a doctor." I made sure I was still out of reach from Al.

His eyebrows raised. "How did you get through any illnesses? You should've seen a doctor now and then." I shook my head no. He put his hands up in front of him. "I'm not going to hurt you. This will help, I promise."

I stared at him for a few minutes. I had two choices: I could let it heal on its own, which could take about a month, or I could trust this man and it could be healed now. I just had to trust whether or not he was good. But what choice did I have? *If he's evil and injects something poisonous, you will die a fast death, but if he's nice, you'll live.* I rolled my eyes at myself. I looked over at Al and nodded my head. "Okay," I said. Al came over and stuck the needle into my shoulder and hit the plunger; cold liquid squirmed its way through my arm. He did that four times. After a few minutes, my shoulder started to feel numb and I slowly put my arm down and moved my shoulder. It hurt a little bit, but most of the pain was gone. I looked at him with wide eyes. "It worked." I could hear the awe in my voice.

Al smiled and started putting everything back in his bag. He zipped it up and walked toward the door. "Try not to put too much pressure on it for the first twenty-four hours." I nodded and watched him close the door behind him. Digging through my duffel bag, I grabbed some clothes and made my way to the bathroom.

I stayed in the hot, steamy shower for an hour, loosening up my muscles and scrubbing my dirty body; I now smelled like cucumbers. My stomach growled, reminding me that it'd been awhile since the last time I'd eaten, so I dressed quickly and walked down the stairs. One of the maids had been cleaning by the time I made it downstairs, so she led me to the dining hall. Jake was already sitting down with a woman I recognized immediately and as I walked in the room, both of them looked my way.

Aileen gave me a look I couldn't decipher, so naturally I ignored it.

Jake stood up and moved the chair out next to him. "Mia, are you hungry?"

"Yes," I said, sitting down. Jake loaded my plate with salad and bread, and I looked at it, wishing it were something else. I'd never liked salads—too many greens—but I forked it up and started eating. I was half way through my salad when the door opened, and Aedan, the man from the Jeep, and Gregory walked in—Gregory had showered, his hair dripping water on his shirt. Aedan sat down at the head of the table while the other man sat next to him. I looked over to the empty chair next to me, but Gregory sat across from me. Once again, annoyance flooded through me. I tried to catch his eyes, but he avoided my gaze. *Maybe next time you shouldn't slap him.* A plate loaded with food was set in front of him. My jaw dropped. Why couldn't I have his plate? Looking down at my dinky plate, I frowned. As I looked over at all the other plates, I noticed only Aileen's plate and mine had salads and bread while the men had plates loaded with pork, potatoes, green beans, and bread. I picked at my salad, wishing it would magically turn into pork and potatoes, but of course, it didn't.

"Mia," Aedan said. "I want you to stay here until we can get you back to your father."

My head snapped up. Panic started to crawl up my throat and black spots appeared in my vision as my head felt heavy. I tried to swallow a couple of times, but each time was harder than the next. I didn't want to go back to my father. Ever. I looked over at Gregory, hoping he would say something, but he just paid attention to his food. "My father is probably dead."

Aileen gasped, though it sounded a little fake, and every head at the table turned in my direction, except Gregory's—like he was avoiding the conversation on purpose. I would make sure he knew how much I hated him for it later. "Now, we don't know that for sure," Aedan said.

"Even if he is still alive, I'm not going back." I would stand my ground. If somehow they could get him out alive, I would not go back. "How do you even know I'd be safe here?"

"Our army will protect you," Aedan said with confidence.

"It didn't protect me in Gildonia," I said. "So how can I trust you?"

"Mia," Gregory said, his voice quiet and monotone. "It would be safest for you to stay."

My heart thumped painfully in my chest, I could hear it pounding in my ears. How did no one else hear it? "What?"

"I agree," Jake said. "You would die out there on your own. It's better if you stay here, knowing you have protection."

I started shaking my head no. There was no way I was going to stay here. They couldn't make me. "I'm not staying here." I looked at Gregory pleadingly.

"Mia," Aedan said. "Why would you want to be out there? Why are you afraid of staying here?"

Because I know what you really are, and you're just as sick as my father, maybe even worse. "I have a better chance of staying alive out there." Aedan's cool expression dropped, now turning cold.

"Now, Mia, stop acting like a child." His face turned red and his eyes shined with anger. "If your father's dead, you have to lead."

"I thought you just said my father's still alive?" I was stalling so I could think my way out of this.

"Mia," Gregory said. I turned to look at him, and my heart sank. His face was completely expressionless. "He's right. You need to stay here. You'll be fine. I promise."

My body started to shake. Was he really saying what I thought he was saying? "Gregory, can I talk to you in private for a minute?" I pushed out my chair and got up, not giving Gregory a choice in the matter, and left the room. I made my way down the hall, stopping at the front door; turning around, I tapped my foot until Gregory stood in front of me. "What are you doing?"

"Mia, listen," he said. "They're right, and you know it."

"No they're not," I yelled. "Staying here will get me killed or turned over to Kieran, and you know it."

"That's not true," Gregory retorted. "They have more men here than they did in Gildonia."

I wanted to wring his neck. "Why are you siding with them?" My heart pounded even harder in my chest and I wouldn't be surprised if it pounded its way out of my chest. "You're supposed to be on my own side. What happened to 'Trust me, Mia'?"

"I'm on my own side," Gregory said calmly.

My heart was now swimming somewhere in my stomach. "What do you mean?"

"I've always been on my own side," he said carefully. "I think it would be best to go our separate ways."

I thought getting punched in the stomach with a hammer wouldn't have hurt as badly as this. I should've known he would do this. This whole time my tiny brain, as he'd referred to it, had decided to think about trusting him. And now, here he was, handing me over like I'd known he would. I put my hand on my side to keep from falling over. "Fine. If that's what you want." Tears clouded my vision. I shouldn't have been hurt by this. I shouldn't have been on the verge of tears because he would leave me behind. My heart shouldn't have dropped in my stomach from the look of relief displayed on his face.

"It is," he said. "And remember, everyone has to do something that makes them uncomfortable.

"I'm sorry I slapped you," I rushed out. "I was mad, but I didn't mean to let it get that far, and I've regretted it since the moment I sat down in the Jeep. I don't want you to leave. I need you."

Gregory fisted his hands. "Mia, look, it would be better if we went our separate ways."

"Why?" I could feel a tear slide down my face. "Why are you doing this?"

Gregory moved toward me, but I moved back. I couldn't have him touching me. Gregory stopped and dropped his arm. "Mia, this is for the best, and you know it."

I swiped angrily at the fallen tears. "Leaving me is for the best? Fine. If you hate me that much, you should have left sooner." I pushed past him and up the stairs. As soon as I got to my room, I slammed the door. I flew to the bed and let the dam break and I couldn't control the tears that flooded out of my eyes.

CHAPTER EIGHTEEN

I didn't know how long I had stayed in the bed. The tears had finally dried up an hour ago, leaving me exhausted. I wanted to feel embarrassed, but I didn't. It shouldn't have hurt that bad, and I should've known he would end up leaving me to fend for myself. I stared up at the ceiling. It hurt to keep my eyes open. I kept thinking back to the day we'd first met and how rude he had been to me. *You knew this was going to happen one day.* Rubbing my swollen eyes, I knew my face looked a mess; if I looked in the mirror, I would see a blotchy, red face with sad eyes. Soon I would get my shit together and escape on my own, but I would give myself this time. Nobody needed to save me, I could do this on my own, and I was determined to do it.

Everyone kept trying to get in, but I'd locked the door and ignored them. I had no plans on seeing anyone because once I stepped outside of this room, I would have to listen them go on and on about a plan to get my father. But the thing was, I didn't trust them. Any of them. That was what I learned from Gregory leaving, I could trust no one but myself, and from here on out that was what I was going to do.

Darkness seeped in through the soft, pink curtains. I'd been lying in this bed for hours. Sitting up slowly, I cradled my head between my hands—*time to woman up! Get your sorry ass out of bed and get ready to make a plan*—and slowly made it off the bed and into the bathroom. I turned the shower on, stepped in, and let the hot pellets of water hit my body; I stayed in the shower until the hot droplets turned into cold droplets. By the time I was dressed and had made it back into my bedroom, night had officially fallen.

"Mia?" I jumped at the voice coming from the other side of the room. Aileen was sitting on the bed. How did she get in? I stayed rooted in my spot, not wanting to get close to her.

I cleared my throat. "Yeah?"

"How are you feeling?" she asked, smiling at me.

Trying to fake a smile, I nodded my head. "I'm fine."

Aileen stood up from the bed and came toward me. "Whatever you say." She stopped right next to me, placed an arm around my shoulders, and led me to the bed. "Let's sit down. I brought up some food, and I figured we could talk."

I walked with her over to the bed and sat down. On the bed, a tray full of meats, cheese, and fruit was arranged, and I picked up a grape and popped it in my mouth. Aileen sat down next to me, but I didn't look at her.

"I'm truly sorry about your mother."

I nodded but kept my mouth shut. I knew they'd been friends, but I didn't have anything nice to say about anyone. Shoving a couple more pieces of turkey in my mouth, I stopped myself from telling her what I really thought of my mother. Deep down, I knew I should have been upset about what had happened to her, but from the crying fest I had earlier, I had nothing left in me that cared. Maybe that was how I was supposed to survive all of this—shut my emotions off.

"I'm sure we'll be able to get your dad away from them." She put her hand on my shoulder and squeezed. Quickly, I stood up and walked away from the bed; I didn't want anyone to ever touch me again. *Being a little dramatic, are we?*

I looked at her. "How exactly do you think we'll do that?"

Frowning at my question, she rubbed her hands. "I'm sure the men will figure something out. They always know what to do."

"Right," I said sardonically. "Let's bring back the man who put us in this position to begin with."

"What do you mean?" She tilted her head at me curiously.

"Oh, come on." I started to pace the room. "We wouldn't be in this situation if my father actually did something. I wouldn't be running for my life if it weren't for my father, your husband, and all the other ignorant Ambassadors."

"Mia, you don't know what you're talking about." Aileen stood up from the bed and smoothed down her red dress.

"Then why did Kieran and his men come after my family?" I asked vehemently. "Why am I running for my life? We both know it's not because it's a fun game."

"You no longer have to run for your life. You're safe here." She smiled. The smile looked forced, or maybe I just hoped it looked forced. She should have realized this place wasn't safe for me.

"No I'm not," I said. "They'll come for me. Kieran wants me badly enough that he will use every resource he can to get his hands on to get to me."

"It won't happen."

Was she not listening to me? I wasn't playing this game with her. "I would like to be left alone."

Aileen sighed. "Fine, but you will come down for dinner in an hour. My husband would like to have everyone present. We'll be discussing what will come next." She stared at me for a long minute before walking out of the room.

Their next step was going to be very different from my next step. I had to figure a way out of there, and I had a gut feeling that something wasn't right. Running over to my duffel bag, I shuffled through it and noticed a few long hunting knives at the bottom of the bag. Thank you, Gregory, for not taking all of the knives. A pang hit my chest when I thought of him, but I quickly ignored it. I would never think of him again. *Sure you won't.* So I looked through the other items that a certain person had put in my bag: brush, scissors, a box of dye, and a fake pair of glasses, and I started to smile. A plan formed perfectly in my head and now I just had to wait until everyone was asleep before I could move forward with it. *Do you really think you can do this on your own?* Of course I could. *Good.* It was time for me to save myself; no one else would.

After an hour of planning and getting things ready for tonight, I made my way down to the dining room. Aedan, Aileen, Jake, and two other men I'd never seen before were already sitting at the table. The table was loaded with food: a roasted ham, baked potatoes, corn, green beans, and salad. *I'd better get actual meat this time and not just salad.* I needed energy, and that meant a good, healthy meal. Conversation stopped as I made my way over to my seat, and I could feel eyes burning into my skin as I sat down.

"Mia," Aedan said merrily. "I'm glad you could make it down for dinner."

Like I had any choice. I nodded my head and started filling my own plate before anyone else could, filling it with as much meat, potatoes, and corn as I could. As I finished loading it up, I looked up from my plate; everyone was staring at me, so I shrugged my shoulders. "I'm hungry."

"I bet you are," Aedan said. "Why don't we all eat."

The table was silent as we ate. I ate as much as I could, stuffing my face until I was so full I thought I might puke. I didn't know when I would be eating like this again, so I figured it was a great time to try and gain a few pounds of fat. Gregory should have food like that. *Thought you weren't going to think about Gregory ever again.* I ignored myself and hoped Gregory had food to eat. And a place to stay. What was he thinking? Did he regret leaving me? Was he happy? A part of me—okay, a huge part of me—hoped he was rethinking his decision to leave me behind. *I think you've obsessed enough about him already. He left. Without you. Now get over it!* I rolled my eyes at my inner…voice? Subconscious? Was I officially going crazy?

"Mia," Aedan said, interrupting my thoughts. "We were able to communicate with your father."

My head shot up. Fortunately, I didn't have anything in my mouth at the time otherwise I was sure I would have choked on it. Did that mean they'd talked to Kieran? Making deals without my permission? I took a bite of a piece of bread, swallowed, and felt the bread slowly making its way down my throat, the rough edges scratching along the way. Reaching for my water, I took a big gulp to help the bread further along. "You have?"

"Yes," he said. "It looks like he's in terrible pain. He'll be lucky to survive another day. We're thinking of everything we can do to get him out."

I'd say let him rot, but everyone would frown upon that idea, so I just nodded my head. I wondered if they really believed they could get him out alive.

"I wonder," Jake said, "if Mia has any ideas for how to help her father?"

My eyes shot to Jake. Jake's face was content, but his eyes danced with mischief. I didn't like Jake; something about him felt familiar. Even though I'd never met him when his parents came to visit, I knew I'd seen him before. "I don't know." When I peeled my eyes away from him, I focused back on my plate. I pushed my plate away and sat back in the chair. What I needed to do was get back to my room and wait for everyone to fall asleep before I could escape.

"No thoughts on how to help your father?" Jake asked. "Don't you want to see your father again?" I looked back at Jake and glared at him.

"Jake," Aileen said. "Leave the poor girl alone. She's been through a lot. She doesn't need any more hassle. Actually, I think we should let her get to sleep early tonight. She probably hasn't had any decent sleep since the attacks started."

I could have hugged her. "I would really appreciate it if I could be excused. I am exhausted."

"See," Aileen said standing up from her chair. "Why don't you men discuss how to save Andrew, and I will see Mia to her room."

"I can make it there on my own," I said. "I don't want you to go to the trouble of helping me."

Aileen waved me off. "It's no trouble at all." She moved toward the door to the hall. "Come along, dear."

I got up from my seat, ignoring the men, and followed Aileen up to the room. She opened the door for me then followed me in and closed it silently behind her. Curiously, I looked over at her, waiting for her to say something, but she just went to the bed, bent down, and started crawling under it. *What the hell is she doing?* Her long legs were the only things now visible. Every other part of her body was under the bed. "Umm…Mrs. Wibert?"

"One moment, dear." Her words were muffled, coming from under the bed. A few moments later, she slowly moved out from under the bed, dragging a long, flat box with her. She got up and put the box on the bed, then wiped all the dust off her body. Intriguingly, I walked over to her and looked back and forth between her and the box. As she opened up the box, my mouth dropped open; I couldn't believe what I was seeing.

"These are for you," she said, motioning to the box.

"Why?" I stared down at the contents in the box: two small handguns, four hunting knives, three stacks of money, and a few IDs. I picked up the IDs and went through each of them. On them was the same picture of me, but I had a different name and age for each. I didn't understand.

"You and I both know you can't stay here," she said sadly. "You're in more danger here than out on the streets."

"Why are you helping me?" Putting the IDs back down and staring at the other contents, I didn't understand her change of heart. "Why all the stuff? Just before dinner you were all for me to stay here and said I was safe here. Why the change of heart?" The three stacks of money, plus what I had with me from before, could seriously buy me a new life.

"I had to say that." She sat down on the bed next to the box. "This house is constantly watched and overheard. I had to make sure no one knew what I was planning."

"Wait, I'm confused." I looked at her sharply. How could I trust her? "How do I know if you're telling the truth?"

"You'll just have to trust me," she said. "Aedan knows you were planning on running away, by the way."

"I don't know what you're talking about." My heart started thumping faster in my chest.

"There are cameras in the room," she said. "He knows what you're planning, so he had men come in and confiscate your stuff while we were at dinner."

I ran to the closet and went toward the back where I'd hidden my stuff earlier. Sure enough, it was gone. They were spying on me? I felt violated. Thank God I never got undressed in here. I walked back out of the closet, furious. "Why?"

"Why what?" she asked.

"Why spy on me? Why take my stuff? Why keep me here?" The questions spilled from my mouth, one after another.

"Keep your voice down," she hissed. Aileen stood up from the bed and walked over to the bedroom door, leaning her head up against it with her ear pressed snugly to the crack of the door and doorframe.

"You didn't answer my questions." I crossed my arms over my chest. I was on the verge of panicking but tried to hold on to every string of anger.

"Shhh," she said. We stood in silence, me with my arms crossed, and her with her ear up against the door. Finally, she breathed a sigh of relief and walked back over to me, standing right in front of me. "I want you to listen to me carefully, and if you respond, you will keep your voice down. Otherwise you will get us both in deep trouble. Do you understand?" She waited until I nodded my head before she continued. "My husband is a paranoid son of a bitch. When we heard things were getting rough out in the poorer regions, he put cameras up all over the inside and outside of the house. He at least had the decency to keep them out of the bathrooms. Anyway, he wanted to catch those who talked about what the rebels were doing. He became obsessive. Your father didn't worry about it. He never thought anything like this would ever happen. Aedan kept telling him things would go terribly wrong if they didn't stop it from the beginning, but your father never listened. This has been happening for months. With your father being captured Lorburn is in crises. So Aedan will do anything, and I mean anything, to get him back. Including sending you in place of your father."

"He plans on giving me up?"

"Yes," she said with a frown. "I disagreed with him, and he called me a traitor. I would never betray my husband, so when he called me that, I was so hurt. I just didn't agree to sending an innocent girl to her death so that her father could live. Then again, we don't know anything about how Kieran works so we wouldn't know for sure if they would even let your father go if we sent you. So I told him I wasn't a traitor and I would always stand behind him. He told me I had to prove it to him. So when I arrived to your room before dinner, it was all an act. He watched the whole thing." She pointed to a small, round black device up on the ceiling. "And when I left, he had this smug, superior smile on his face that I just wanted to smack off. And that's when I knew for sure I had to do the right thing."

"Isn't he watching now?" I couldn't take my eyes off the device.

Aileen laughed softly. I looked over to her and saw her smile. "I was able to get it turned off."

"Oh," I said. "How did you do this?"

"I had some help, and that's all you need to know." She moved back to the box, and leaned over to the pillows and pulled out my backpack from behind them. I was so relieved to see it. She looked over at me with a smile. "I had someone bring this back."

"So what's your plan?" I started to get excited. Someone was really helping me. I didn't trust her, but I couldn't say no to her help.

She raised her eyebrow at my excited tone. I shrugged my shoulders and smiled. I was going to leave this place and had a partner. Hope bloomed in my chest. "Well." She started stuffing all the contents from the box into my backpack. "Around midnight I have someone coming to get you. You'll both sneak out of the house through a hidden passage. Aedan and his men have no idea where the path is so the two of you will be safe. There's a tunnel you will take that leads straight to the station. The individual coming to get you already has the tickets for a train ride to Minonia. There will be someone in Minonia picking you both up, and then you will bide your time before making it back to Gildonia. It is important you go back home. I know you're only seventeen and you're afraid you'll fail. But you won't. I'll meet you in Gildonia in a month. Try not to alert anyone you're there. It's important you get back home and find that slip of paper I hid in a book long ago. Remember the night of the party?" I nodded my head. "That paper is very important. Find it and wait for me. There are fake IDs for you so you can travel without alerting anyone."

I was speechless. I'm pretty sure my mouth was hanging open, but I didn't care. I didn't know what to say. "What's on the paper?"

She smiled. "You don't need to worry about that right now."

I already knew I'd obsess over it. But if she wasn't going to tell me, I'd just have to wait. "So, who's supposed to help me?"

"You can't know until the moment they arrive," she said. "I can't tell you, just in case the plan doesn't go through. I need you in escape mode and thinking only in that mode. It's the only way you'll survive."

I nodded my head. "I understand." I actually didn't, but whatever. "Are you sure this plan will work?"

"I'm hoping it works." Tears formed in her eyes. "It worked one other time, and I'm hoping the results are the same." She wiped away a tear and zipped up the backpack. *What the hell was that about?* Setting the backpack behind the pillows, she slipped the box back under the bed and then made her way to the door, turning back to me. "You leave in a few hours, so you should probably get some rest. It will be a very long night for you." I nodded my head. "Be safe, my dear."

"I will," I whispered to her disappearing back. Walking over to the closet, I rummaged through clothes that were hanging up until I found a pair of stretchy black pants, a long-sleeved black shirt, and my black leather jacket. I changed into the clothes, put on my white sneakers, and slipped into bed.

The room was dark, and the only thing visible was the red dot that was flashing at the top of my ceiling. *Looks like the camera's back on.* It took awhile before I could fall asleep; I was too anxious to get out of here. The house was completely silent and I wondered who Aileen had gotten to help me. My heart kept hoping it would be a certain-person-I-wasn't-going-to-think-about, but I knew that was unlikely. That person was long gone by now. I looked back up at the camera and counted the red flashes until my eyes finally closed.

CHAPTER NINETEEN

I woke with a start. I wasn't sure what had woken me up. My heart pounded painfully in my chest, begging to be let out. Rubbing the dew from my eyes, I looked around the quiet room. I didn't remember much about the dream, but what I did remember was running for my life. I was constantly running away from something, I just didn't know what that something was. Sweat dripped down my face; I used the bed sheet to wipe it off. Slowly, I slipped out of bed and had to wait a few minutes before I could walk: my head felt light and dizzy. It took a few minutes and deep breaths to help push the dizziness away.

I didn't know what time it was, but I was parched. Quietly, I opened the bedroom door and made my way downstairs and into the abandoned kitchen. A light would have helped me locate a cup, but I didn't want to meet anyone in the middle of the night. After opening and closing a few cupboards, I finally found a cup. Filling it with ice from the ice box and water from the sink, I made my way out of the kitchen and headed back to the bedroom. On the opposite side of the stairs, in large bright red colors the numbers read 1:37. Carefully, I made my way back up to the room, trying to figure out what was wrong. Something at the back of my mind kept nagging me and I just couldn't put my finger on it.

Softly, I slipped back into my room and shut the door behind me. As I leaned my back against the solid wooden door, I took a sip, the ice-cold water trickling down the back of my throat. It felt amazing, so I gulped the rest of the water and headed back to bed.

I sat the cup down and started to get into bed when I realized I was wearing sneakers. Why would I wear sneakers to bed? *Think, Mia, think.* Then it hit me. It was one thirty-seven in the morning. Aileen's mystery person was supposed to come get me at midnight. Something must have happened. Hurriedly, I pulled back the pillow and sighed in relief when I saw the backpack. What happened to the person coming to get me? I tried not to panic. Maybe they were delayed? *Or maybe Aileen lied to you.* I shook my head. I didn't trust her, but my gut told me to. I decided I would just have to escape on my own. *And how exactly? You don't even know where the secret tunnel is.* I willed the voice in my head to shut up—I really needed to stop talking to myself. Sitting on the bed, I closed my eyes and tampered down the brewing panic. There was no time for me to lose my head, because I had to stay focused on getting out of the place.

After sliding the backpack on my shoulders, I made my way to the door and tried to breathe as quietly as I could as I leaned up against the door, trying to hear any noise. It was silent. With my ear pressed up against the door, I stayed for five very long minutes, just in case someone was walking around. I didn't need to be caught.

Finally, I opened the door—thanking the heavens that it made no noise—and made my way to the stairs. Stopping, I listened: nothing. My heart pounded away painfully, and my hands were slick with sweat. *I can do this*, I repeated over and over again, before taking a deep breath, and started walking down the stairs. Every time a step creaked, I cringed.

When I got to the last step, I let out the breath I'd been holding, and walked slowly and quietly toward the front door, and peeked out the window next to the door and almost groaned out of frustration. Six men perched outside the front door talking and I definitely wouldn't be able to sneak by them. Turning around, I walked slowly back toward the stairs. *Where to now, smart one?* I bit my lip and tried to think. Maybe I could try the kitchen? Silently, I walked past the stairs, on my tiptoes, toward the kitchen.

"Where do you think you're going?" a deep voice asked from behind me. I jumped and turned around quickly, running into the hall table. Something fell off and smashed to the ground. A light turned on, and Aedan and Jake were standing in front of me.

"I…ah, I was thirsty," I finished lamely.

"With a backpack?" Jake asked, amused.

"I always sleep with a backpack," I said. "Since I've left home it's become a habit. You can't trust people out there."

"Sure," Jake said, raising his eyebrows.

"Didn't you already get something drink?" Aedan asked, squinting at me like he had a hard time seeing me.

"I wanted more?" I said, hating that it came out more as a question than an answer.

"Jake," Aedan said. "Go get Mia something to drink."

Jake licked his bottom lip before walking past me. Aedan and I stood in silence. I kept my gaze away from him, but I could feel his branding my skin. I wrinkled my nose.

"Nervous?"

I looked at him. "No, just tired." *I think it's time to get away from him.*

"You shouldn't be roaming the house so late," he said. "Never know when something might happen. I figured you would know that already, seeing how you barely escaped in the first place."

"I thought you said it was safer here." I pushed my hands into my pocket to keep Aedan from seeing them shake.

He ignored my comment. "How exactly did you escape?"

"What do you mean?" I tilted my head to the side. I knew what he meant, but looking stupid would be the only way to stall him.

"Everyone is trying to figure out how you escaped," he said. "We were all in your father's office when the attacks started, but you weren't. Luckily, a few of us were able to get to safety. How did you manage to leave without being noticed?"

Agathy never told anyone? *Smart woman!* "I was with Tyler in the library. I was helped out of the house," I said. I wanted to ask what had happened to Tyler, but I didn't think he would've told me.

"How?" he inquired.

"How?"

"How did you get out without anyone noticing? I would assume someone would have been noticed smuggling you out." He stepped closer to me and narrowed his eyes even further while his brow wrinkled.

I stepped back an inch. My hands clenched my stomach. I could feel the sweat start to pop up on my skin. I swallowed nervously. "Someone made a diversion, and I was able to slip out the back door unnoticed. I guess I was lucky."

"I don't think you're being very honest with me," he said, taking another step closer to me. "But I doubt you'll tell me. Why is that?"

I looked over his shoulder to see Aileen walking silently behind him. She had a finger pressed against her mouth. "Why is what?" I asked, looking back at Aedan.

"Why won't you be honest with me? I've never been dishonest with you."

I snorted. "Yeah, okay."

Aileen picked up a large vase, lifted it up, and slammed it against Aedan's head. His eyes rolled back, and he dropped to the floor like a sack of flour. I looked up at Aileen's calm face. Did she really just do that? *Maybe I can trust her after all.*

"Is anyone else down here?" she whispered. I didn't understand why she was whispering. She'd made enough noise hitting Aedan over the head with the vase.

"Jake's in the kitchen."

Panic slashed across her face, but it was gone as fast as it happened. "Follow me." She grabbed my arm, and we headed back up the stairs.

"Why are we going upstairs?" I asked at the same time Jake spoke.

"Where are you two going?"

We both turned to see him standing at the bottom of the stairs, his face composed, but his eyes gleaming with excitement. My body stiffened from his intense stare. We were just a few steps away from the top.

"I'm taking Mia back to her room," Aileen said. She started to walk back up the rest of the stairs.

"Stop," Jake said. She and I both looked down at Jake, who had made his way up to us so quietly that neither of us had heard him move. He grabbed my other arm. "Why don't I bring her up?"

"I can do it," she said.

"You should take care of Father," Jake said, pulling me roughly toward him. "He seems to have hit his head on a vase and is lying unconscious on the floor."

"Oh dear," Aileen said, her voice dripping with false surprise. "He really shouldn't drink so much."

"Mother," Jake said. "Go help Father."

She cringed at his tone and looked my way. Her nostrils flared, and I could see a sheet of sweat gleaming on her forehead. I wasn't sure what or who she was so terrified of, but it sent cold chills down my body. She slowly let go of my arm. "Mia, never be afraid of the dark; the dark will be your savior when you least expect it." With that, she walked down the stairs. I watched her retreat, thinking over her words. What dark?

Jake pulled me painfully up the rest of the way and into the room. As he slammed the door shut, he threw me across the room and I didn't have time to catch myself before I fell firmly onto the floor. My right shoulder slammed into the hardwood floor, and I cried out in pain. Jake kept the light off, but I could see him pull something out of his pocket, punch something in, and lift it to his ear. He turned around to face the door, giving me an opportunity to try to get out of reach. I made my way silently to the bed and slid underneath it, squeezing my eyes shut as the bed frame pinched against the exposed skin on my back. I let out a breath as I scooted all the way to very back of the bed. But when I tried to roll on my side I didn't fit, so I stayed on my stomach. It would have been smart if I'd taken my backpack off and got a weapon out before I slid under the bed, but I hadn't thought of that. Now I had no way of getting to one. I was stuck—pretty tightly—under the bed.

"It's time," Jake said. I wasn't sure who he was talking to, but I didn't want to find out. I could only see his feet walk around, closer to the bed. "Mia, where are you?" he asked tauntingly.

I tried slowing my breathing down so I wouldn't be so loud. My heart wanted out of my body—I wanted out of my body. *Well, way to get yourself cornered.* I, once again, ignored myself.

"Oh, Mia, where are you?" he asked at the same time I could hear a loud scream come from somewhere in the house. "Come out come out, wherever you are." More screaming started up, along with thumping. I started to shake. What the hell was going on? "Come on, Mia, do you really want me to find you? Because no one's coming to save you, and if I have to come get you, you're not going to like it." I could see his feet as he walked around the bed. I fisted my hands, my nails biting into my skin. "Alright, I guess I'll just leave and come find you later. I think my help is needed downstairs, anyway." I watched as his feet moved away from the bed. The door squeaked open, screaming floating into the room, and then silence as the door shut.

For a few minutes, I didn't move a muscle. When I couldn't hear anything, I started moving out from under the bed. My legs were the first to come out, and when I finally pushed the rest of myself out, I sighed. As I started to get up, something solid slammed into the side of my head, knocking me off my knees. My head slammed into the floor, and stars danced in my dark vision.

"I really can't believe you fell for that." Jake laughed. He grabbed the collar of my shirt and pulled me up toward him until we were face-to-face. "Kieran will be so proud of me." I fisted my hand and slammed it into his right ear. He yelped and let go of my collar. I kicked at him, heard him grunt, and crawled away from him on all fours. Jake tackled me to the floor, knocking the breath right out of me. He shoved me over until he was straddling my hips.

"Stop!" I screamed, shoving my hands into his face.

He grabbed both of my wrists and pulled them over my head, pinning them to the ground. "Do you really think you could take me?" He bent his head, and his nose hit my neck, making me jump. He started to sniff my neck. "You smell fucking amazing. Luckily for me, Kieran said I could have a taste once I got you."

Fear pierced through me. I lifted my right leg and kneed him in the groin. He grunted and fell to the side. "Get off of me!" I screamed. I tried to push myself away from him, but he got back in the same position.

"You bitch." He grunted, taking my head between his hands and slamming it into the ground. I screamed from the needles of pain puncturing my head. I kicked at him, but he had slid down my legs to pin them. One of his hands went back to pinning my wrists while his other started to roam up my shirt. "I'm going to take what I want." He slammed his lips against mine. I opened my mouth and bit down on his lip until I could taste the metallic, warm blood dripping into my mouth from his lip. He bit back harder, and I felt him draw blood. I kicked with my whole body, trying to get him off of me, but his hand reached under my bra, grabbing on to my breast. Tears formed in my eyes; I wasn't strong enough to get him off, and he wasn't going to stop. I tried to push again, and this time he finally flew off. I heard him grunt and yell, "What the hell," then saw his body fall on the ground. A large body came into my view, but I couldn't tell who it was in the dark. I tried to scoot my body back, waiting for the person to attack me.

"Mia?" His voice broke the silence, and I cried out in relief.

"Gregory?" My voice wobbled.

"I'm here." He bent down and picked me up, cradling my body in his arms. He moved over to the bed, still holding me. "Are you okay?" I shook my head and buried myself further into him. I had been so close to losing my innocence in the most horrible way, I didn't think I'd ever recover. His arms tightened around my body.

"What's going on?" I mumbled. I could still hear screaming and commotion coming from other parts of the house.

"Jake's working for Kieran," Gregory said. "I was supposed to be here at midnight to get you, but Kieran's men were all over the place."

"You're the person who Aileen said was coming for me?"

"Yes." He started to set me down on the bed. I didn't want to let go, but I did so grudgingly. "You have to believe I didn't want to leave you, but I had no choice. I met her yesterday. She told me it was important for you to come here and that, no matter what, I had to make sure you did. So I thought the best way to do it was be a dick and push you away. And will you look at that?" He smiled. "It worked."

I rolled my eyes. "Was part of your plan to leave me here?"

"Actually, no."

"Then why did you leave?"

"Mr. Wibert threatened to hurt you if I stayed." Gregory cupped my face. "I couldn't let him hurt you, so I agreed to leave. But what he didn't know was that I was already making plans to break in and get you." He moved his hand over my bloody lip, wiping away some of the blood. Anger bloomed in his eyes.

"How did you and Aileen meet up about our escape plan?"

"She saw me before I left and told me the plan. I agreed with her and told her I would do anything to get you out of here," he said. "What I didn't know, until around midnight, was that Jake was one of the rebels."

"How did you find out?"

"I overheard some of the men talking about Jake being Kieran's lap dog. Once I knew that, I knew you would be in greater danger. I've been trying to sneak in all night without anyone noticing, but it hasn't been easy. It wasn't until Kieran's men came in that I was able to sneak up here to get you," he said.

"Maybe next time you could warn me ahead of a time, and you wouldn't have to be a dick." I crossed my arms together to stop the shaking.

I could see him roll his eyes. "Like you would ever go with it."

We both turned toward Jake, hearing him stir. "We should probably get going," Gregory said. His thumb swiped once more at my mouth before he grabbed my hand, and walked us to the door. Jake's voice stopped us in our tracks.

"You're not getting out alive," Jake said. "Kieran always gets what he wants."

Gregory shrugged his shoulders, but I stopped him. "Jake has something that communicates with the people downstairs." Gregory let go of my hand and went to Jake. I heard another grunt as Gregory smashed something.

Gregory walked back over, grabbed my hand, and opened the door. "Let's go."

CHAPTER TWENTY

The hallway was completely darkened when Gregory opened the door. "Why is it dark?" I whispered as we made our way out of the room and Gregory shutting the door behind us.

"I cut the power," Gregory said. "I figured it would be easier this way." I nodded my head, doubting he could see me.

Screams traveled up from downstairs, along with bangs and groans. Aedan's men must have gotten here and were fighting back. We slowly made our way down the stairs, keeping our backs to the wall. My hand started to sweat in Gregory's as my fingers dug into it, helping me keep my hold on him. "How are we getting out of here? The front door?" I asked, peering down the stairs. The door stood wide open. With all the chaos around us, no one would even notice us slipping out.

"No," Gregory said. As we got to the last step, he turned us into the room closest to the stairs and shut the door. "It's too dangerous for us to walk out the front door.

There might be fights going on in here, but I bet there are still men set up outside."

"Oh," I said. I never thought of that. "So how are we getting out of here?"

"We are still going with the plan Mrs. Wibert set up." Gregory moved across the room, pulling me with him.

As a thought occurred to me, I tugged on Gregory's hand, stopping him. He glimpsed over at me, his eyes roaming my face. "Are you okay?"

"Aedan keeps cameras up to watch the comings and goings of the house." I looked up at the ceilings, trying to find the small black devices, but with the room being so dark, I couldn't find any.

"Don't worry about that," he said. "When I cut the power, the cameras stopped working."

"Are you sure?" I didn't want to go so far only to find out we were being followed.

"I'm positive. Now let's go before anyone decides they want to come in here." He moved us to the bookcase and let go of my hand. I quickly wiped my hand on my pants, trying to get as much sweat off as possible before he touched it again.

Gregory tore through books until finally stopping when five flipped out sideways like a flap. I tried to peek over his shoulder, but I could barely see anything. Gregory skated his hand inside the bookshelf. After a few moments, Gregory pushed on one of the sections of books, and a secret passageway opened up to us. I beamed up at him. If we weren't on the run for our lives, I would be truly amazed. This must have been the tunnel Mrs. Wibert had talked about. Gregory motioned for me to go first, so I stepped in. A blast of cold, musty air hit me in the face, and I almost smiled. Almost. I stepped further in and looked behind to watch Gregory pulling the shelf back to conceal us.

"Is there any light?" I squinted around, barely able to distinguish anything.

"In a sec." He shut the shelf completely, came toward me, and grabbed my hand. "We have to go through another door before we can have any light."

"Why?" I asked, trying to keep up with his long strides. "How far do we have to go?"

"Mrs. Wibert said it was a little ways down." Gregory started to pick up his pace. "She said it wouldn't be safe if we had a light on in this part of the tunnel."

"Oh," I said. We both walked in silence for a little bit. Well, he walked—I jogged. "So, where did you go?"

"Huh?"

"Yesterday morning when you left," I said. "Where did you go?"

Gregory raked his hand through his hair. "Mrs. Wibert had me hide out at one of her maids' house. The maid was happy to do it. She was planning on leaving tomorrow as it was. She fed me and gave me a bed to sleep in. I was lucky."

"Oh," I said. I wanted to feel terrible that he had to hide while I stayed behind feeling betrayed. If he had let me in on any details of the plan, I may have a felt a twinge of guilt. But I didn't. I still felt a little peeved by the secrecy and the way he acted.

"What are you thinking about?" he asked.

"When can we slow down?"

"Once we get to the other door, we can slow down." He gripped my hand tighter. "We have to put as much distance between us and them as possible."

"But I thought Aileen said no one knew about this tunnel." I could hear myself whine. *Very mature, Mia.*

"She thinks no one knows, but we can't really rely on what she thinks," he said. "I have a feeling Mr. Wibert knows more about this place and just pretends he doesn't. But once we get to the other door, I'll be able to block it."

"How?"

"You'll see," he said.

I shook my head and kept up with him. Twenty minutes later, we made it to the other door. I wanted to hug the floor and never get back up. Putting my hands on my legs, I tried taking deep breaths. Gregory opened the door and ushered me through and then shut it behind him. Pulling down the lamp that was hanging next to the door, he lit it and handed it over to me while he locked a bunch of locks and finally moved a metal cabinet in front of it. He grabbed the lamp, and we started walking forward at a much slower pace. We began speaking at the same time.

"How far will we be walking?" I asked.

"Are you going to tell me what you were thinking about back there?" he asked.

We looked over at each other, and I raised my brow. Gregory spoke first. "Mrs. Wibert said it's about a day's walk down here. It'll take us straight out of the city and right to the station. It should be about nightfall by the time we get there, so we should be able to catch the last train without any notice."

"Okay," I said.

"So," he said, looking at me. "Are you going to tell me what you were thinking about back there? Or are you going to ignore my question?"

I kept my head down. Did I really want to start a fight between us? "What are we?"

"Huh?" he asked, clearly confused.

"We bicker and only get along half the time," I pointed out. "I know only very little about you, and you know very little about me. So my question is, what are we? Are we friends? Acquaintances? Because it would really be helpful to know before we continue on."

"Does it matter?" He growled.

"Yes," I said, matter-of-fact. "It does matter. I don't know if I trust you. I don't think I ever fully trusted you. If we're in this together, there should be trust. And lately, we've really only been living day by day. So once again, what are we?"

Gregory shook his head, clearly annoyed. He didn't say anything, but I kept my mouth shut, waiting for him to talk. It was ten long, silent minutes before he finally opened his mouth. "I don't know what we are. But seeing how Kieran knows both of us, I'd say we are both in deep shit. So, it would be best to stick together. Help each other out."

He had a point. Kieran now knew who he was. And Gregory did save my life three times, so it looked like kicking him out of my life would be a bad idea. "I agree. And I think we should start all over."

Gregory scrunched his brows. "What do you mean?"

"Let's start over," I said. "Let's pretend we never met and this is our first time. Let's forget about what happened in the past and just look forward."

"That's a stupid idea."

I sighed loudly. "Why is it a stupid idea?"

Gregory smirked. "Because no matter how much you want to start over, we'd never be able to. Plus, I like remembering all of the times you've fallen flat on your face. It's quite comical to see." Gregory laughed, and I turned my glare toward him, pelting him with invisible knives. "You know, you're quite cute when you get angry. It's almost fun to get you to this point."

I ignored the lone butterfly fluttering in my stomach. "You're such a jackass," I said, but I couldn't help but smile.

Gregory reached over and pinched my cheeks. "What is that? Is that a smile? I don't think I've seen one on that face before."

I shoved him away from me and shook my head, trying to fight the smile.

After a few hours of walking, Gregory finally let us rest. I sat down and leaned up against the wall.

"Here." Gregory handed me a bottle of water.

I took a long gulp and drank the rest in the matter of seconds; I was so parched. I drank the water greedily without realizing that we might be sharing. I looked up to see him drinking his own bottle. My stomach growled. It wasn't a quiet growl—it was a wake-my-neighbors growl. Gregory looked down at me and smirked, handing me half a loaf of bread.

"Where did you get the water and bread?" I asked. I bit into the bread, moaning in delight. Wishing I hadn't drunk all of my water so I could have something to wash the bread down, I took another bite. It was like Gregory read my thoughts, because he tossed me another filled bottle.

"Take it easy on that bottle," Gregory said as he opened his new one. "There are only a couple left. Mrs. Wibert had left a backpack of food and water for us at the second door."

I hadn't even noticed Gregory carrying a backpack until now. He sat down next to me, his knee bumping up against mine. "She must have been down here when I went to kitchen for water the first time." Gregory looked at me questioningly, so I explained, "I had woken up from a nightmare and made my way downstairs to get a cup of water. Every time I had a nightmare when I was younger, Agathy would bring me water to drink. She would say, 'Drown your nightmares, my dear.' I'll never forget that. Anyway, I went downstairs and got some water. When I went back upstairs, I noticed the time, but it didn't hit me right away that you were late. It took me until I went back to bed, noticing that I was still wearing shoes to bed that you were late. So, I made my way back downstairs again to run away on my own, thinking you were never going to show up, and Jake and Aedan caught me. Jake went off to the kitchen, and Aedan stayed back to talk to me. That was when I noticed Aileen walking behind him. She eventually grabbed a large vase and smashed it over his head. She must have been coming from here when she got back. She must have overheard us." Gregory just shrugged his shoulders and ate on. "I'm glad you thought to look around for a backpack."

"She told me she would leave supplies," he said between bites. "I guess your backpack is filled with weapons, money, and fake IDs?"

I looked up at him in shock. "How'd you know?"

"Because mine is the same," he said with a smile. "She must have thought about food and water after she gave you your backpack and remembered to put it in mine."

"I'm so happy she eventually remembered." I smiled. She'd really helped us. I hoped nothing happened to her. "Did she tell you who we were meeting up with?"

"Yeah," he said, dusting his hands off. "Someone named Emma Farraday. Do you know her?"

I shook my head. "No."

"I don't either, but Mrs. Wibert said Emma knows we're coming. So I guess when we get there, we wait to see if someone approaches us, and hopefully it'll be her."

I didn't like that idea. "What do you think happened to Aileen?" I was afraid to know the answer.

"I don't know," he said. "I didn't see her when I came in. We just have to hope that she was able to escape in time."

"Okay," I said, frowning. She had helped us so much that it was painful not to know if she'd gotten out in time. "How long are we resting?"

"Just a little bit longer," he said. "We need to make up time and get to the station before the train leaves. Otherwise, we will be in deeper shit."

"Okay," I said, standing up. I did a few stretches, trying to avoid looking at Gregory's amused face. He just didn't understand how hard it was to keep up with his long legs.

My short legs hated me at the moment, but thankfully they were cooperating. We started walking again in silence, both deep in our own thoughts.

By the time we made it to the end of the tunnel, I was drenched in sweat, my legs burned, and my stomach was eating its way out of my body, but I was so happy to be out in the fresh air. It was dark out, and since we were both dressed all in black, we were hard to notice. We walked toward the station, which was crowded with people. The train had just pulled up, and people were coming and going through the train doors. I noticed a few soldiers in blue walking around the station, so I kept my head down and held on to Gregory's hand. Gregory gave me a surprising, supportive squeeze and guided us to one of the lines to enter the train. People were slowly making their way on.

"What are we going to do about tickets?" I whispered.

"I already have them."

I nodded and faced forward. The hair on the back of my neck prickled, and tingles ran up my scalp. It felt like someone was watching us, but I didn't want to turn around to look. *Paranoid much?* We were only a few feet away from the entrance when we heard the yelling and screaming. I peeked over to see a man and two women being dragged away by soldiers, fighting and screaming. I looked over at Gregory to find his face set in anger. It was our turn to get on the train, and it took a few pulls to get Gregory to move forward.

The ticket master took our tickets and let us through. We walked to the very back of the train until we'd made it to the very last room. I went straight over to the chairs, sat down, and smiled: my legs thanked me too. Gregory shut the door behind him and sat down next to me. I bent my head and leaned on his shoulder. It wasn't until the train started moving that either one of us started talking.

"I'm hungry," I said, my stomach growling in agreement.

Gregory chuckled. "Alright, I'll go find us some food."

Gregory stood up and walked to the door. I looked out the window and watched the fields of grass fly by. When the door opened a few minutes later, Gregory was holding two trays filled with food. "I figured you would eat all of this," he said, motioning to the food.

I smiled up at him. "Yes, I will." He handed over the tray, and we sat there, eating in comfortable silence.

CHAPTER TWENTY-ONE

I was out of breath. I didn't know how long I had been running, but I knew it'd been a while. Sweat dripped down my forehead and onto my cheeks. I kept swiping at it, but it seemed the more I tried to wipe the sweat away, the more there was. My hair was up in a tight ponytail, but some loose pieces kept flashing across my face while others stuck to my sweaty skin. My legs were burning. They were tired, and I just wanted to find a bed and crawl into it. I couldn't even remember who I was running from.

I kept looking over my shoulder to see if I could see the person I was running from. All I could make out was a black shadow slowly coming toward me. I looked back forward just as I slammed into a hard, muscular chest. Hands cupped my upper arms and my eyes locked onto the naked chest, which was softly littered with dark hair. My eyes slowly made my way up from his toned abs, to his toned pecs, and to his strong, square jaw. Finally, I made it to his eyes—eyes the color of grass right after a downpour. His mouth moved, causing my eyes to look at his delicious lips. I wanted to kiss them. Half of his mouth smirked and I licked mine in anticipation. I looked up at him, his face now serious. His eyes roamed me, taking in every inch of my body. I wanted to keep staring into the depths of his eyes.

"Gregory," I said breathlessly. "What's happening?" My heart pounded so fast that I swore it was going to turn into a train and leave my body. I was sweaty. Why was I sweaty? Something wasn't right.

"Shhh," Gregory said, his rough, calloused finger sliding down my soft lips. "Let me take care of you." His hand softly caressed my cheek and slowly slid down, down my neck, onto my shoulder. He squeezed it and when I looked down, I was horrified by what I was seeing.

"My clothes," I said, trying to cover my naked body with my arms and cross my legs. "What happened to my clothes?"

"Shh." Gregory lifted my head so my eyes could meet his. "Let me take care of you."

I backed away. Something was very wrong. How had I ended up here? How had I lost my clothes? "What's going on?"

"Nothing," Gregory said. He stepped closer, our naked thighs caressing each other. I shivered at the contact. "You are where you need to be."

"What does that mean?" I asked. I was about to take a step back when the place shook. I grabbed his arm to keep my balance, but the place started to shake faster. "What is that?" I yelled as I looked around, spotting the shadow looming closer. The shadow? Then it came back. The running. The shadow was dangerous and it was coming closer and closer. I positioned myself in front of Gregory to protect him from the shadow, but he acted like he didn't even notice it. He started to trail kisses down my neck, murmuring that I was where I needed to be, whatever that meant. The shadow was moving faster, an arm reaching out toward me. I squeezed my eyes shut and screamed.

I jolted awake, my forehead slamming into someone else's. My eyes popped open, and I was looking into those same green eyes. Rubbing my forehead, I moved back and looked around; I was still on the train. Hastily, I looked down and let out a relieved sigh: I was still clothed. I felt Gregory move back to his seat next to me. I looked over at him to find him studying me.

"Are you okay?" he asked, pointing toward my forehead.

"Yeah," I said, dropping my hand. "Where are we?" I asked. The train was stopped, and I could hear people moving around in the hallway.

"We've stopped in Centonia," Gregory said. He stood up and stretched, his shirt rising just enough to see his V. "They're refueling the train and picking up and dropping off passengers. We've been here for a good half hour. I was going to wake you, but you looked so peaceful. It's nice to see you quiet and not mouthing off. Well, that was until you started talking in your sleep."

I watched him move his way to the door. "What do you mean talking in my sleep?"

"You started mumbling something, but I couldn't figure out what you were trying to say, and then you started rocking back and forth." He opened our compartment door. "So I started shaking you, and then you woke up screaming. Are you alright?"

There was no way in hell I would tell him what I had just dreamed. "It was a nightmare. Where....um...where are you going?" I cleared my throat. That dream kept flashing in my mind.

"The train will be stopped for another ten minutes, so I was going to look around and see if I could find out what happened to the Wiberts." With that, he exited the compartment before I could say anything.

Getting up from the chair, I moved toward the door and shut it. My body protested when I stretched my arms over my head and bending down toward my feet; I needed a massage. I walked around the empty room for a few minutes until I was officially bored. If Gregory could leave and find out information, why couldn't I? Opening the door, I swiftly exited and moved my way down the hallway, passing a few compartments. Two men, who looked a little bit older than me, were in a heated argument and blocking the way.

"Excuse me," I shouted, trying to move around them.

"Move it," one of the guys said. He had tie-dyed hair and dark blue eyes. He was a little taller than me, but not by much. His arms were as thin as mine, and his clothes ripped. I looked over at the other guy, who was the complete opposite of the first guy. His hair was blond, and he had hazel eyes, towering over both me and Tie-Dye.

Tie-Dye pushed me out of the way, hard enough to knock me off my feet and I hit the floor hard. "What are you, five years old?" I yelled, getting back to my feet and wiping dirt off my backside.

"Mind your own business," he said with a scowl. Blondie just looked at me curiously. He seemed to be richer than Tie-Dye, and I hoped he wouldn't recognize me.

"It became my business when I couldn't walk down the aisle," I said.

Tie-Dye continued to scowl at me until finally he looked at Blondie. "Stay out of my way next time," he said, and then he stormed off.

I started to turn back toward my compartment when Blondie began to speak. "Wait, do I know you?" I picked up my pace and ignored him, but Blondie just followed me. I stepped into the compartment and closed the door in his face. I had just made it to my seat when the door opened and Blondie stepped in.

"Umm…can I help you with something?" I wrung my hands together, hoping Gregory would be getting his ass back here soon.

"Nope, not at all," he said, taking the seat across from me.

I gaped at him. "What are you doing?"

Confusion crossed his face. "What do you mean?"

I pointed to him and then to his seat. "Why are you sitting there?"

He pulled out his ticket and held it up. "Because it's my seat."

"I'm sorry, what?"

"My ticket is for this room. You do know that people share rooms, right?" He peered at me through narrowed eyes.

I didn't know that. Why hadn't Gregory warned me? "Yes, yes I knew that." I turned away from him and looked out the window. The view showed dead brown grass, and the sky was overcast. Great, the weather matched my mood.

"So, where are you going?" Blondie asked.

I looked over at the door, hoping Gregory would walk through. But nope, he wasn't there. "Umm…Minonia." *Way to be smooth.*

"Ah, family?" he asked.

I looked over to him. "I'm sorry?"

"Are you going there for family?" he asked, curiosity covering his face.

Say nothing. "Um, no." I looked back over at the doors. *Didn't I just say "say nothing"?* I ignored my inner self.

"So are you by yourself?" he asked.

I rolled my eyes before looking back at him. He was starting to get on my nerves, and I didn't know why. He was just curious and being friendly. *Stay paranoid. Nothing good can come from talking to him.* "No, I'm with someone."

"Oh." He stretched out his legs and crossed them at the feet. "Your brother?"

Just ignore him. "What's with all the questions?" I snapped. *I said ignore him, not me!*

He put his hands up in front of him. "I'm sorry. I like to get to know people I share a room with. It helps pass the time, and you always come out making a new friend."

My sudden annoyance vanished. I was being mean to someone who didn't need it. I usually saved it for Gregory. "No, I'm not here with my brother." *How did he know you were with a male?* I looked at him closely. Something about him nagged at me and he seemed to be sitting there casually, but his eyes were on alert. "Why did you ask if I was with my brother?"

He shrugged. "I figured you would be with your brother."

"Why not a sister?" I asked. *Where the hell is Gregory?*

"Usually, girls always travel with their brothers. Kind of dangerous if it's just two girls."

I was officially being paranoid. *But still, something isn't right about him.* "Oh. I'm sorry. It's been a long day, and I haven't slept very well for the past few days…or maybe weeks. I honestly don't know. Days seem to run together."

He smiled. "It's fine. So what's your name?"

"Her name's Melinda," Gregory said from the doorway. I breathed out an annoyed breath. Melinda? Really? I watched him close the door and sit next to me.

"Melinda?" Blondie said, and I nodded. "It's nice to meet you." He held out his hand for me to shake.

I took it gingerly, murmuring, "Nice to meet you."

Blondie held on to my hand a little bit longer before letting go. "I'm Darren."

I smiled softly at him and pointed toward Gregory. "This is Tony." Gregory coughed next to me, either to laugh at my stupid name choice or warn me I might have to pay for giving it to him.

"So, you are both going to Minonia?" Darren asked.

"Sure," Gregory said, staring down Darren.

"So why were you arguing with that guy out there?" I motioned toward the door. Gregory gave me an accusatory stare, but I just shrugged my shoulders and ignored him.

"We were both getting on the train, and he tried to take my ticket." Darren put his hands behind his head and closed his eyes. "Thankfully you were there to stop us from putting on a terrible show."

I rolled my eyes. The tension in the compartment could've been cut with one of the hunting knives that were currently hiding in my backpack. I looked over at Gregory—who was staring daggers at Darren—grabbed his hand, and squeezed it. Hard. Gregory gritted his teeth then continued to squeeze my hand a bit harder. Gregory raised a brow innocently and smiled wickedly. His eyes darkened. I looped my arm in with Gregory's and faced Darren. I lay my head on Gregory's shoulder and sighed. I could feel Gregory stiffen. "So, Darren, why are you going to Minonia?"

He looked back and forth between Gregory and me before answering. "I live there with my wife. I've been busy traveling for work." He scratched the side of his head. "How long have you two been together?"

I looked over at Gregory and giggled. He closed his eyes and shook his head. "What has it been sweetheart? One, two years? We're celebrating our anniversary to see his family."

"That's nice," Darren said.

"Isn't it?" I smiled sweetly at him. I turned to look at the horrified expression on Gregory's face, and my smile grew. So this was how I made him uncomfortable? I leaned up and kissed his cheek. When I moved back, he glowered at my wink.

I lay my head back down on Gregory's shoulder, ignoring how nice it felt to have someone to lean against. Honestly, it was nice to have someone to share this terror with. Gregory was strong, smart, and scary at times. A person you would want on your side. I'd been hard on him. Yes, he annoyed me, but he never stopped protecting me. Was it coincidence that I'd met him that day after school? Or were we meant to meet? Did we have a destiny linked together? Or was I over-thinking it? Could this "adventure" turn us into friends? I looked up and into Darren's eyes.

"Yes?" I asked, raising an eyebrow.

"Nothing." Darren smirked. "You just look like someone I know."

"Sorry to disappoint," I said. "But I've never met you before. I'm one hundred percent sure about that."

The train started moving, making our bodies rock back and forth with the motion. Gregory's shoulder was rock solid, but I kept my head on it. Staring down at our combined hands, I started humming a song Agathy had taught me when I was little. She told me that this song was from way back before Lorburn was split into different regions. I loved the song. I hummed under my breath and could feel Gregory taking a deep breath and letting it out.

"What's that song?" he whispered in my ear.

I looked at him—we were much closer now. The last time we had been this close, he'd kissed me to get me out of a panic attack. I bit my lip, remembering the way it had made me feel to kiss him. I let out a shaky breath. "Agathy taught me the song. It's called, *You Are My Sunshine.*"

He smiled. "I like it."

I smiled up at him and started humming it again. He leaned his head back against the chair and closed his eyes. My head fell back onto his shoulder, and I kept humming the song that once used to calm my nerves. Now I had a whole set of new nerves, and I couldn't figure out if it was because of this truce between me and Gregory or the trip to Minonia.

I hummed until I could hear his breathing even out. Slowly, I lifted my head off his shoulder to look at his face; he was asleep. He looked so peaceful when he was sleeping. His face had smoothed out all of the glowering wrinkles. I smiled as I put my head back on his shoulder carefully and swept my gaze up toward Darren, who stared at me. Smirking at me, he closed his eyes. Restlessness crawled through my stomach; something wasn't right about him. Deep down I knew he knew me, but why he didn't come out and say anything, I had no clue. He either worked for Kieran or for the army. I'd bet money on the former. Either way, he would be too dangerous to be around. Gregory and I would have to change our plans and find this Emma Farraday another day. It wouldn't be safe for her to find us along with Darren, but how would we sneak past him? Was it even a coincidence that he was in the same compartment as us?

I couldn't sleep knowing that we had a follower. I would watch over Gregory while he slept; he needed his sleep if we were going to start running again.

CHAPTER TWENTY-TWO

An idea of how to get away from Darren popped into my head. It wasn't the greatest plan, but I knew it could work. I needed to figure out a way to let Gregory know without alerting Darren—Gregory had slept through the rest of the trip. The train conductor announced that we would arrive in Minonia in ten minutes, which meant I only had ten minutes to let Gregory in on the plan without Darren finding out. I'd hoped Darren would've left the compartment sometime during the trip, but he never did. I didn't mind when he was sleeping; it was during the times he was awake that I felt uneasy. He would just stare at both Gregory and me, analyzing us. I tried to ignore the stare, but I could feel his eyes burning holes into my body. He didn't try to talk to me, which I was especially happy about.

I looked up at Gregory; he looked so peaceful and not annoying. I think I preferred him that way. I grabbed his arm and shook a few times. Nothing. Finally, after shaking his arm and almost ready to shove him off of his seat, he bolted up. His eyes went to the door before they made their way over to me. He sat back in his chair, rubbed at his eyes, and then raked both hands through his hair.

"What's going on?"

"We're ten minutes out of Minonia," I said.

Gregory nodded his head and yawned. "You should have woken me earlier."

I shrugged my shoulders. "You needed the sleep. So, I was thinking about something." *Can't wait to hear how smoothly you tell him your plan. My bet—you fail epically.*

"About what?"

"Well, I know we're supposed to be meeting up with your aunt," I said, trying to choose my words carefully. "But I was thinking maybe tonight could be our night."

Gregory looked at me like I had grown horns on my head. Casually, I touched the top of my head, just in case. Nope, no horns, which meant I had failed at communicating with him. I gave Gregory a stare and moved my eyes toward Darren and then back to Gregory. Five times. I did it five times, and Gregory still looked confused. This was harder than I had thought.

"What do you mean?"

I cleared my throat. Let's try this again. "Wouldn't it be easier to go search for her tomorrow during the day? When it would be easier to locate her?" I just stared at him, not moving my eyes from him. Trying to speak to him with my mind.

Gregory looked out the window, watching the black sky fly past. He was quiet for a few minutes. I looked over at Darren, who was now staring intently at the both of us. Damn. If Gregory didn't understand what I was trying to say, then we were doomed.

I looked back over toward Gregory. His eyes caught mine, and he nodded his head so slightly that it would have been easy to miss. He knew. I would have cheered right there and then, but since Darren was in the compartment, I wasn't able to. Killjoy.

"You're right," Gregory said. "It would be rude to show up at this hour."

"Maybe we can get a sweethearts suite at the local inn?" I wasn't sure if they had one of those, but seriously, it sounded nice. There would be a big bed. With clean bedding. A large bathtub. And food to di—

"Maybe," Gregory said, interrupting my thoughts.

I smiled and sat back in my chair. As Gregory stood up and stretched, I, of course, looked at his exposed toned stomach and V. What girl wouldn't? And I was a girl. But what I made sure to do was keep the drool from falling out of my mouth. If it weren't for Darren in the room, I swear I would have launched myself at Gregory. This was a definite change from wanting to kill him every five minutes.

I peeled my eyes away from Gregory when Darren started coughing annoyingly, loud. I looked over at Darren, who was wiggling his eyebrows.

"Yes?" I asked. I could feel the blush creep up my face. I was caught.

"What's with the hostility?" Darren asked, his voice clouded with amusement.

I took a deep breath and let it out very slowly. I needed to be nice. I needed to be nice. I needed to be nice. *Just because you say it three times doesn't mean you'll listen to yourself. For example, you never listen to me when I have sage advice.* I wasn't sure if this whole talking to myself thing meant I was crazy or sane. But I was probably straddling that line. "I'm sorry." Not sure who exactly I was apologizing to. Him or me. "It's been a very long trip, and it's gotten me edgy."

"I accept your apology," Darren said. He stood up and stretched, and I rolled my eyes. "Now if you will excuse me, I must use the little boy's room. I don't want to have to stand in line at the station once we stop."

Gregory and I watched as Darren made his way out of the compartment, Gregory made sure the door was completely shut before speaking. "You apologize to a complete stranger but not me?"

"You and I never apologize to each other. Because neither of us cares enough about each other to be concerned about what the other is feeling." Gregory narrowed his eyes, and I shrugged my shoulders. "I'm usually nice to people. It's hard when I'm around you. So, how long do you think he'll be gone?" I asked. I moved and started to grab our things from under the seats. Gregory walked over to Darren's seat and started rummaging through his things. "What are you doing?" I yelped.

"Shh," he said. I raised an eyebrow at him, but he just ignored me. After what felt like years of Gregory going through Darren's personal items, Gregory finally withdrew a small black gadget. "I knew it."

"Knew what?" I peered at the small object. "What is that?"

Gregory walked over to the window, opened it up, and threw the object out of the window. My jaw dropped. "What are you doing?" I looked anxiously at the door.

"That was a recording device," he said, shutting the window and going back over to Darren's belongings, putting everything back in its original place. "He's been recording us since he's been in here."

"I don't understand." I stared blankly at Gregory.

"He's been following us since Inonia." Gregory started putting his backpack on. He'd been following us since Inonia? *Are you really that surprised?* "I saw him the night we first got to Inonia. And then again when we were at the train station. It wasn't until I saw him in the compartment that I put two and two together. I don't know why he's following us, but we're not going to wait and find out. He knows who you are and has been playing with us."

"Won't he notice his recording thingy is missing?" My stomach churned at the thought that he'd been following us.

"He won't take it out while we're still with him," Gregory said.

“How can you be sure?”

“He doesn’t know we’re on to him. So he isn’t going to flash it out in front of us. I have a feeling that he’s out there—” Gregory pointed toward the door “—communicating with his people.”

“We can’t get caught. We can’t have him be the reason we get caught.” I started to pace back and forth. This was not good. I really shouldn’t have been surprised at this point. We had the worst luck in the world. Or at least I did.

“I know.” The train started to slow down. “Which is why are leaving now.”

“How?” I looked at him suspiciously. We’d been down this road before, and it had ended with my arm being in a sling.

Gregory looked over to the window. I glanced over then back to Gregory. I dropped my head in my hands and whimpered. I actually whimpered. Out loud. He was crazy. First we had to jump off the back of a moving train, and now we had to jump out of the window of a moving train. Would I ever be able to ride a train without having to jump off of it while it was still moving? “Please tell me you are just joking.” *Please.*

He shook his head, and my stomach sank. “If we do it now, he won’t notice we went out the window. I’ll open up the door a little so he can think we went out that way, which will make him search the whole train.” He smiled. He actually freaking smiled. It was a crazy-person smile. Seeing how I kept talking to myself, we were both crazy. I didn't like it. Not one bit. "At least this time the train won't be going so fast, so neither of us should get hurt."

"Well, that's great to know," I said dryly. I bent down, grabbed my backpack, and slipped it on.

"We should probably get going." He moved to the light switch on the wall next to the door and switched it off while opening up the door just a crack. I could hear people talking excitedly outside of the room. I was jealous of them, I wanted to have a normal freaking day and doing normal freaking things. And ride a train without jumping off of it. Gregory moved his way over to the window and stealthily opened it. The train was going much slower this time, but that didn't mean this wasn't going to hurt.

Gregory looked at me expectantly, so I moved to him. I put my hands on the windowsill, and with Gregory's help, I was sitting on the sill with my legs dangling over. I took a deep breath and jumped forward off the train. The wind whipped at my face as my body hurtled toward the ground. My feet slammed into the gravel, but I was able to keep my body upright. I looked over to see Gregory holding on and shutting the window at the same time. I walked forward toward his airborne body, and he landed smoothly a few feet away.

"Now what?" I asked as I made my way to him.

"We walk the rest of the way." Gregory moved off the tracks a few feet, and I followed him, knowing that maybe if I survived this whole Kieran situation, I could tell an awesome story. It wasn't awesome at the moment though.

"Okay," I said.

Gregory and I walked for forty minutes before we could see the lights of the station. We made our way into the deep, tall grass helping us hide our cover as we walked around the other side of the station. My feet kept slipping on rocks, making me stumble and at one point I fell down, scraping my hands in the process. Gregory was nice enough to help me up. "Thanks," I mumbled.

Voices danced in the air as we got closer to the edge of Minonia. I was ready to find a place to stay and sleep for a week. Forget everything that had been going on and just bury myself in a comfortable bed. Preferably with Gregory serving me grapes. I smiled as I pictured him in a toga feeding me grapes. It was an admirable sight.

As we stepped up next to a large building, Gregory held up his hand. People were laughing and hollering while music played in the background. It sounded like a party was going on. Different smells of meat wafted in our direction and I started to drool. I thought my body might have floated in the air and followed the smell, but my body didn't move an inch. Quickly, I wiped the drool from my mouth and grabbed my grumbling stomach. Gregory looked over at me with a smirk. I shrugged my shoulders. I was always hungry.

Gregory put his finger to his lips and moved down the building, bending under a window so that he wouldn't be seen. Following him, I did the exact same thing until we were all the way to the edge of the building. I stood watching as Gregory peered around the wall, I checked behind us—no one was in sight. I thanked the heavens that nobody had followed us and asked for food. And a shelter. And all this mess to be over with. But unfortunately, no one answered.

"There seems to be a festival going on," Gregory said.

"What do we do?"

"We might be able to go through it without being noticed."

"Are you sure?" I had a nagging feeling that we would get caught. Because let's face it, we'd been caught so far everywhere we've gone. Luck would be great to have on our side.

"Yeah," he said. "There are so many people out partying. Most likely, they all have been drinking, so it should be easy to walk through and find somewhere to stay."

I nodded my head. "Okay."

Gregory put his hood up and reached in his back pocket, pulling out a black hat. Placing the hat on my head, he pulled it so far down that my eyes could barely see out. I raised an eyebrow that he couldn't see as he stepped back. "It will help us blend in."

"Right."

"Ready?"

I nodded my head. Gregory walked around the wall of the building with me on his heels. I got right up next to him, our arms slightly touching.

Gregory had been right. Some type of festival was in full swing. The place was lit up, and people were gathered around talking, dancing, and laughing. Cheering erupted farther down the road, and as we got closer we walked past vendors that stood every five feet, selling food, brightly colored beads, furry hot pink and dark green hats, and a type of feathered scarves. *Who will wear those?* We passed a bunch of women and young girls wearing beads and the scarves around their necks. Everything looked tacky, but it was like no one cared. I didn't get it. *That's because you aren't from here.*

There were just as many kids out as adults. My jaw dropped as we passed two women walking completely topless, men whistling at them as they walked by. My cheeks burned, I could never do that. *That's because you're no fun.* I tried to keep my gaze off of them, but it was like I couldn't control my eyes. It was a strange sight. This was something I definitely wouldn't see back home. As we walked further into Minonia, women were dancing with snakes on their shoulders, men threw sticks lit with fire in the air, and women grinded on men while children watched in fascination. It was official: I didn't like this place. Too much chaos. Beads of sweat started forming on my forehead, as my shoulders tensed. I clasped my hands together and swallowed down the unease that started to trickle up.

In the middle of the road, people were cheering, booing, and yelling out names. Gregory moved forward into the crowd, and I had to grab his jacket so I wouldn't get lost in the wave of people. My hand slackened as we got to the front. Two men were punching each other, blood spurting all over the pavement. I could hear people yelling, but everything turned into one giant white noise. With each hit the men threw, I flinched. How could people be cheering them on? I felt sick. Nausea reared in my stomach, I took a couple of swallows to keep it from coming up. I looked over at Gregory, and my stomach dropped. He was enjoying it. He was laughing. He bounced from foot to foot as he gestured fake punches. How could this excite him? People were yelling and jostling behind me. I wanted out but couldn't move. I was horrified that this was what Gregory found fun. Wasn't it enough that we were literally running for our lives? Did he have to be excited about fighting? *You don't really know him. Why are you so surprised?* For once I didn't shut myself up. I was right. I didn't know him.

I looked over at the two men just in time to see one of them grab the other and slam him to the floor, the man's head bouncing off the pavement. A sickening crunch echoed in the streets as it hit, and I flinched while everyone—including Gregory—cheered. I stared at the man just lying on the ground. He wasn't moving, and blood was coming out of his mouth and nose; his eyes were wide open. He should have moved by now. *Not with a hit like that.*

I wanted to cry for this man lying lifeless on the ground. I wanted to run. I wanted to puke.

I pulled on Gregory's arm and stepped up on my tiptoes so I could reach his ears. "We should get going." I wanted to get out of here and find somewhere safe. And maybe puke.

Gregory looked at me, elated. "It might be better to stick around. Maybe find out information."

I shook my head. "Shouldn't we do that tomorrow?" I really, really wanted to leave.

Gregory didn't answer me as his attention focused on the announcer.

"Ladies and gentleman," the announcer said. "We need more fighters for tomorrow night. If you feel you have what it takes to be a champion, step right up and sign up tonight."

Gregory looked excited. "I think I should do it."

"What? No!" I grabbed his hand and tried to drag him out of the area, but he didn't budge. "We need to get out of here and find somewhere to stay. I'm tired and hungry, and this is just all too overwhelming." *And I don't want to see your dead body on the ground.*

"Oh, come on," he said. "We should have some fun while we're here."

I gapped at him. "Are you serious? We should have some fun? We are on the run for our lives, and you want to have some fun by fighting? Well, how about when we run into everyone who is after us you can fight them!" I placed my hands on my hips, trying to look intimidating.

"No one will recognize us," he said, raising his voice. I watched as his eyes flashed with irritation and his face tightened.

"Fine," I said. "You go and be stupid and fight. I'm going to find a safe place to hide. Because I don't have a death wish." I screamed the last part in his face. People glanced over, but I ignored them. I turned around and walked away from Gregory. Every part of me wished I would pull him with me, but I knew I was too weak to physically pull him along. *Maybe you shouldn't trust him.* I ignored my annoying inner sidekick and moved along. I was so angry. What had gotten in to him? *He just doesn't care about you. You are running for your life. He is helping you. He could stay here and blend in and no one would notice or care. Maybe he's tired of running.* I gulped. I didn't want to think that.

I pushed my way through the crowd, bumping against others. It was stifling trying to get through. I heard grunts as I finally made my way out and looked around. There were way too many people out. I didn't know which way we came from or which way to go. The streets were completely packed with people, and I was only a short distance away from the crowd when my shoulder was yanked back. I fell slightly backward but caught myself from tumbling all the way to the ground. Looking over my shoulder, a man stood behind me and I could smell—almost feel—the fumes of alcohol rolling off his tongue. His eyes were bloodshot, and I noticed a long, slim scar on his right cheek.

"'Ey, girl," he slurred. "'Ere ya goin'?"

Takinga step back, his hand slipped from shoulderand slid slowly down my arm. Chills danced up my spine and as I stepped back again, and his hand dropped away from my arm. I moved backward even further, keeping my eyes on him.

"'Ey, I asked ya a questin!" he yelled.

I kept moving backward until I was far enough away from him and then turned around and ran down the street. Covering my ears with my hands—to block out the noise—I continued running, bumping into people in the process. I ignored their nasty looks and made my way down an alley that was empty. Halfway down, I sat down on the ground, with my back up against the side of a building and I let out a breath and buried my head into my hands. This was a nightmare. How could I ever think I could survive living like them?

My head shot up as I heard footsteps running toward me. Gregory grimaced as he got closer to me. He stopped and kneeled in front of me. "Hey."

"Hey." I looked at him suspiciously. Was he going to try and make me go back? Because I would fight him before that happened.

"I forgot. You're not used to this kind of stuff."

"This happens?"

He nodded his head. "I'm surprised you never heard stories about the festivals. It used to happen all the time in

Gildonia, but things started to get really heated, so it stopped a few years ago."

"Why did it stop?"

Gregory shrugged his shoulders. "I should have warned you or something. I just got really into it, remembering the days I used to go to the festival. We've been running for what seems like forever, and I thought we both needed some fun. I wasn't thinking. I forgot about everything for a few minutes," he said. "We should find someplace to stay."

"How long does the festival go on?" I asked.

"A week," he said. "But I don't know when this one started."

I gulped. "Maybe if it's going on a few more nights, we can go." I could be nice. This was the first time Gregory seemed like he was enjoying himself. Of course, I wouldn't watch the stupid fights. But maybe I could get a hat or scarf or something.

Gregory smiled. "That sounds like a deal. And I promise we'll have fun."

I grimaced. "I'll hold you to it."

"We should go."

"Okay," I said. We walked down the rest of the deserted alley. I was ready for a place to sleep.

CHAPTER TWENTY-THREE

As we made our way down to the end of the alley, we could still hear the laughter and hollering from the other end. Gregory stopped and glanced around the corner before he walked over to the next street. It was much quieter, the sounds from the festival muffled from the looming buildings. Only a few people mingled in the area, still I kept my head down and watched my feet take one step at a time, wanting to be as inconspicuous as possible.

Gregory stopped and tugged on my arm. Looking up from my feet, I noticed we were standing in yet another alley, with buildings looming high over us on both sides. Gregory glimpsed around, first at the buildings and then at the alley, trying to figure out where to go next. He must have made up his mind because he led us down the middle. The alley seemed more foreboding than any of the others we'd been in. As soon as we walked into it, it seemed all the noise from a couple of streets over were cut completely off. As I strained to hear the festival, I couldn't. When I peeked up at Gregory, his shoulders were tight and his hands were clenched in a fist: I took it as a bad sign. Wanting to get out of there as fast as possible, I kept up my pace with Gregory's.

Every time I heard a squeak or a crunch, my head would whip around and my eyes would dart all over the place, looking for the object or person that had caused the noise. I had a feeling we were going to get murdered, but no one came jumping out at us. My hands were sweaty and I crossed my arms, bunching the sides of my jacket in my hands. My muscles tensed and my heart raced. I could feel sweat dripping down my face. It wasn't particularly warm out, but I was sweating like I was walking through a desert. My heart thumped erratically in my chest; something didn't feel right about this alley. Chills crawled up and down my spine while the hair on the back of my neck stood up. My gut screamed at me to get away from there as fast as possible.

I didn't even realize I was running until Gregory shouted something at me, his voice muffled. Gregory grabbed my hand and stopped, keeping a firm grip on it. I slipped forward, my knees hitting the ground; I didn't even feel the pain. I looked up at him trying to catch my breath. He wrinkled his brow and bit his lip, looking worried. "What?" I asked. I looked behind us to see if someone was after us.

"What's wrong?" Gregory asked. He cocked his head to the side, his voice tense.

I looked back up at him. "Huh?" I slowly made my way back to standing, wiping the dirt from my knees: a small hole formed in the left knee of my pants.

"A minute ago you picked up your pace and started running. I've been trying to talk to you since, but you wouldn't respond. Are you okay?"

I shook my head. "Something's not right."

Gregory furrowed his brow. "What do you mean?"

"I don't know," I said. "Something just isn't right. I know this is going to sound weird, but it's like my gut's telling me something's been wrong ever since we walked into this alley." I started to pace back and forth. Couldn't he feel the danger in here? Was I going crazy? *Probably.*

"What would be wrong?"

I looked behind us again as I paced. Just as I turned my head to look at Gregory, something black slithered across my peripheral. I turned quickly to see if I could make it out clearly. I didn't know how long I stood there staring, but I couldn't make out anything. Gregory lightly touched my arm, causing me to jump. I put a hand on my chest and could feel my heart trampling inside. "Yeah?" I almost shrieked.

"What is going on?" His concern grew. *I wouldn't blame him; you're going crazy.*

I closed my eyes as I tried to take a deep breath. I didn't know what was happening. Maybe I was going crazy. My chest tightened, and it was getting difficult to breathe. My hands shook, and my body felt like it was ready to collapse. Opening my eyes in horror, I realized I couldn't breathe, so I picked up my pace, trying to catch my breath. I clawed my neck, my fingernails digging deep into my skin, and I bit my lip until I tasted blood. My gaze darted all over the alley and I could hear Gregory's voice, but I couldn't differentiate what he was saying. I put my hands on my head, looping my fingers around large chunks of hair and pulling. *Breathe, Mia, breathe.* I couldn't. Tears welled up in my eyes and dripped past my eyelids. How was this happening? Gregory grabbed me by my shoulders, stopping me. Tears were streaming down my cheek. My heart twisted as if a hand was in there helping it.

"Mia, what is going on?" His eyes were full of worry.

"I...I can't breathe," I made out between gulps. I put my arms around my upper body, rocking back and forth.

Gregory helped me to the ground and shoved my hair back. "Mia, look at me."

I looked everywhere but at him. Whatever was happening could be contagious, couldn't it? And it would be bad if we both ended up dead. Gregory shook my right shoulder.

"Mia, look at me now." I flinched at his sharp tone and looked up into his eyes. "You're panicking. You just need to get your breathing under control. Everything will be fine. So take a deep breath with me." Gregory took a breath in and let it out, and I did the same. I followed his lead. We breathed in and out for five minutes, but it felt like hours.

My body seemed to finally calm down. My chest slowly eased out of the tight hold, and my shaking seemed to stop. I was able to breathe again. A few more tears slipped from my eyes. Gregory swiped them gently from my face. "Are you back?"

I smiled feebly. "I think so."

Gregory stood up, helping me up too. He took my hand, and we started to walk again, much slower this time. "So tell me something."

I felt exhausted. I could feel my eyelids get heavy. *Drained and officially crazy.* "Tell you something?"

"Yeah," he said. "I want to know more about you."

Keeping my focus on what was in front of me, my brain working slowly, I thought for a second. "I had a favorite doll." *It's so sexy to tell a man you used to have a favorite doll. Maybe next time you can tell him you wet the bed until you were ten.* I ignored myself.

"A favorite doll?" he asked.

I looked up at him. I could see a slight smile on his face. "Yeah. I got her on my fourth birthday from Agathy. My parents never believed in giving presents, or even love for that matter. The doll was the first gift I ever received. I named her Madeline, after my favorite book."

"Madeline?"

"Agathy had some of these really old books from a very long time ago—the library back home didn't even have any of these books. Anyway, one of them was called Madeline, and it was my favorite. She let me keep the book, and I always read it, even now, well, before everything had happened. I didn't care how old I was when I read them, I loved the book. Madeline had become my hero. When things got bad with my parents, I would hide myself in the closet with the doll and the book and just hold on to both. Like I was holding on to my life." I frowned. I would never see that book or doll again.

"What's wrong?" Gregory asked.

"It's nothing," I said. "It's just that I won't ever see that doll or book again."

"You never know," he said. "It could still be there waiting for you when we get back."

I nodded my head not saying a word. "Tell me something about yourself."

Gregory was quiet for a few minutes. I started to think he wouldn't say anything, but he surprised me. "I had a dog once. I found him as a puppy when my family moved away. He was the only thing I'd cared for in a long time. He was so scrawny. You could see his bones through his skin when I found him. I fed him and gave him plenty of water. I named him Angus; he had this strength in him that kept him alive. He shouldn't have been able to survive, but he did. He was a fighter. He had this rich, golden brown fur, and his eyes were as blue as the sky."

I smiled. Angus sounded sweet. "Where is he?" I didn't remember seeing him at Gregory's place.

"He's dead," Gregory stated. A frown formed on his face.

I gasped. I wasn't expecting that. "I'm sorry."

Gregory shrugged his shoulders. "It's fine. It taught me not to care for anything but myself."

I nodded. I ignored the giant drop in my stomach, which was probably my heart, and cleared my throat. I hated when my body acted weird when he made comments like that. "So, how long is this alley?" It felt like it was never ending.

"We should be getting close to the end," Gregory said.

"Good." I tried going for nonchalant. "I'm ready for some sleep."

Gregory just nodded his head, lost in his thoughts. The end of the alley was deserted, along with the streets we were now looking at. The buildings were falling apart. Gregory and I walked forward, then went left and walked for a while before coming up to a half-collapsed building. Gregory let go of my hand and glanced through the window. I looked behind us to make sure no one had followed us. It appeared we were in the clear.

"Come on," Gregory said as he walked through the door of the building, I reluctantly followed. Why were we staying in this building? It could kill us while we slept. I crossed over the debris of wood and bricks one leg at a time.

I had to duck under wood beams. A couple of times I tripped on a brick, but I always managed to keep myself upright. Gregory led us to the very back of the building, and the farther we went, the likelier we were to get crushed to death. At least no one would find our bodies. Gregory opened another door and went through, and I stayed right on his heels; he closed the door behind me and sat down in front of it.

"We should probably stay the night," Gregory said, rubbing his face.

I looked around the room. It was dark outside but even darker in here, I could barely see. I went to the wall opposite Gregory and moved down slowly to the floor. I stretched out my legs and kept my eyes on my feet, which were sore and needed a rub. "I was thinking about something."

I could feel Gregory's eyes on me. "What?"

"I was hoping you could show me some fighting moves."

"You want me to show you how to fight?"

I looked up at him. "Yeah."

"Why?"

"Well, I think it would be good for me," I said nervously. "I need to learn how to defend myself, especially since we seem to always be in the middle of a fight. What would happen if something happens and we get separated? I need to be able to save myself."

"I agree," he said.

I stared incredulously at him. I thought he'd say no and we'd have to fight about it. "Really?"

"Yeah," he said. "You need to learn to defend yourself."

I smiled. "Thank you."

He gave me a tight smile, causing my smile to dim. "No problem."

I looked back at my feet. I wished I could read his mind. *No you don't.* Yes I did. *No you don't.* I had no idea what I wanted to know.

Slipping off my backpack, I set it down next to me then slid down to my side and lay my head on it. Hoping I could catch some sleep, I closed my eyes—knowing sleep wouldn't come anytime soon. I wanted to say something, anything. "I care about you," I blurted out. I slapped my hand over my mouth. *Way to go.* That wasn't supposed to be said aloud. That wasn't supposed to be said at all. What was wrong with me? Deep down I knew I cared about it him, even if it was just a little bit. I squeezed my eyes shut and crossed my fingers, hoping he was asleep. My whole body was strung tight as a bow, waiting to hear what he would say, if he would say anything at all. I heard him let out a long breath. Maybe he wouldn't say anything at all and pretend he hadn't heard anything. That, of course, would hurt just as badly as if he just plainly rejected my statement.

"Mia," he said. I held my breath, waiting to be hit in the stomach with a bar. "I care about you too."

"Okay."

"I didn't want to care about you," he said. My heart started to race as my stomach dropped. Not something I wanted to hear, but he kept talking. "You're annoying and whiny. I just wanted to help you get somewhere safe and away from me. I didn't want trouble. I knew if I stayed around you for very long, I would find myself feeling bad for you, eventually something close to caring. I haven't cared for anyone since Angus. I would take random girls back to my place." I definitely didn't need to know that. "And they'd always try to be the one to get something more out of me. I've closed myself off to everyone, until you. You were on my mind way before I helped you escaped. Ever since you bumped into me that morning, I just couldn't shake you. I tried to ignore it. Then I saw you in that dress outside of your house, and I couldn't stop staring at you. You have no idea the effect you had on me. Then it wasn't until I caught sight of you in that bar, with those idiot friends of yours, that I knew I was done. It was like you kept haunting me. I tracked you from the minute you stepped into that place. I don't even know what compelled me, but I changed seats just to have a better angle to look at you. And I was terrified and pissed off in that moment as I stared. You had this look of a broken person. Someone who was just done with life and ready to give up. I just didn't understand how someone from your social standing could look so broken. I'd never noticed it from the times before.

"Then, the next day, when I saw you with the bruises, I wanted to go apeshit on the person who did that to you, which confused me even more. Then I understood why you were broken and barely hanging on for dear life. I understood why you wanted to get away. I understood how much you hated those people. But once I got to know you more, I knew you had to be the one to run Lorburn. You're smart, considerate, and understanding. You want to see a change, and that's what this Nation needs. That's why I think you need to go back and claim your spot. I understand how much you don't want to go back, because of the memories and fear. But one day you'll have to confront those fears, or those fears will ruin your life, and you don't want that to happen."

I was speechless. I didn't think I had ever heard him say so many nice things at once before. About me. Everything he'd said went straight through my heart. The good and the bad. He saw through me. I was broken, but now I was slowly on the mend. "Wow." I didn't know what else to say.

"But don't let that all go to your head," he said. "You're still the biggest pain in the ass, and you make me want to slam my head against walls at time."

I smiled and placed my hands over my heart. "My heart."

I could see him shake his head. "Smartass."

"Yes, but I wouldn't be the person you cared about if I didn't make snide remarks."

Gregory laughed. His laugh, beautiful to hear. So masculine, so free. "We should probably get some sleep."

"Shouldn't we take turns to watch?" I asked as I positioned my backpack as a pillow.

"We'll be fine," he said. "No one followed us."

"How can you be so sure?" I shivered thinking of my dream of the shadowed person.

"Don't worry."

I closed my eyes and listened to his breathing, my own evening out. We'd officially moved past whatever we were before and were now friends. It finally felt good to say I had a friend. We annoyed each other and yelled at one another, but what friends didn't?

CHAPTER TWENTY-FOUR

"Get me out of here!" I screamed, pounding on the walls. I didn't know where I was, except I was in a small four-by-four room, the walls and floor made up of steel. A bucket was the only other object in the room. I didn't know what had happened. I couldn't remember how I'd ended up here. Flashes of running filtered through my mind, but I couldn't remember who or what I was running from. I sat on the freezing, solid ground, the cold seeping into my pants and tank top. I hugged my knees to my chest, trembling. Need to get to Gregory. *The thoughts kept floating up like bubbles in my head, but I couldn't recall who Gregory was. My heart was trying to tell me that he was someone important, but who was he? Even if I could remember who Gregory was, how would I get to him? There were no doors to let me out of this room. How had I gotten in here? Tucking my head in my arms, I tried to keep my breathing even, and I rocked back and forth, not wanting to panic.*

"Mia, are you ready to talk?" My father's voice filtered through the air.

My head popped up and I gasped as I stared at my father, who was standing in front of me. What was he doing here? He was supposed to be dead. Dead? He looked exactly the same as he had when I'd last seen him, which was when? His light brown hair was gelled back, and his brown eyes glared into mine. He was still tall and well built. The only difference was a horizontal scar across his throat. "Dad?"

"Mia, I asked you a question," he said while jabbing a finger in my direction. His nostrils flared, and his lips were pulled back, baring his teeth.

"I don't understand what's going on," I said, my voice wobbling.

"Are we really going to go through this routine again?" he asked. He leaned his back up against the wall and sighed. "Why did you do it?"

"Do what?" I looked around the empty room, trying to figure out what was going on, but came up blank. I couldn't remember anything. It was like someone had stolen my memories.

"Why did you kill your mother, Mia?" He shook his head. "How could you be so cruel?" His demeanor changed. He was no longer enraged. He was more somber.

Tears formed in my eyes. I didn't kill my mother, did I? He's lying! Now wake up! *But I was awake. I shook my head. Nothing made sense. My father slowly paced around the tiny room. Tears cascaded down my face. "I didn't do it."*

My father just shook his head. "Yes, you did, and you know it. You killed her right after you slit my throat." He pointed to his throat, which was now dripping with blood. "Did you have fun doing this?"

More tears fell. "I…I…I didn't do anything."

My father pointed a finger at me. "Yes you did! You gave me to those animals so you could save your own life." He walked over to me, his demeanor changing back to rage, swinging his hand up. "You are not worthy of living in this place, you little bitch." His hand swung down and slapped me hard across the face. Stars exploded beneath my eyelids. My head bounced back and hit the wall.

"I don't know what you're talking about!" I screamed, trying to cover myself as he kept hitting me. He started shaking my body roughly and I tried to move away, but he kept a solid hold on me.

I jolted up, breathing heavily and drenched in sweat. A hand touched my shoulder, but I flinched back and the hand disappeared. Light was shining through the window, illuminating the room: brick, wood, and trash littered the floor. Wiping my eyes, I tried to get rid of the tears, but they kept coming. Arms encircled me, and I tried to get out of the hold, remembering my father hitting me.

"Shhh," a familiar, warm voice whispered in my ear. "It was just a dream. You're okay."

I closed my eyes and reopened them. I was still in the messy room and not the steel one. Letting out a sigh, my body relaxed into Gregory's.

"Another nightmare?" he said.

I shook my head and bit my tongue from saying a sarcastic remark. He was genuinely being nice. "I don't want to talk about it. Not now."

"That's fine," he said. We sat in heavy silence for a while; my dream kept popping up. Did I feel guilty for leaving my dad behind? *There's nothing to be guilty about.* I shook my head.

Gregory never said a word. It seemed he was waiting for me to say something first. As I turned around to face him, he lifted his hand, wiped my hair behind me, and gave me a small smile. "Are you feeling better?"

I nodded my head. "Yeah. Just a nightmare."

"Sure you don't want to talk about it?" he asked.

I narrowed my eyes at him and grabbed the sides of his face and peered all around. He tried to get out of my grasp, but I held on. I looked at every inch. "That's weird."

He furrowed his brow and tilted his head. "What?"

My eyes widened, and I crinkled my nose. "You look the same, yet you're acting different." Gregory pressed his lips together and narrowed his eyes. "Are you the same? Is someone invading your body?" I let go of his face and smiled.

"Ha. Ha. Ha," he said dryly. "You're very funny."

I clasped my hands together. "I know."

Gregory sat back against the wall across from me. "On a serious note, do you want to talk about it?"

I looked down at my clasped hands, my smile disappearing. "I couldn't wake myself up. I kept telling myself to wake up, but I couldn't."

"What was the nightmare?"

"I was in a small, cold room with nothing but a bucket. Then my father appeared out of nowhere, blaming me for killing my mother and him." I gazed into his eyes. "Is that my way of telling myself that I'm feeling guilty for leaving them for their deaths?"

"I don't know. It could be your subconscious showing you how you really feel," he said seriously. "Some of it might be guilt, but some of it might be fear. You've endured a lot from your parents. You might be scared that one day he'll come after you. But for now, just think of it as a nightmare. Because that's all that it is. Try not to succumb to the guilt. You have nothing to feel guilty about. I'm sure your father had resources and knowledge of what was coming, and he could've gotten you to safety. But he didn't. So don't blame yourself. You had no control over any of it."

I nodded. But that didn't change the way I felt.

"I was waiting for you to wake up," Gregory said. "I'm going out and doing a food run."

"And let me guess, you don't want me to come," I said, crossing my arms. I was getting tired of being left behind to wait for him to do everything. I wanted to help.

"It's like you can read my mind," he said. He stood up and walked to the entrance of the room."

"I want to come."

He pinched the top of his nose and was silent for a minute, keeping his back to me. "I bet you do, but it'll be faster if it's only one of us."

"Then why can't I do it?" I asked stubbornly.

I heard him take a deep breath in and let it out very slowly. "Do you want me to make you a list?"

I rolled my eyes. "You're a little sexist, do you know that?"

Gregory shrugged his shoulders. "As long as it keeps you safe, I'm fine with that." He opened the door and stepped out of the room. He turned toward me. "You should be safe here. We weren't followed last night, but that doesn't mean you can go skipping around outside. Stay in here and don't make a sound. We don't need anyone accidently finding you."

"Skipping? You really think I would go outside and skip and pretend I don't have a care in the world? How dumb do you think I am?" He ignored me by shutting the door in my face.

I stood up and walked to the door, sliding the lock into place. Footsteps clanged against the floor as Gregory made his way to the front. Shuffling back over to my spot, I lay back down, curling up into a ball. I was afraid to close my eyes—I didn't want to have that dream again. Chills skipped up my spine just thinking about it.

As much grief I gave him, I really wouldn't know what I would have done if I hadn't had Gregory with me. A part of me was anxious for him to come back already—okay, a large part. It was dangerous for both of us to be out there, and I didn't want to be stuck here if he ended up getting hurt. I didn't know what it meant when the lone butterfly in my stomach made friends with others when Gregory looked at me. And it didn't matter what kind of look it was: angry, annoyed, content, happy. I liked that he looked at me and that was the problem. Yes, I'd lust over him—anyone would—but this was going way past lust. I didn't have time to catch feelings. For anyone.

I was thrilled that he'd agreed to teach me how to fight so I could defend myself. I hoped we wouldn't get separated, but I couldn't take any chances. Plus, it was time I pulled my weight. I had to be strong for myself, because I couldn't be a victim to this horrible situation. My eyes slowly closed and as I drifted off to sleep, my parents' faces kept floating through my mind. As the dreamland took over, I was lucky enough to dream of nothing.

I jolted awake. At first I didn't know what had woken me, but then I heard it again. Creaking steps echoed through the building, coming from the opposite of the door. When I grabbed both mine and Gregory's backpacks, I quietly made my way to one of the hidden corners in the room. Fisting the backpacks, squeezing until my knuckles turned white, I could hear more creaking in different areas on the other side. More than one person stood on that side. I tried to keep my breathing quiet. My heart raced, and I tried to talk myself down from having another panic attack. I jumped when someone yelled on the other side and bumped into the wall. The voice was muffled, I couldn't hear what the person was saying, so I quietly made my way over to the door and put my ear up against it. The voices were still muffled, but I could now make out what they were saying.

"What do you mean you lost them?" a deep voice asked.

"It wasn't them," another guy said. "It was him. I followed the guy, and I swear I saw him go into this building. I did what you said. I radioed it in and waited until you guys got here."

"There is no one upstairs," a different voice said. It didn't look like there was an upstairs when we came in last night, but I'm glad we didn't go up there.

"Tucker, you should have taken him out before he even got here," the deep voice said.

"What if he isn't the one we're looking for? And if he is and we took him out, how would we find the girl?" Tucker said.

"Well, now you've lost him," the deep voice said. He seemed to be in charge. "And we have no idea where either of them could be."

"Sir," the third voice said. "What if someone stayed behind and waited him out. I'm thinking he probably spotted Jackass over there and realized it would be better to escape. He might have left something behind that's valuable to him. He might take a chance to return and get it." Yeah, maybe like me.

I started to shake. Someone had spotted Gregory, and he'd gotten out before they could get him. But I didn't understand why they weren't checking this room. They had checked the whole building but this room. It didn't make sense.

"Tucker," the man in charge said. "You get to stay behind, and this time, if you see him detain him until we can get here. Do you think you can handle it?"

"Yes sir," Tucker answered.

"Alright, Smith, let's go." I could hear boots leaving the room and after a few minutes, I was sure they were all gone but Tucker.

I stepped away from the door quietly and made it back to the corner. There was a window in the room, but it was too high for me to climb up without making any noise. I needed to think of a plan. Maybe I could sneak past the guy, or use one of the weapons I had in the backpack on him. Could I really go through with killing someone with a gun or a knife? Could I even use a gun or a knife? Maybe I could at least injure him. Unzipping the backpack, I pulled out one of the knives; I had a better chance with a knife than a gun, I had no idea how to use a gun.

An hour later, I was squatting in a corner with a knife in my hand. I kept going over different plans. They all had the same result: I'd end up injuring myself and getting caught. A loud boom came from the other side of the door, shaking the building. With both backpacks on my back, I stood up and moved from the corner. The explosion came again and again. I moved toward the door and eased my ear against it. The roars sounded much louder that time. I heard a "What the hell" from Tucker just before a loud blast when off, shaking the building firmly. Debris fell from the ceiling, covering me in dust. The building moved again as another blast went off, this time brick falling down along with the dust. Quickly, I covered my head as bricks fell toward me. My hands flinched out in pain as a heavy brick smacked me across the knuckles. The place was going to collapse. I couldn't hear anything on the other side of the door except for fragments falling to the ground. If I wanted to get out of this place alive, I had to act now.

Just as I reached for the lock on the door, a brick smashed through the window above me. I covered my head—too late—and looked behind me to see what had happened. Gregory was perched on the windowsill with a long rope dangling through the window. *How the hell did he get to the window?*

"We need to get you out of there," he said simply. *Well, no shit.* I gave him a look, but he ignored it.

I ran over to the wall and grabbed the rope. The building was slowly collapsing, and bricks were jutting out. Stepping on the few bricks that were jutted out, I made my way up to the window. It took a few tries to get near the window, and Gregory pulled me the rest of the way up. I sat on the windowsill and looked down. It wasn't a very big jump—I'd jumped worse—but glass covered the ground. I looked over at Gregory, and all he did was nod, so I jumped. Luckily, I was getting use to jumping because this time I landed on my feet. Gregory jumped right behind me. He pointed to our left, and we ran down the street, keeping in the shadows of the buildings around us.

We didn't stop running until we were a few blocks down. I gulped down air like it was fresh water. I looked over at Gregory, who was also huffing and puffing. He was holding a duffel bag on his shoulder. I wanted to ask him what was in it, but I couldn't get words out between breaths. Gregory let us rest for a few minutes before pushing us forward. We ran all the way to an abandoned underground station and down the stairs: it was dark and musty. Neither of us spoke as we made it to the bottom, slowing down in the process. We walked the platform until we hit the end, where Gregory jumped down onto the tracks. He held up his arms to help me down, which I greatly appreciated, and we made our way in the dark.

I was hot, thirsty, and hungry. Not to mention exhausted. We'd been walking the tracks for at least a few hours. We didn't stop once. I wanted to stop. I tried to stop, but I couldn't. I knew we had to get far away from whoever we were running from this time. This was officially tiring. I wanted to burst out in tears. I was angry. I shouldn't have had to run for my life every second of every day. I should have enjoyed what my life had brought me. This wasn't fair. Not at all.

"Mia?" Gregory asked, breaking through my pitying thoughts.

"Yeah?" I asked.

"Are you okay?"

No. "Yes," I said. It wouldn't be fair if I took it out on him. He had nothing to do with this. *Except he led someone back to your hideout.* "Are we going to stop soon?"

"Yeah," he said.

"So what happened back there?" I tried to keep the anger out of my voice. I was really trying hard not to kick him. I kept repeating in my head it wasn't his fault, but technicality it was. "I didn't realize someone was following me until I got to the end of the alley. I knew I should have turned in a different direction, but I knew they would search the buildings, and I had to hide you."

"I don't understand."

"Well," he started. "I went in and moved a giant cabinet in front of the door. It was able to completely hide the door; they would've never noticed there was another room unless they knew beforehand."

"Why didn't you just get me so we could've run?" I asked. It seemed like the logical thing to do.

"I thought of that, but we wouldn't have made it out in time. I heard him call in for backup. I barely got out of the building before they arrived. It was best to keep you hidden away until I could come back for you."

"Oh." I could have died if he hadn't come back. I wouldn't have been able to move the cabinet from the door. He should have just grabbed me, and we could have chanced it.

"I bought some explosives from a guy at the market. He sells them under the table. I threw a few at the building, giving me enough time to come around and get you. It wasn't the smartest plan, but it worked."

And I would have died if it hadn't. No big deal or anything. "Yeah."

"But I have some good news," he said, stopping. I stopped next to him, trying not to narrow my eyes at him. He smiled.

"What's the good news?" This wasn't his fault. I was just hungry. *It was kind of his fault.*

"I found Emma Farraday."

I narrowed my eyes even further. My arms tightened at the sides of my body. I wrinkled my brow as I raised my voice. "How?"

"When I was at the market, I was eavesdropping on peoples' conversations. Then this woman appeared next to me, staring at the apples. There was something familiar about her like I'd seen her before, but I couldn't figure out where. Her eyes stood out. I just stared at her until she whispered my name. Then I stared at her for a completely different reason. She continued to pick apples while she whispered to me. She'd been at the train station all night looking for us but couldn't find us. She remembered Aileen specifically telling her where to meet us, but she thought maybe she'd heard wrong. I asked her for her name, and she said her name was Emma Farraday. I asked her some questions to verify if it truly was her, and it was. We made a plan, and we're meeting up with her tomorrow."

I smiled. For his sake. Something didn't feel right. Something nagged at me. "Why not now?"

"She said she had things to do today and wouldn't have time to talk with us. She said she had important information to give us. We made plans of meeting up and then went our separate ways."

My smile dropped from my face faster than a bullet. I turned away from him before he could see my frown. Something didn't add up. What were the chances of him bumping into Emma and then have someone tailing him? If we had arrived last night like as planned and met up with Emma, wouldn't she have given us a place to stay and any information we needed? No, something was very wrong. Gregory seemed so sure it was the right Emma. With everything she'd told Gregory about Aileen, she sounded authentic. Why did my gut scream at me to not trust her?

Gregory and I started walking again. I stayed silent, lost in my thoughts, but I could feel the lightness radiating off of him. I didn't want to burst his happy bubble, but he needed to be cautious. Now wasn't the time to get sloppy. "Hey Gregory," I said, looking over at him.

"Yeah?"

"How can we trust this Emma person? Doesn't it seem like it was more than a coincidence that you had someone following you right afterward?"

Gregory was quiet for a few minutes. I watched as a frown appeared on his face. After a while, he spoke. "I don't know. Maybe we're just thinking too much into it because of everything we've been through. Maybe not. But we won't know until we actually meet up with her." He didn't seem all that concerned about it, which, of course, made me even more nervous. The last time he had been like this, I'd ended up trapped in a house and making plans to escape.

"And you want to do that?" I asked.

"What other choices do we have?"

"None, I guess," I said. Aileen told us it was important to meet with this person. That she would help us get back to Gildonia.

We walked forward in silence. Gregory eventually led us over to the left side and stopped in front of a door. He pushed it opened, and we both made our way through. It was small enough to be a janitor's closet, which it probably had been at one point. Gregory shut the door behind him, and we were engulfed in darkness. Sliding my hands up on the wall, I used it to help me sit down and I could feel Gregory do the same as he sat next to me, our thighs touching. The zipper on the duffel bag squeaked as it opened, a light appearing a few seconds later. Gregory sat the flashlight down in front of us, then proceeded to take out food and water. We ate and drank in silence.

My eyes started to droop as the food settled in my stomach. I leaned over and put my head on Gregory's shoulder, sighing. At first his body stiffened, but then it gradually relaxed. I shouldn't have been putting myself in this position, but I was tired of sleeping on the floor.

"So what do you want to do about tomorrow?" he asked.

"I think we ought to be careful when we meet her. Stay on our guard." I slid my eyelids shut.

"Okay."

"Are you going to keep yapping, or can I sleep?" I asked through a yawn.

I might not have been able to see him, but I knew he rolled his eyes. "You're quite crabby when you're tired."

I ignored him and let the darkness cloud my vision.

CHAPTER TWENTY-FIVE

My knees were slightly bent, and my hands were positioned up in front of my face as Gregory and I stood facing each other. Gregory came at me, and I moved my arms quickly to block his hit. Pain zipped down my arms. I wasn't doing very well.

When we woke up, Gregory told me it was best to start practicing every morning. That way, if we got into any entanglements, I'd be able to kind of protect myself. I agreed. We ate and then started practicing. I sucked. Gregory was kicking my ass. One time he literally kicked at my ass but not hard enough to hurt. I was drenched in sweat and ready to take a break, but it seemed he could go on forever. Bruises were already forming on my arms. At first, Gregory didn't want to hit me. He wanted me to attack him. I disagreed. If he didn't hit me, how was I supposed to know what it felt like? And how was I supposed to learn how to block if he wouldn't come at me? We argued for over an hour before Gregory gave in, mumbling something about my "stubbornness," and, of course, I reacted by jumping on his back. Gregory kept pointing out everything I was doing wrong and showing me over and over again how it needed to be done. He didn't lose his temper once. I, on the other hand, was thoroughly frustrated. When I tried to punch him, I couldn't get enough force behind it. I was too slow, and he easily blocked it.

"Now this time, when I come at you, duck and kick my leg," he said.

I nodded my head. He came at me fast. I tried to duck in time, but I was too late. He grabbed my waist and tackled me to the ground, a loud thud bouncing around the small room. I gasped as my breath whooshed out. His legs pinned down my legs, and his hands grabbed my arms and pinned them over my head. I blew out an irritated sigh. "I'm never going to get this."

Gregory smiled down at me, and my eyes narrowed at him. "It's going to take time before anything becomes familiar to you."

"I want to know it now."

"I know, but it doesn't work like that," he said. He got off of me, holding out a hand to help me up.

"Well, it should." I wiped off my pants and placed my hands on my hips.

"We should stop for today." He moved toward our bags.

"What? Why?" I walked over to him, my hands on my hips. "I'm nowhere near ready."

His brow furrowed. "Why are you so impatient about this?"

"I don't want to go to Emma's place unprepared."

"Do you really think something will happen?"

I didn't know what would happen once we met up with this Emma person; it could be a nice chat, or it could be a fight. But every time her name popped up, I kept thinking back to what had happened the day before. It was way too coincidental. I didn't want to go in unarmed. I knew we had weapons, but that might not be enough. We needed strength too. "Honestly, I don't know. I just feel like something will go wrong. Like maybe we should forget about going to see Emma and just run."

"Where would we go?" he asked. He stood staring me down with his hands on his hips.

"I don't know." I started pacing the small room. "But somewhere. What about Destonia? No one would think of us going there."

Gregory shook his head. "I'm sure the rebels and the army are both there. Emma is our only choice."

"Why?" I snapped. "Why is she our only choice? Why can't we make our own choice for once?"

"Because we don't have choices!" he yelled back.

"Yes we do!" I shoved him, but he only moved an inch. "We can run and go find somewhere else to stay. We can find a different way back to Gildonia. We don't need anyone's help. It can just be the two of us. I don't trust easily. I'm just now starting to trust you. Who knows when I'll trust her?"

"You're being ridiculous." He shoved his hands through his hair.

"How am I being ridiculous?" I gritted my teeth. My body tensed as heat flushed through every limb and made its way up my neck.

"How exactly would we do it? Do you plan to walk there? The trains have to be crawling with soldiers by now. I don't know about you, but I don't plan on walking all the way back to Gildonia. It would be months before we even stepped foot there again. We need help, whether you like it or not."

"We could take a bunch of food with us," I said. I actually liked the idea of walking. Maybe by the time we arrived, the fighting would be over and everything returned to the way it was before.

"We wouldn't survive," he said bluntly.

"How do you know? How do you know we'll survive now?" The more he disagreed with me, the more I wanted to hit him.

He stared at me for a long moment. "I'm going out." He walked past me and to the door. "You might want to get some rest. We're seeing Emma tonight." With that he walked out the door and slammed it behind him.

So that was that? I didn't even have a choice in the matter? Why didn't he just go by himself, then? I sat down against the wall. Leaning my head back, I closed my eyes; I believed we could do it. We could have a nice walk. Get to know each other better. Find out what really irritated him so I could have a weapon to use against him when he pissed me off.

***

I had to keep running. I looked back behind me. The shadow was closing in on me. I raced forward, faster. Keep running! My lungs burned, and my legs were tired. I tried to keep moving, but my legs were slowing down. The shadow was on my heels when I looked back around. I looked forward just in time to see the wall I was about to crash into. I couldn't stop the momentum of my run in time, and I slammed into it. My head banged on the concrete, snapping backward. My body dropped like a bag of potatoes. My head pounded, and as I gently put my hands on my head, I flinched.

I kept my eyes closed tightly. I wanted to cry, but no tears formed. I tried to keep my breathing even.

"Mia, get up off of the floor," a voice said behind me.

I slowly opened my eyes and sat up. I turned around and faced Kieran. "I'm glad you decided to turn yourself in."

I blinked slowly, trying to get the stars out of my vision. "I didn't?" It came out more like a question than an answer. Where was I? I looked around. I was back in the four-by-four cell I'd been in last time. Haven't I always been here? No. How did I just answer myself? Because you're sleeping, and I'm you. *I clutched my head. I was crazy. I'd officially lost it.*

"Of course you did," Kieran said, peering at me. "You wanted to save your father, so you decided it would be best to become my wife."

Wife? What? Where was my father? This is a dream. *"I don't understand." I wasn't sure who I was talking to—Kieran or myself.*

"Well, maybe if you stopped throwing yourself at walls, you would remember better." Kieran chuckled to himself. "Now it's time for the ceremony." He walked toward me, grabbing my arm.

"What ceremony?" I tried to yank my arm back. His fingers dug into my skin, his nails drawing blood.

"Don't play dumb." He dragged me with him toward the other side of the wall.

I tried to keep my feet firmly on the ground, but he was much stronger than me. "No!" I leaped forward and punched him in the face. His hold weakened enough on my arm enough that I was able to pull it out of his grasp. "Don't come near me!" I shrieked. I put both hands up in front of me. Position yourself like how Gregory showed you. *Who was Gregory?* You know who he is, you just need to wake up! Like now! How? I don't know. Try ramming your head against the wall again.

"This was our deal," Kieran said. He walked toward me, holding his hand out.

I looked over at the wall. Would I wake up if I did what I'd told myself to do? I ran past Kieran and went headfirst into the wall.

I jolted up. My head pounded. The room was dark, guessing I must have fallen asleep earlier. Gregory wasn't there. I looked around the room and wondered if Gregory had come back earlier or if he had been gone the whole time. Just as I was thinking it, Gregory walked through the door. Shutting it behind him, he sat down against it; holding two large paper bags in his arms. He wouldn't look at me.

"How long have you been gone?" My throat burned as I talked. I needed water.

"I came back about three hours ago, and you were dead asleep," he said, going through the bags and avoiding my gaze. "So I went back out to get some stuff."

"What did you get?"

Gregory pulled out some dried meat, chips, and an orange soda, handing them over to me. He pulled out his portion and started to eat. "Well, food, a different pair of clothes, and some things for the road."

I perked up. Was he going to agree about finding a different way? "Things for the road?" I tried to say it as nonchalantly as I could, but it came out way too excited.

Gregory finally looked at me with a raised eyebrow. "Well, you may have had a point earlier. So, I got some stuff for the road: more food, water, and some medicine. It's for plan B."

I stiffened. "What's plan A?" *Something you're not going to like.*

"I still think we should meet up with Emma. She's our best bet. But if we get a bad feeling from her, we'll leave."

"How would we do that?" I tried to keep the irritation out of my voice.

"I was thinking we leave our stuff behind here. No one knows we're down here, so we won't have to worry about anyone taking it. We'll still meet up with Emma, but like I said, if things feel off, we'll come back here. We'll wait it out and then find a way back to Gildonia."

I grumbled about ditching plan A but sucked it up.

"I take it you're happy with the plans," he said sarcastically.

I nodded my head. "I don't have any other choice, do I?"

"Nope." He took a bite of his dried meat. "Now we should eat. We're meeting up with Emma in a few hours."

"Why so late?"

"It would be better if very few knew of our presence."

"I'm glad you thought of that." I bit into the meat, almost moaning. "I never would have."

"She actually told me it would be better to do it that way," he said.

I frowned. I didn't want to do anything she wanted us to do, but I didn't want to start another argument with him, especially if we were to be on our way soon. "Okay."

"You're not happy about it, are you?" he said.

Damn. "I didn't say anything." I stuffed chips in my mouth. I looked at Gregory, who just rolled his eyes at me. "So, where are we meeting up with her?" I said between bites.

"In that alley where you had a panic attack."

I looked over at him, my eyebrows raised. "Wouldn't, I don't know, men who have been looking for us be there?"

"They should be gone."

If I were one of those men, I would have stayed put. People always go back. "Right."

"She'll be waiting for us there. Then we'll go with her to her place." He wiped off his hands and went for his drink, taking a long pull.

"Why couldn't she just tell you how to get to her place? It seems like it would've been better that way."

He shrugged his shoulders. "She said she knew the best way to get there without being noticed."

I bet she did. "I still would've liked to just meet her at her place. We could have scooped out the area first and seen if it was a trap. Now we'll never know."

Gregory smiled at me.

"What?" I asked uncomfortably.

"You."

"What about me?" I pushed my hair behind my ears.

"You're adapting to the runaway lifestyle."

"Is that a bad thing?"

Gregory shrugged. "I think it's good. Not the whole running-for-our-lives situation but that you're easily adaptable. Well, not that easily adaptable, because you complain and stomp your feet when you don't get your way."

I narrowed my eyes. "I don't stomp my feet."

Gregory reached forward and lightly touched my face. "Whatever makes you feel better."

I stilled at his contact. His eyes bounced back and forth between my eyes and lips. I licked them nervously, tasting the salt from the chips. His thumb moved softly over my bottom one, and I stayed perfectly still. What was he doing? I had this sudden urge to kiss him. His mouth parted as he concentrated on his thumb as it swiped back and forth on mine. I moved an inch closer and ruined the mood. My soda spilled all over me, and I jumped up from the cold liquid seeping through my pants. I stood up and jumped around as I tried to dry myself off. Gregory went back to eating and ignored me.

After I'd determined I was dry enough, I sat back down, but this time opposite Gregory. He kept his attention on his food. I really wanted to know what he was thinking.

"I'm sorry."

I looked up at him, my heart racing against my chest. Was he sorry he almost kissed me? Was his very first apology to me going to be for almost kissing me? "For what?"

"For how your life has been. No one should've had to go through what you've gone through."

I shrugged my shoulders and took a sip of the orange soda. "Is it really a surprise that people would retaliate against a Leader?"

"Not that," he said.

"Not what?"

"I'm sorry you were born to a cruel father. Someone who was supposed to be there for you, protect you, and love you. I'm sorry that you had to live in fear for most of your life. You should never be afraid of your own home. Family's everything. Family's supposed to be there for you, always. I'm sorry you never knew what it was like to live in a happy home, where parents showered their children with love. Love from a family is different from all other types of love. Love from a family is a love that will be with you forever. It's a love that, no matter how many fights you have with them, will always be there. And I'm sorry."

Tears formed in the corners of my eyes. I blinked a few times until I knew I wouldn't shed any. Where was this coming from? I almost wanted our fighting back. "It's not your fault."

"I know, but I have that love. Grew up with that love. And you've never experienced it. It pisses me off to know you grew up terrified of what would happen next. No child should be terrified of their own home."

I looked down. "I don't have a home." It was true. I didn't. I had never thought of Gildonia as a home. My home was always with Agathy, and she was gone now. I only had myself. And Gregory. I looked up at Gregory. His beautiful lips were frowning. "I lost my home when Agathy died. I only have myself. And you. I don't want to lose you." *No matter how many times he's pissed me off or annoyed me.*

"You won't," he said.

"Then I want you to make me a promise." I sat up.

"What?" He looked at me suspiciously.

"Promise me that, no matter what, I won't lose you. That if it comes down to life and death, you will always pick your life over mine." Gregory opened his mouth to say something, but I put my hand up and in front of me. "Never choose my life over yours. Your life is just as precious as mine. I want us to both survive and live to very old ages. But as I've found out, that's never promised. So promise me that I won't lose you."

Gregory was quiet. He captured my eyes and held them captive for what felt like hours. "I don't think I can make that promise."

I closed my eyes and leaned my head against the wall. "Why not?"

"Because for some unknown reason, you've wiggled your annoying ass into my life, and I can't let you get hurt," he said.

He had such a way with words. "Then we might have a slight problem." A laugh bubbled up in my chest. I opened my eyes and started laughing. Gregory narrowed his eyes. "We will both be jumping in front of each other. I guess that could work out in our favor though. I jump in front of you, you jump in front of me. Over and over again, and the person coming after us might get bored." I started laughing harder. It took a few minutes, but I finally controlled my laughter. Gregory was shaking his head.

"You're crazy," he said blankly.

"I'm starting to think so," I said with a smile.

Gregory shook his head again and smiled. "We should get going."

"Were you going to kiss me?" I blurted out. Gregory instantly froze. I shouldn't have said anything. "Earlier, I mean. Before the soda spilled all over my pants?"

Gregory rubbed his face with both hands. "Is there any way you will drop this?"

"Nope."

"It was a moment of weakness," he said. I could feel the pieces of my heart start to crack. It shouldn't be cracking, but there it was, cracking. "A moment that won't happen again. Or at least until you turn eighteen. I'm six years older than you. I shouldn't be kissing you. I shouldn't be thinking about kissing you. It was a moment of weakness."

Gregory stood up and walked out of the room. I guess that was my cue to leave too. So I had to wait three months before he would kiss me again? I didn't want to wait three months.

CHAPTER TWENTY-SIX

Gregory and I entered into the pitch dark and freezing tunnel. Pulling my leather jacket closer, I crossed my arms and sniffed; my nose was cold and running. We'd been walking in silence for over an hour, we didn't want our voices to bounce off the walls. We stayed close to the edge of the tracks. In case anything or anyone came toward us, we could slink deeper into the shadows.

I wished we'd had more time in the room that now lay behind us. We hid the duffel bag, with the extra food and clothes, under a loose floorboard. I wanted to go back, but I knew we had to give Emma a chance. I hated the idea, but I sucked it up. I didn't want to understand how Gregory wanted The Emma Plan to work, but I did. She could help us tremendously.

I wondered how Aileen knew Emma. Aileen didn't seem to be a person who had connections here.

I wished we'd found out what had happened to Aileen and Aedan. I hoped Aileen had made it out, but doubt clouded in. I also hoped Jake hadn't made it out. He would be one less person I'd have to worry about coming after us.

What kept filtering through my mind were my parents. I started to feel a loss, knowing I'd never see Mother again. I hoped she didn't suffer before she died, but I did wonder if she'd had time to think about the kind of mother she was and if she regretted it. My father was still alive that much I knew. Otherwise we would've heard something. And I couldn't help but think this was his karma. As much as I hated them for everything they'd done to me, I didn't want either of them to suffer. But I still wouldn't turn myself in. There was no way Kieran would let my father go if I turned myself in. He was smarter than that. He needed to contain both of us or he wouldn't be the Leader of Lorburn.

"Mia?" Gregory whispered, breaking through my thoughts.

"Yeah?" I whispered back.

"Do you hear that?"

We stopped walking and listened. At first I thought he was just hearing things, but then I could hear it. There was a slight clinking moving closer toward us, slowly but surely. I looked over at Gregory. "What is that?" I whispered.

Gregory shrugged. He put his finger to his lips and moved in front of me, grabbed my hand, and started walking forward. The farther we moved, the closer we got to the noise. A light ahead of us bobbed up and down. The clinking grew louder and louder. Voices bounced off the walls, along with the clinking. I ran into the back of Gregory as he stopped. Tightly, I grabbed his jacket. We quietly stalked into the shadows and crouched low to the ground as the voices became clearer.

"You think she's alive?"

"Nah, she's most likely dead." The voices belonged to two men.

"How would you know?"

"No one has seen her since Leader Aedan's house got hit," the other one said. "She probably was killed there, and Kieran and the men are just lying."

"I don't know." There was a long pause. We could hear the shuffling of their feet. "You gonna join the rebels?"

"Bobby, you know my answer."

"Still no?" Bobby asked. "Why not? I heard they have great things."

"I don't care."

"So why are we searching for this girl?"

"Maybe she survived."

Bobby laughed. "You seem set on the girl being dead. Are you doing it for the bounty? It's a shitload of money. Maybe I'll get lucky and find the bitch."

The men passed by us. I inched closer to Gregory, tightening my hold on his jacket. *Please don't see us, please don't see us, please don't see us.*

"I want to do what's right."

Bobby snorted. "And what's right?"

"I don't know yet."

The voices trailed off as the light went with them. My body shook. Kieran had put a bounty on my head? Not very surprising. We crouched until the light, clinking, and voices had completely disappeared. Gregory pulled us up, and we started to move. He slid an arm around my shoulder, holding me close as we walked. His warmth spread through my clothes. Plan B sounded more appealing the further we walked.

By the time we made it to the stairs that led us out, panic started to settle in. We'd be out in the open and anyone could discover us and turn us in. Emma could turn us in. Gregory stopped me before we walked up the stairs. He opened his backpack, pulling out two guns. He handed over a gun, placing the cold metal in my hand. My fingers closed over the handle as I watched Gregory slide his in the back of his pants, his jacket falling over it. I followed his lead, the cold penetrating through my shirt. Before we left the room, Gregory showed me how to use the gun. Sure, I listened intently and watched exactly what he did, but I wasn't sure any of it would stick in my brain.

Night had fallen by the time we made it out of the station. No one was around. We walked into the darker shadows of the buildings, our progress slow and quiet. It took us a bit to get to the alley, but once we made it, I let my body relax a bit. We looked around, but there was no one there.

"Where is she?" I whispered. I rubbed my hands up and down my arms.

"We might be early," Gregory responded. He didn't sound so sure.

I went over and sat next to a dumpster. Gregory followed, standing in front of me. "So what, do we just wait to see if she shows up?"

Gregory looked down at me. "We'll stay until the sun starts to rise, and then we'll leave." He looked back up and around.

I was frozen. I kept wiggling my nose to keep it from running. My ears burned each time a piece of hair flapped by them and I had to blink away the tears that formed every time wind rushed by. We had been there eighty-seven minutes and counting. I'd been bored enough to count. My arms held my knees to my chest, my head leaning on my arms. My toes were frozen—I could no longer move them. I wanted to complain, but I didn't want to waste my breath. I kept my eyes closed. I couldn't keep watching Gregory search the alleyway. It was too exhausting to watch. He seemed so set on this plan working.

"Someone's coming," Gregory finally said. We'd been silent since I'd sat down. I jumped at the sound of his voice.

I opened my eyes and looked up at him. "Is it her?"

Gregory didn't answer me right away. "Yeah," he finally said.

Slowly, I untangled myself and stood up. I positioned myself next to Gregory and bounced on my toes to keep warm. I rubbed my hands back and forth, blowing into them now and then. A woman walked toward us, but her face wasn't visible. Her hood was up, and she faced the ground. Just as she got a few feet away from us, she finally looked up. Her eyes caught mine, and my breath got stuck in my throat. My jaw dropped.

"Emma, you're late," Gregory said, not noticing my reaction.

"I got held up." Her voice came out like sugar; her eyes never left mine. "I'm sorry I'm late. I hope I didn't worry you guys."

I couldn't move my eyes from her. This couldn't be real. It just couldn't. My chest tightened and my stomach dropped. My scalp prickled as I shook my head back and forth. My bouncing stopped. Gregory looked back and forth between us, finally noticing my reaction.

"Emma, this is Mia," he said. "Mia, this is Emma."

Emma held her hand out to me, but I couldn't take it. "You're not real."

"Mia—" Gregory started, but Emma interrupted him.

"I am."

I stepped back, shaking my head. "No."

I stared into the same blue eyes I had known my whole life. Her hair was different, but her eyes were the same. Her nose still had a small crook to it, and her lips were still full and pink. "You're supposed to be dead."

Gregory looked back and forth. "What's going on?"

I ignored him. "You're supposed to be dead. Not standing here with a different name and...and..." I motioned my hand to her hair and worn-out clothes. "And looking different."

Gregory looked at Emma then back at me, understanding dawned on his face.

"We should discuss this later," she said. "We need to get out of here. It's not safe." She started to walk back the way she'd come. Gregory shook his head and followed her. I took a deep breath. I could leave or follow her. I followed.

She was alive and well. She had never once tried to reach out to me. To warn me. I had thought she was dead. My parents had told me she was dead. Seeing her up close and personal hurt. She'd left me behind with our parents. She didn't care about me. She only looked out for herself. How could she have left me behind?

We walked through the deserted streets, the festival nowhere in sight. We stayed to the shadows and crossed into different alleys. I made sure to keep each detail of the way in my head so I could remember how to get back to the station. I shot daggers at the back of her head. Not the real kind, though.

I felt disgusted looking at her. There was no love in me for her. She'd lied and left me. She'd left me with them.

"Get in," Emma said as we made it to her small hut of a house. I couldn't bring myself to call her Meghan. The name she was born with.

Her place was tiny but nice: there were two couches, a chair, and a coffee table facing a small fireplace. She went over to the fireplace and set a fire. Gregory and I stood next to the door, and I looked around. To the left was the living room, and on the right was the kitchen and in front of us was a hallway. Two doors lined one wall and one door was on the other. Two bedrooms and a bathroom? Hopefully one of those bedrooms had a window. I wanted to have an alternative exit plan.

"I need to use the bathroom," I said.

Emma looked over at me. She gave me a slight smile and pointed down the hall. I narrowed my eyes at her. "The second door on the left is the bathroom."

I started walking away the minute she started speaking. I slipped into the bathroom and quickly looked around: a tub, a toilet, a sink, and two doors took up the space. I opened one door, revealing a closet. Quietly, I shut it and went to the other door. A deadbolt was locked at the top, so I unlocked it and opened it. I was staring out at a backyard. I smiled, quietly shutting the door but keeping it unlocked. Just in case. As I flushed the toilet and turned on the water, I looked in the mirror. I was a disaster. Dirt, dust, and mud were caked on my face and in my hair. I needed a shower. Why hadn't Gregory told me I looked terrible? I shut off the water and headed out of the bathroom.

Gregory was sitting on the couch with a cup in his hand. My sister was sitting next to him, laughing. I narrowed my eyes and cleared my throat. Both sets of eyes focused on me. My sister stood up.

"I know we can't be here too long," I said, "but I was wondering if I could take a quick shower. I'm quite a mess." I waved my hand over myself.

Emma smiled. "Of course you can. I don't want you guys to think you have to leave. You'll be safe here." She moved ahead of me.

I raised my brows but didn't comment. Like I would believe her. Reluctantly, I followed her as she walked into the bathroom and turned on the light. Pulling out a white towel from the closet, she laid it on the counter next to the sink. "Do you need anything to wear?"

I nodded my head. She left the bathroom and a few moments later came back with a pair of blue pants and a white shirt. "These should fit you just fine." I nodded my head and waited for her to leave. She just stood there. "You don't know how happy I am to see you." Tears sprang in her eyes.

I pointed to the shower. "I should probably get showered."

"Of course," she said. She looked me over for another long second before turning and shutting the door behind her.

Turning the shower on, I undressed quickly, and dove under the hot spray. I let the water fall over me, taking away the dirt and grime. I wished it could take away the fear. I was terrified. And angry. For years I wished to see my sister again, I cried for weeks after she was dead, but finally getting that wish terrified me. It felt wrong. And now she's here, alive. What kind of person faked their own death? I didn't believe she was here to help. It felt more like a trap.

I shampooed and conditioned my hair and loaded my body with soap. Once I was all cleaned, I shut the water off and wrapped a towel around my body, drying off. I dressed quickly and rummaged through the drawer until I found a hair band and I pulled my hair up into a bun and tied it.

I walked out of the bathroom, the steam following me. Gregory sat alone in the living room. He met my eyes and smiled. "You look fresh and clean."

I glared at him. "I am. Thanks for not telling me how gross and disgusting I looked."

He shrugged his shoulders. "I knew you'd find out eventually." I rolled my eyes at him before walking over and sitting down next to him.

"Where's Emma?"

"She had to step out. She told me I could shower after you."

I looked him up and down. "Yeah, you should."

Gregory poked me in the side, causing me to laugh. He left, and I was left alone in my dead sister's house. I sat in the living room by myself for ten minutes and counted.

Gregory finally walked out, all shiny and new. I smiled at him as he sat down next to me.

"Has she come back yet?"

"No," I said. "Gregory, I don't trust her."

He searched my face. "Honestly, I don't either."

My eyebrows rose. "Really?"

"There's something off about her." He raked his nail against a spot on the couch.

"Yeah," I said. We sat in silence for a few minutes, lost in our own thoughts. "When did she leave?"

"When she came out of the bathroom. She said she had to get something."

I didn't like that. "There's a back door."

"I know. I checked the bathroom. I presume you unlocked the door?"

I smiled at him but didn't say anything. The front door opened, and Emma came through holding two large paper bags.

"I got some food. I figured you guys must be starving." She walked over to us and started emptying the bags. She pulled out baskets of fried chicken, cups of mashed potatoes, and rolls, along with a few bottles of orange soda.

She handed over the baskets, and we all started eating. I wasn't about to give up free food. I moaned in delight as I bit into the chicken.

"We should start talking," Gregory said at last. I looked over at him and glared.

CHAPTER TWENTY-SEVEN

"I agree," Emma said. "We should talk."

I looked over at Emma. "So, let's talk."

"How are you doing?" she asked, searching my face.

"I'm fine." I just wanted this over with.

"How did you and Aileen talk?" Gregory asked.

"She helped me escape those horrible people years ago, and we stayed in contact ever since," Emma said. "My parents got what they deserved. Aileen told me about Mia needing help and I told her I wanted to see you, Mia. I thought you would want to be safe."

"How could I be safe with someone who abandoned me?" I asked.

"I'm so sorry I left." Tears swam in her eyes. "I never wanted to leave you behind, but Aileen said she could only get one of us out."

"So you decided it would be best to leave me behind?" Anger bubbled up in my chest.

"I didn't want to leave you," she said, "and when I heard you were in trouble, I knew this was a chance for me to help you."

"And how exactly are you going to help me?" My body shook from the anger.

"You can stay here." She stood up and paced. "I have enough room."

"If you haven't noticed, there are people after me," I said dryly.

"I know, but they won't get you here," she said excitedly.

I narrowed my eyes. "How can you be sure?" Gregory asked.

"I know some people, and they've promised to help," Emma said. "We have so much to talk about. How your life was when I left. What my adventure was like getting a new life. How you endured this trip. How you two—" she waved her hand between me and Gregory "—met. I want us to become sisters again."

My jaw dropped. Was she serious? *Just making up for what she did.* I closed my mouth and gritted my teeth. "You want to know how my life was like when you left?" I tried to control the waves of anger.

"Yes." She either didn't notice my anger or ignored it.

I stood up and pointed my finger at her. "My life was HELL! My parents—not yours, but mine—beat me. There were times I wished I was dead, but I never actually died. I guess it would look bad if they went too far and had two dead kids. I had no one but Agathy, and she's gone. She died because of the asshole who's coming after me."

Emma started pacing back and forth. She seemed anxious, but I was so angry that I didn't register it. "I'm sorry I left you behind. But I needed to save myself. If you had been in my shoes, you would have done the same thing."

"I wouldn't have!" I yelled. I wouldn't have been surprised if people came to her house, worried about all the yelling. "I would've stayed behind and tried to protect you until you were old enough, then we would have both escaped."

"That would've never worked." She laughed nastily.

I dropped my hand as realization hit me. "Mom and Dad knew you ran away. That's why they hit me worse than ever. They were afraid I would do the same thing. So they frightened me into staying. How did Aileen help you?"

Emma stopped pacing. "What?"

"How did Aileen help you?" I fisted my hands.

"Aileen and her son both helped me. She needed help but didn't trust her husband."

I froze. I could feel Gregory's body stiffen next to me. "Jake helped you?"

"Yes," she said. "Actually, he's the reason I got here safely. He helped set me up in this house. He's been an angel to me."

My anger shifted into panic. I looked over at Gregory with wide eyes. "Does Jake know I'm here?"

"No," she said. "Aileen told me not to tell anyone. Only a few people know you're here."

She obviously doesn't understand what not telling anyone means. "Who are the others?"

"You don't know them," she said. "But you can trust them. They promised they wouldn't tell anyone. They know how important it is to keep quiet."

"I thought Aileen told you not tell anyone." I tried to keep my voice from shaking. I kept wiping my hands on my legs to release the nervous energy.

"I had to tell my husband and the others will help you."

"You're married?" I didn't mean to ask, but the question slipped out of me.

She smiled. "Yes, he's a wonderful man. He makes me feel so happy and safe. Actually, he should be home in a little bit. He really wants to meet you."

I didn't want to meet him. I wanted to get back to the small room in the underground station.

"Jake is part of Kieran's army," Gregory said.

"I heard," Emma said.

Gregory met my stare as I turned to him. I couldn't tell what he was thinking, but the frown and fisted hands meant his thoughts weren't happy ones. I looked down at my shoes. How had she found out about Jake? Did that mean Aileen was still alive? Wouldn't it have been risky of Aileen to reach out to Emma? I looked over at Emma, who seemed very anxious. Time for plan B. "Maybe we should leave for the night and come back at another time." I moved toward the door, but Emma beat me to it, blocking me.

"Please don't," she pleaded. "I really want to catch up with you. I've missed you so much. It's been so hard living a peaceful life, knowing my baby sister has been going through hell. I've been saving money so I could come and get you. I just don't have enough yet. And now that you're here, I don't have to worry about you anymore. Please, why don't you both sit back down and finish your meals. Why don't we talk about something lighter?"

Is this bitch serious? Gregory and I shared a look. *We're going to rush her and get out of here,* I said with my eyes. Gregory sat down. I needed to work on communicating with my eyes. I wanted to yell at him to get up. We needed to leave. But I held my tongue and walked back to the couch, glaring at him. He just shrugged and started to eat. He chose to stay here for food. *The bastard.* I dropped down next to him, "accidently" jabbing him in his stomach. Gregory emitted a groan, and I smiled. Emma sighed in relief and sat down in the chair across from us.

"So, Gregory," she said. "Tell me about yourself."

"I'm from Gildonia," was all he said. He stuffed another piece of chicken in his mouth. I wanted to laugh at her. I sat smiling smugly at her. *Aren't we being a little childish?* I didn't care. Gregory had barely told me anything about his life; there was no way he would tell her. I wanted to go, "Nana nana boo boo." *Very childish.* I sipped on the orange soda, letting the bubbly goodness trickle down my throat.

Emma looked at Gregory, waiting for more. When she realized he wasn't giving her anything else, she turned her attention on me. *Here we go.* "Tell me more about you. I want to know you."

I bit into the chicken. "I don't trust you enough to tell you about myself." I swallowed my food. Was it very ladylike to talk with my mouth full? No. But did I care? No.

Emma sucked in a breath. She looked like she had just been slapped across the face. Wiping my hands off, I looked over to Gregory, who was also finished eating. "I'm sorry if we have to eat and run, but we should really get going."

"What? Why?" Emma cried out.

Gregory and I stood up, and I followed him as he moved toward the door. "I don't trust you, *Emma*." I waved between Gregory and myself. "We don't trust you. We may have the same blood, but to me that doesn't mean anything. You've been dead to me for years, and that will never change. I don't consider you a sister right now. My sister is dead in the ground. The only person in this room I trust is Gregory. He's helped save my life over and over again, and he didn't even know me. He's done it out of compassion, something you wouldn't understand."

Emma stood. "I don't want you to leave. You haven't even met my husband. Please, please stay. I'm so sorry. So sorry. I just couldn't take it anymore. I couldn't take the constant abuse. I had to save myself. But at least you had Agathy there for you. I was alone. I might have had help getting out of the house, but I was all alone. It wasn't until I met my husband that I felt safe." She had started crying, tears streaming down her face. "I hate myself for leaving you behind, I really do. But what else was I supposed to do? I'm here now, trying to help you. Help keep you safe. You're shrugging it off, and that hurts. It hurts so deeply. I don't like my baby sister giving me a look of disgust and hate, but I know I deserve it. So please, let me make it up to you. Please?" Her silent tears turned into sobs.

A trickle of guilt started in my stomach, but I focused on the anger and held on. She seemed she wanted to help me and her words felt genuine. Putting my face in my hands, I groaned. I didn't know what to do. I knew I shouldn't trust her. My gut screamed at me to run, but I ignored it. Could I forgive her for leaving me behind? As I removed my hands, I looked at Gregory, who gave me a sympathetic smile. I opened my mouth to speak when the front door opened. My eyes locked on the man who entered the house and my heart stopped. My blood ran cold: ice cold. Emma's face lit up and she smiled, throwing her hands over his neck and kissing him. She let him go quickly and faced us. Her smile faded as she saw my face. I could feel

Gregory get close behind me, the tension radiating off of him.

"What's wrong?" Emma asked.

"Who is that?" Gregory asked slowly. His voice was like steel. He gripped my arm and pulled me behind him.

Emma looked between her husband and us. "Mia, Gregory, this is my husband, Darren. Darren, this is my sister, Mia, and her friend, Gregory."

Darren smiled slimily. "Nice to see you two again."

Emma looked confused. Her eyebrows were drawn as she looked at the three of us. "You've met them already?"

"We were in the same compartment on the train. I'm glad to see the two of you here."

"Why is that?" Gregory gritted out.

"It's easier if you two are here."

"What do you mean?" I asked, staring up at Darren.

"Sweetheart, remember what we discussed?" Darren asked Emma. She nodded and left the room.

"What's going on?" I asked.

"Do you know," Darren started, "how hard you two are to track down? You've made everyone's lives difficult." Darren pulled out a long gun from his coat. He whipped it around as he talked. "But we're finally at the end."

Emma came out of the room holding ropes. She avoided my eyes as she went to Darren. "What would you like me to do with these?" Emma asked Darren.

I stared in disbelief at my sister. This had all been a set up. Had Aileen been in on it, too? "Emma, why are you doing this?"

"Search them and remove any weapon you find. Then tie them up," Darren instructed Emma.

"And what makes you think we would let her come near us?" Gregory asked. I could feel the anger rolling off of him.

Darren smiled. "You wouldn't make it out of the house alive if you fought. It's surrounded. And if you don't come quietly, I have orders to shoot Mia."

"Why would you shoot me?" I asked. Wasn't keeping me alive the point?

"I can shoot you without killing you," Darren said simply.

I looked at Gregory then back to Darren. "I'll go."

Gregory groaned. "No, you won't."

I ignored him. I didn't want to get into a fight with him at the moment. "But Gregory gets to go free."

"Mia, so help me," Gregory gritted out.

Darren smiled. "Deal." He turned his attention back to Emma. "Please tie her hands behind her back."

Gregory pulled me toward him. "What are you doing?"

I smiled a sad smile. "I'm jumping in front of you." I pulled myself out of his grasp and walked toward Emma. Placing my hands behind my back, I felt the twine rope tighten against my hands as Emma tied it. Emma grabbed my arm and pulled me out the door. I wouldn't look back at Gregory.

"Why are you doing this?" I asked. Tremors ran up my spine.

"I'm trying to help you," she said.

"By turning me in?" I ask incredulously.

"Believe it or not," she said, "this is your best chance at survival."

I fisted my hands and stayed silent. Sweated beaded on my forehead as I watched two black Jeeps park on the street. Four men got out and approached us. Emma handed me off to one of them.

"So, you're Mia," the man said. He smiled, his pearly white teeth shining. He had chocolate-brown skin and perfect straight teeth. He was almost the same height as Gregory. He was beautiful. Too bad he was my enemy.

He leaned in until his lips were next to my ear. "You should know, there are plenty of people who are rooting for you." He stood back up and smiled.

I raised my brows and prepared to speak when a loud crash came from behind me. The man holding my arm pulled me away in time to see six guys bringing Gregory down. My heart raced as they tackled him to the ground. I strained against the man holding me and screamed for them to stop. But they didn't. I watched as they beat Gregory until he went unconscious and then loaded him up in one of their Jeeps. I could feel tears tumble down my cheeks. Darren stepped in front of me with a triumphant smile on his face.

"We made a deal," I choked out.

"Deals are meant to be broken."

I saw red. Instead of trying to get out of the rebel's hands, I gathered as much spit as I could in my mouth and blew it out at Darren. It landed on the upper part of his nose and left eye. His face turned red as he wiped it away. His fist I didn't see coming. It hit me so hard across the face that pain bloomed like a flower. I blinked and my vision blurred. I blinked and black dots formed. I blinked one more time, and there was darkness.

The End.

Acknowledgements

I first want to thank my best friend and sister-in-law for reading this book over and over and over again, and will more than likely read it again. My dad who encourage me to write it, no matter how I felt about it, and who still encourages me to focus on my dreams. To my parents who have encouraged me to keep writing and to focus on what I love, instead of what others love.

I want to thank Murphy Rae who edited and gave me some pointers that will make the story flow much easier. Also, I want to thank her for the beautiful cover design that I would have never been able to come up with! I want to thank the rest of her team, Kerry for proofreading and Wendi for formatting. I was clueless when I first finished this book and didn't know what to do next. So, thank you all for helping me take a step further to achieving a dream!

Lastly, I want to thank all the readers who have given this book a chance. I hope you enjoyed it and will be ready to read book two when it comes out!